THE MYSTERY OF MONKTON HOUSE

Sienna Stevens Mystery Series

By

P.J. YARDLEY

In memory of my parents, Tom and Monica.
Your spirit lives on.

"The person who follows the crowd will usually get no further than the crowd. The one who walks alone, is likely to find himself in places no one has ever been."
— Albert Einstein.

CONTENTS

ACKNOWLEDGEMENTS

To Hal Duncan and Debi Alper for your keen eye.

To my family, thank you for believing in me. Your constant help has been a boost.

Becky and Chris. You're the best. You've kept me going from the beginning.

And last but not least, a massive thank you to husband Jon for his constant love and support in bringing this book to fruition. Got there in the end!

CHAPTER 1

Nearly there.

My stomach clenches in anticipation.

No one else can see it.

It glides towards me, hiding amongst the clouds and floating in and out of the atmosphere. Putting my hand up to shelter from the sun's rays beaming through the glass, it fluctuates and swirls in front of us.

A whisper as soft as baby's breath. 'Find her. Find her.'

I place my hands over my ears to block out the incessant murmuring.

We drive towards the main road and turn off into a narrow lane, arriving at a concealed opening. A wooden five-bar gate with a 'No Entrance' sign is slung haphazardly across the railing and hidden by the old oak tree. The gate is stuck fast in the ground, its base embedded in dried mud and grass, and the trees merge to form a canopy of woody branches. I open my car window, revealing the darkness of the forest.

Silence, apart from the wind rustling amongst the tall oak trees. Dad steers us down the rutted lane, muttering to himself as the overhanging branches scrape against the glass.

'Do us a favour and shut the window,' he says. 'Look at the state of this. All their money and they won't pay for a decent road.'

'Welcome to the haunted forest,' whispers my younger sister Bella, flicking through the pages of her running magazine.

The road widens, and the forest disappears. We turn a corner and face a large mansion shrouded in a grey haze. The sun has vanished and clouds lower over the building, covering it with a film of rain.

'Why is it always gloomy out here?' asks Mum.

Dad shrugs and pulls up. The entrance has imposing, high, wrought-iron gates with intricate designs of leaves and flower petals curled along the top. Fastened to the stone pillar and angled down towards a control pad is a security camera. Dad presses in the numbers. The gates squeal open and we continue along a winding driveway. Cherry blossom trees flank the road and petals float towards the ground, creating a snowy pathway. Apprehension grows in me as we drive towards the building. A flock of ravens, screeching and cawing, circles around the roof. I stare at the ancient grey granite stones covered in moss. The criss-crossed bars across the sash windows give the appearance of a prison. Dad parks the car and we climb out.

Desolation hangs over the place. Paint is flaking off the wooden window frames and creeping ivy covers the wall. We walk up the wide steps towards a stone arch engraved with the words 'Monkton House' curved above the thick oak door.

'Spooky,' groans Bella.

'Grow up,' I snap.

My sister, at fourteen, is two years younger than me and doesn't believe the house is haunted. Every time we visit, she teases me about it.

The moment we enter, the stench of decay overwhelms me. The door opens into a large foyer, its walls covered in polished wooden panels. A chandelier droops from the vaulted ceiling, emitting a faint light. An ancient, blackened fireplace is positioned on the left and contains a large floral arrangement. In the middle of the room, a winding staircase separates in two. To the left, tapping away on a keyboard at a wooden polished desk, is a receptionist wearing a navy blue outfit. We stand in front of her and she lifts her head, pointing to the visitor's book. Dad signs our names, opens the internal door, and we enter.

In the distance, ethereal shapes glide along the polished floor. Dressed in long brown gowns, hoods conceal their faces. My mouth puffs out an icy breath as goose bumps cover my arms. My heart beats faster when the whisperings, low and warm, flood my ear.

'Secrets. Keep out. Secrets,' they chant.

'Mum, Dad, stop. Who are they?' I ask, as my family carries on ahead, following the receptionist, the clacking of her high heels echoing on the wooden floors. I try to catch up with them as a potent odour of mustiness and damp, masked by lavender air spray and perfumed flowers, surrounds me. Endless, dimly lit passages, plain wooden doors, and statues of saints greet me. In the distance, a wailing drifts along the corridor.

'Did you notice them?' I mumble to Bella, grabbing hold of her arm and pointing toward the figures.

'What are you rabbiting on about? Honestly, Sienna. Why do you bother? Whenever we're here, you act weird. Are you trying to scare me and stop me from visiting Nan?' she says, rushing away and leaving me on my own.

They admitted Nan Ria to this care home two weeks ago. Strangely enough, that was the same time my new friend, Charlotte O' Toole, arrived in my life and the visions began.

Rounding a corner, I see an oversized crucifix of Jesus, similar to the ones at school, made of plaster, his loincloth soaked in reddish-brown blood. There are holes where nails pierced his hands and feet, and red liquid streams from the crown of thorns.

My eyes are heavy with tiredness. Heat burns my body as sweat drips down my nose. I'm transported to another time. A period of death, stoning, the pressure of the crown piercing my head. I stare at the cross, and the tingle fizzes along my spine. As I gaze up, Jesus slowly opens his eyes, and the intense stench of coppery blood clogs my nose. Buzzing fills my ears as dizziness overpowers me, and I hold the wall to steady myself.

'Wake up, scaredy-cat, stop daydreaming,' says Bella. Mum standing by her side and studying me.

'Didn't… didn't you notice that?' I point upward at the statue and rub my eyes.

They stare at each other.

'What is it this time?' asks Bella.

'Those strange images I've told you about? They're here and…'

Mum interrupts me. 'If this place upsets you, stay at home next time. We'll have to make an excuse to your nan.'

'No, it's not that,' I say.

'Hurry up and follow us.'

As I trudge along the gloomy passage, Dad opens the door and Bella rushes into the room.

'Hi, Nan.' She places the bunch of sweet-smelling freesias on the bedside locker.

'Is that my Bella? What have you've been up to? Do you have the lead role in the school's dance performance this year?' She watches as my sister pirouettes around her bed.

Nan's room faces the forest, and I watch a flock of blackbirds fly over the trees, settling near the stony edge of the lake. They cast a shadow on the room.

'Ravens,' says Dad. 'Damn things need shooting.'

'What was that, James? Can't stand those birds. Inspecting me with their black, beady eyes. They harbour secrets.' A frown appears between her eyes as she gazes outside.

I walk over to the window and pick up a cat ornament from the old-fashioned oak sideboard.

'Put it down,' whispers Mum. 'There'll be hell to pay if you break it.'

Photos of Dad playing the violin in his school uniform and collecting his degree from Oxford University are propped on the bookshelves. An antique oak wardrobe by the side of the window blocks out the light, making the room darker.

Bella strokes Nan's hand.

'Nan, you have beautiful skin. What's your secret? I bet you're not a day over twenty-one; what do you think, Sienna?' she asks, twisting around and sticking her tongue out at me. I try to suppress a laugh, which ends up in a coughing fit.

'I was born in 1932, which makes me eighty, isn't that correct, James?' she asks.

Dad's eyes crinkle at the corners as he pats her hand.

'Still have my wits about me; now where are my toffees?' she asks him. He laughs and wags his finger.

'It's not a good idea to eat them with your dentures.'

She opens her mouth and pulls them out.

'Yuk,' I say, spotting the chewed food coating her teeth. Dad pushes me towards her.

'Say hello to your nan.'

I gaze at her twisted mouth and the arm hanging by her side from the stroke. Depression sweeps over me, thinking about her living in this creepy place.

'Earth to Sienna, where are you now?' asks Bella, snapping her fingers in my face. My parents are staring at me and I'm miles away again. As I bend over and kiss her cheek, Nan reaches out her bony hand and grabs my arm.

'How's school?' she mumbles as a trail of saliva dribbles from her mouth.

She asks me the same question every time. I used to describe the classes, teachers and even the girls, but realised her memory was fading after she repeated the question three times in a row. Nan contributes to my school fees but Mum isn't happy with me attending there. My parents argue about this problem because, unlike Dad, Mum didn't have a private education. She believes state schools are just as good.

My father pats my arm, interrupting my thoughts.

'Be a love. Stop daydreaming and make yourself useful.' He moves me out of the way to reach Nan. 'Up you get; you're slipping under the covers. Those pillows need sorting out.'

'I'll make you comfy,' says Bella, talking to Nan and helping Dad lift her.

Meanwhile, Mum is putting her clean clothes in the drawers.

'What's wrong with your hair, Sienna?' asks Nan, grinning at me.

'Nothing,' I say, smoothing my crinkly hair flat with my fingers.

'Cut those curls off, your hair is too thick and frizzy,' she cackles. 'Now, Bella, *you* remind me of myself at your age,' she purrs, stroking my sister's glossy locks.

'Oh, Nan. Sienna can't do anything about her ginger mop, can she?' Bella grins at me again.

Nan squints at me. 'Who are you?'

'It's me, Sienna.'

'At first we didn't realise what she was up to,' Nan says. 'We followed the others for a laugh.' Her eyes are closed and she's rocking backwards and forwards, holding her arms across her chest.

'What did you say? Where did you go for a laugh?' asks Dad. He stares at us and scratches his head.

'What's wrong with you?' Nan asks, twisting her head to scrutinise me.

'Me? I'm tired, too much studying.' I look away, puzzled by the change of subject.

'I hope you appreciate it's my money paying for your education.'

'I do,' I say. 'School is er…'

'Don't mumble child, what did you say? Oh yes, school.' Nan then turns to face Dad.

'He picked the lavender, didn't he, James?'

Dad slumps on the chair, wipes his hand over his face and sighs.

'Do you want a glass of water, Ria?' asks Mum, moving over to the water jug on her bedside locker.

'No, keep away, I can manage it myself. I'm not senile.'

'I'll do it, it's no problem.'

'Keep away, Tracey Stevens. I see you're still wearing those ill-fitting charity clothes.' She laughs and turns to Dad. 'Where am I again?'

'Let's get a vase,' I say, looking at Mum.

We open the door. Outside her room is a cupboard bursting with bits and pieces – sticky tape, scissors, spare bulbs – and next to it is a sink. A low guttural moaning resonates through the walls and I check Mum's face. She's removing the cellophane from the flowers and hasn't heard a thing.

'Mum, why does Nan treat me differently from Bella?' I ask, reaching for the crystal glass vase.

'She can't help it. Her Alzheimer's is worsening, and now, with this stroke, it's not surprising she's miserable.' Mum sighs and fills the vase with water.

The murmur of voices from her room drifts over to me.

'James. What's wrong with your eldest daughter? Away with the fairies most of the time she's here. As for her mother...'

'What?' I shout and spin around, knocking over another dried flower display perched on top of the cupboard. It crashes to the ground.

'Sis, is that you?' asks Bella, dashing out of the room. 'Did you hear her? Listen, she's confused and doesn't understand what she's saying. Go on in and I'll arrange the flowers.'

I storm into the room, and the muttering stops.

'Ah, here she is. Sit down, love,' says Nan, patting the bed and smiling at me.

How she changes. Is she pretending to be friendly towards me or is this mood change part of her illness?

'Have you been learning anything interesting at school?' she asks.

'My friend and I are researching a topic for our school project. Oh, and Mum found a couple of old books in the charity shop.' She turns her back to me and fumbles with the sheet.

'Where is that Mrs Jones? She told me to call her Kath. People lack respect these days. I'm not using her first name and I want my cup of tea,' she says, and using one hand rings the bell at the side of her bed. 'Do you remember, James, how dark it was when we nearly fell down those steep stairs into the cellar? It was frightening.'

Dad rubs his eyes and stares out the window.

'I brought you these.' I open my bag and hand her the books. 'Did you read poems at school?'

She sneezes and Dad hands her a tissue.

'Get rid of them before the dust triggers her asthma,' he says.

'I thought with your background in education, this might interest you. The picture on the front resembles a girl's school.' Using the corner of the sheet to wipe off the dust, I pass it to her.

A prickling sensation travels over my body. The stench of dead flowers hovers around the room. An unseen energy pushes my hand onto Nan's, covering the photograph.

'Get off me. Watch out for the lilies. You're hurting me. Ow! Ow!' she screams.

'Sienna, you're squeezing her too tight,' says Dad.

I withdraw my hand away in dismay. *What am I doing?*

'Sorry, Nan. I don't know my strength.'

'You're clumsy,' she says and rubs her hand.

'Nan, what's the matter?' asks Bella.

Something had possessed me to grab her hand. But what? The urge to escape is intense; I stand up and glance behind me. Nan's hands are in front of her face, as if hiding. She's old and muddled and often makes strange gestures we don't understand. But pooling between the middle and ring finger is red liquid. She drops her hands. Tears of blood stream down her face.

Dad rings the bell and Kath Jones rushes into the room. She's a large overweight woman with grey permed hair, wearing a cotton apron wrapped around her sizeable breasts and tied at the back. She glares at me and comforts Nan. Meanwhile, a nurse arrives and places a cuff attached to the blood pressure device over Nan's bony arm.

'Too tight, too tight,' she squeals.

Mrs Jones wipes the blood from Nan's face and passes her a cup of tea.

'It's time to go,' says Mum, standing up. 'We don't want your nan overtired. The nurses will help her.'

My sister kisses Nan's cheek while Dad strokes her hand. I wait in line to say goodbye, but she pulls me down with a vice-like grip and whispers, 'Watch out for the lilies.' Her eyes cloud over and stare behind me.

She has forgotten us already and is chatting with her carer.

As we climb into the car, Dad asks, 'Why did you bring those ancient books with you?'

'I thought she would like them. What's wrong with her eyes and what does she mean about lilies?'

'It's high blood pressure and it's a side effect of her tablets. She's a sick woman.'

As soon as we drive away, the heavy air clears and the sun emerges. Yellow daffodils on the grass verge sway as we pass.

At night, I make a mug of cocoa and soak in a hot bath, but Nan Ria's face appears with tears of blood trailing down her cheeks.

CHAPTER 2

Next day in school, I grin as my best mate, Charlotte, or Charlie, plonks herself into the empty seat next to me in class. Her presence sends shivers running through my body. I peek at her and she stares back at me, her dark brown eyes flecked with goldish green streaks, and grins. She's wearing tiny silver earrings in the shape of a skull and chipped black nail polish on her bitten nails. How does she get away with looking like that? The staff are normally strict about our uniform.

During our study period, we work together on a school project. We're hoping to present it the last day of term. After the lesson finishes, we hurry to the canteen before the rush of students. Charlie studies my salad and throws a handful of chips on my plate. The same group of girls who have plagued me with their sarcastic comments now smirk, whisper, and stare at us. Charlie grins back and sticks a chip in her mouth.

'You need to eat more carbs and ignore them, they're losers,' she says, glaring at them.

'You don't know the half of it, but I could do with losing a few pounds, though.' I laugh and grab the rolls of fat underneath my blouse.

'What the hell do you mean? You're not fat.' I watch the frown line crease on her forehead as she studies the group. 'Why do them lot stick together like a pack of hyenas?'

'They've known each other for years – from prep school, tennis club, ballet classes and so on and so on. It's been difficult to make friends here. I'm not bothered about being known as a loner.'

'Ignore them coz you're with me now,' says Charlie.

We finish eating and walk out of the dining room and into the toilets.

'I mean, check me out.' I stare at myself in the long-length mirror and spin around, showing off my uniform with its distinctive cherry-red jumper, a red and black tartan kilt and black blazer. 'This colour doesn't suit me with my ginger hair and makes this stand out.' I drag the curls over my face to hide my birthmark.

'It's tiny, and I didn't notice it till you mentioned it.'

She's being kind, but it's not true. It's a massive red blotch as if someone has slapped me. I open up my books and spend the rest of the day listening to a boring maths lesson. Finally, it's home time and we grab our bags and walk out of the gate together.

'Those comments you made earlier: you're saying you didn't have *any* friends before me?' she asks.

'A few, but they drop me when they realise my interests,' I say, shaking my head. 'Before you arrived, I'd spend time on my own. Matt from my old primary school is cool, though.'

'Is he the guy with the floppy hair who keeps staring at you?'

'Er, yes. Staring at me? I don't think so.'

'God, he's fit! Didn't you notice the girls scowling when he spoke to you?'

'No. What do you mean? His brother is on Bella's sports team. Matt was only giving me a message about the change of venue.'

Charlie stares at me and sticks her hand through her jet black hair, making the tufts stick up.

'I've known him for years,' I say.

'Yeah, right.' She stares at me. 'Come on, let's go home.'

Charlie is fun to be with, and weirder than me. She tells me the meanings of signs and symbols and believes treading on cracks in the pavement is dangerous as they lead to the underworld. A black cat shoots out in front of us; she clutches my arm and spooks me by saying it belongs to a witch.

She lives in one of the newly built, large executive-style homes near to the school. It's grander and more luxurious than ours and resembles a show home with thick cream carpets, mirrored furniture, a spotless kitchen, and a huge American fridge. It's fun staying there, away from my noisy home, without my annoying sister to contend with.

Opening the front door, we walk into a large hallway and she throws her blazer over the banister and drops her school bag on the floor.

'I'm starving. What do you want?' she asks, going into the kitchen and searching through the fridge.

'Anything.'

After a few minutes, I'm handed a ham sandwich and we eat in silence. A sense of contentment flows over me, sitting here drinking lemonade and eating with her. I think about the group of girls who have been bothering me for ages, and place the half-eaten food back on the plate.

'This may seem petty, but my special left-handed pen went missing from my pencil case and the other day I found my new geometry set hidden behind the radiator. The girls shove me in the dinner queue and try tripping me up,' I say.

It sounds pathetic now. She's staring at me and it's impossible to gauge from her expression whether she's annoyed with me or mad with the girls.

'I've pleaded with my parents to allow me to go to the state school, but Nan Ria wants me and Bella there coz she pays for it,' I say.

Charlie's face darkens, and her eyes screw up.

'They don't bother when you're with me, but that day you were off sick…' I struggle to carry on, thinking about all the taunts I've endured.

'I'll deal with it.' She studies me as my phone vibrates with a message from Mum.

Walking home across the empty playing field into the wood, the silver glint of water catches my eye. It always awakens memories of spending time at the lake with my dad. I remember the cool water lapping at our feet and crunching gravel beneath our toes; Dad's finger on his lips, gesturing for me to stand still, his binoculars hung around his neck; the heron standing tall and proud in his slate grey feather suit, his beady eyes studying us as we navigated the slippery rocks; the joy of observing the flash of iridescent blue-green of the kingfisher soaring over the river; the repetitive song of the cuckoo. That was before fear crept into my life.

Opening the door to our three-bedroom detached house, the 'bump bump' of my sister pounding on her treadmill vibrates throughout the walls. Before Bella can pester me, I dash upstairs to my bedroom and flop on the bed, surveying my book shelves. This is my refuge when life gets too much.

My hobby is searching through antique shops, collecting old hardbacks. I love the musty aromas redolent of another time. Once, I made the mistake of inviting a girl from school back home. We went into my room, and she peered at my books, holding them up and sniffing. I knew something was wrong when she sneered at the black obsidian stone, which was supposed to protect me from negativity.

She studied my favourite ink print, *The Peacock Skirt* by Aubrey Beardsley, and seemed interested in my book collection about the Pendle witches. However, the next day at school, her friends clustered around her, pointing at me and laughing. All I heard were the words *"creepy ginger witch"*, as my face burned with embarrassment.

That was ages ago, but now I sit on my bed, pick up the book that frightened Nan and stare at the front cover. My eyes blur and dizziness overcomes me. I'm walking through the entrance hall of Monkton House, but everything is dark and cold. The stairs creak and I'm in the middle of a large room. The spirit's energy surrounds me and whispers:

'They lied. She promised me I would have a room of my own, warm clothes, and enough food. But that has not happened. When I first entered the house, the silence surprised me. Religious statues are everywhere. The woman met me and I could tell she was in charge because the rest of the staff scurried around her. She possesses a powerful confidence and scrutinised me when I met the other girls in the dormitory. Her sour face didn't break into a smile. This place, and all who work here, are gloomy, and darkness exists everywhere. The staff wear the same uniform – a simple black gown. The teachers are all women of various ages, but are miserable. The other girls stare at me with hatred in their eyes. As I prepare myself for bed, I try to speak to the others. I want friends, but they turn their heads to the wall. The sound of sobbing will stick in my memory for ever. Sienna, help me.'

'Sis, come down, Mum wants you,' Bella shouts from the bottom of the stairs.

What happened? Where did I go? Leaving the book on my bed, I hurry downstairs and sit at the dining room table. Mum brings out the tureen of chili con carne and Bella follows with a bowl of white rice.

'Help yourself to the garlic bread,' says Mum. 'James, do you fancy a glass of red wine? Be a dear and bring the bottle in.'

As we dish up our meal, Dad stares at me.

'What's up with the pale face? Have you been studying too much?'

I shake my head and look at the brown mince with deep red kidney beans interspersed among the white flakes of rice. My stomach is in knots, and I can't open my mouth to answer. I put my fork down.

' I er...'

'Yes, she's always got her nose in a book. Haven't you, dear?' says Mum, smiling at me over the rim of her wine glass.

'Why is Nan at Monkton House?'

'Why do you ask? You know she's poorly,' says Mum, looking over as Dad refills her glass.

'It's just I had, erm, a sort of dream about it.'

'What do you mean, Sienna, a sort of dream?' asks Dad, staring at me, a deep crease indented on his forehead. 'I don't want any of that nonsense again when we visit your nan. What possessed you to push down on her hand? It hurt her. Eat up, your mother's gone to a lot of trouble to cook this meal. Delicious, Tracey,' he says, turning to Mum and raising the glass to her.

Bella is staring at me and under her breath whispers, 'Weirdo.'

After our evening meal, I sit in the lounge as my parents switch on the television. Some programme about politics is on but I can't concentrate with both parties arguing with each other.

'Tell you what,' shouts Dad at the screen. 'Pay those care workers a decent wage, get the roads fixed, and I'll vote for you.'

'Oh James, you're on your soapbox again,' laughs Mum, as she snuggles up to him.

'I'm going to bed,' I say, getting up from the chair. 'I'm tired.'

'Good night. See you tomorrow,' says Mum.

'And don't stay up all night reading,' says Dad.

When I get upstairs, Bella's door is open.

'Come in and tell me about your dream.' She's lying on her bed and reading her magazine, *Running Weekly*.

'How do you know I had a dream? It was nothing,' I say, plonking myself down.

'Well, it must be something for Dad to comment on your face. You looked like you'd seen a ghost, though.'

'Did I? Well, I saw Monkton House, but it was different. Like it was years ago. And someone whispered to me.

'What?' asks Bella, sitting up.

'Yes, it was a young girl. She knew my name and told me to help her.'

'Do you know what I think?' says my sister, studying me.

'What?' I ask, hoping she'll say it wasn't real and that I imagined it.

'You're a weirdo. Now get out,' she says, throwing her pillow at me.

I retreat to my room, and everything looks the same apart from Nan's book which is now back on the shelf.

CHAPTER 3

Today, I'm sitting in class on my own, while Charlie is at the dentist. Discussing my problem yesterday with her has given me confidence to challenge the person bullying me. Plucking up the courage to confront her, I follow her into the cloakroom. At first, she doesn't notice me, but a few girls sidle away and block the door. I walk towards my locker, but Octavia stands in front of it, placing her hand on top of the handle.

'Scram, ginger witch,' she says. The other girls laugh and crowd around me.

'Octavia, I want you to stop taking my things right now.' My throat tightens and my voice squeaks in fear.

'Oh, you do, do you?' She sticks her face close to mine. Her mascara has stuck her eyelashes together in clumps, and the powdery blusher on her cheeks is flaking off. She addresses the girls standing next to her.

'Did you know this loser and her creepy friend are studying witchcraft? In a catholic school, too. What shall we do with her, girls?'

'Drown her, drown her!' they shout in unison.

'Down the toilet,' says one girl.

'Tell Father Ignatius.'

'Octavia le... le... leave me alone,' I stutter.

'Aw, didums, why don't you show us a magic spell and make yourself disappear?' she says, joining her friends and making a cutting sign across her throat. Next minute, they crowd around me and wrench my hair. They pick up my bag and throw it at each other. The first slap strikes me from the side while I kick out and connect with a girl's leg. I'm brought down onto the linoleum floor. Lying there with my hands over my head, I spot dust balls and sports socks underneath the bench. A trail of ants clamber over a half-eaten energy bar. I shuffle closer to the wooden frame and rest my arms on the bench, ready to pull myself up, but the shutter on the air vent opens and a sheer silver cloud floats towards me. A sense of calm and resilience comes over me as I turn around and shout out.

'Clear off, Octavia, you're nothing. You don't frighten me.'

The bell rings for the start of lessons and the girls dash out the door while I crawl into the hallway. Matt sees me huddled in the corner and fetches a teacher. I don't tell the staff who the culprits are as it will make things worse. Blood drips from my nose and my face burns from the slap, but at least the kick to my leg fades when I rub it. The first-aider applies a support bandage to my ankle and cleans the blood from my cheek. I hobble into the principal's office and she writes in the accident book, then contacts my parents.

Limping back to class, I notice Octavia smirking at me. Meanwhile, Charlie arrives back from her appointment and whispers, 'What happened?'

I bite my lip and carry on writing. The rest of the day passes with no major incidents. Matt gazes at me, and I avert my eyes, but as the heat reaches my cheeks, my birthmark throbs and my hand automatically reaches towards it.

Finally, the school bell rings, and we stroll to Charlie's house.

'There's a way to get rid of those bullies forever. Come with me,' she says as I follow her upstairs.

Pulling out a suitcase from under the bed, she removes a faded purple velvet fabric bag embroidered with emblems of gold circles and stars. She strokes the silky nap of the material and stares into the distance.

'This belongs to my grandmother, Rose; she's a mystic.'

'You're joking?'

'My dad claims she possesses special abilities, but I've not witnessed anything psychic yet.'

Charlie rummages through the bag and passes me a handful of magazines and books. I study the titles: *Traditional Witchcraft, Folklore of Ireland, Mastering Witchcraft, Occult Behaviours, Herbal Remedies.*

'Have you read these?' I ask.

'Some of them.'

'What's this?' I ask, picking up a necklace of dried beads.

'It's a rowan berry charm. They're supposed to send evil on its way.'

I twirl them in between my fingers, making a clicking sound.

'This is what I want to show you.' She shuts the curtains. From the bag, she takes out a black pen and candle and crumpled piece of paper ripped out of a magazine.

'It's faded and I can't read all the words. Where's it from?' I ask, smoothing the crinkles out of the page.

'It's from this,' she says, showing me a magazine called *Witches Weekly.*

'Why would your gran keep this in her bag?'

'Dunno. She collects weird things and bought these magazines for a knockdown price at a car boot sale in the grounds of Drumbeg Manor, but she hasn't read them.'

'Where's that?'

'Drumbeg Manor? It's a haunted mansion in Donegal, Ireland. My gran loves creepy places. Anyway, we need to do what it says here.'

She stands up and pours a salt circle around me. Taking out a black candle, she lights it. It makes a whooshing noise as the wick bursts into flames.

'They call this a banishing spell. Imagine the person harming you and write their name on this piece of paper,' she commands.

'What are we doing?' I ask.

'Trust me.'

Taking the pen, I write the name Octavia Hamilton-Jones in capital letters on the paper. Clutching my hands, Charlie reads from the piece of torn magazine.

'Biddy Bl… I can't work out the name.'

I peer over her shoulder. 'Is it Biddy Blog or Blum?' I say.

'Don't know, let's just say Biddy.'

'OK.'

'Biddy, join me and lend me your shield,' she says. 'Now, you next, Sienna. Ask her to guard you.'

'Octavia. You will not hurt me again. I ask Biddy to protect me from your wrath.'

I chant, as we repeat the spell three times. Charlie's eyes close. The candle flame is getting higher.

Her mouth opens, emitting an eerie wailing noise. 'Quick, put it out!' she shrieks, opening her eyes.

'What is it? What's wrong? Who is Biddy?' I ask, holding her hand.

When I utter her name, a chill wind rushes through the room, and she materialises: a woman dressed in a dark gown trailing the floor, long sleeves tight at the wrist with white cuffs, little pearl buttons running up to her throat, a lace collar around her neck. Her bonnet has slipped down, showing dark hair parted in the middle, tied into a bun as the necklace of rope tightens around her throat.

I open the door and shout for help.

Charlie's father, Brendan O' Toole, rushes in and stares at us.

'Charlotte! What are you doing? Sit up.' He hauls her up off the floor onto the chair.

'Are you alright, Sienna?' he asks. 'What on earth are you doing with the curtains closed? Are you trying to burn the place down? Oh, I see.' He picks up the magazines and candle. 'Her grandmother is to blame for these strange ideas. Wait downstairs, please, and I'll arrange a lift home.'

'But, I saw…'

He walks away before I ask him what he means and I trudge down the stairs. The enormous gold-plated hall mirror reflects my dishevelled appearance so I smooth my hair. When I stare deeper into the glass, the mirror becomes a sea of water, undulating with filaments of green weeds reaching out, trying to wrap around my neck. Wisps of silky smoke float towards me, transforming into the figure of my sister. I stretch out my hand, but the image bursts into thousands of silvery droplets. Why am I visualising Bella? I rub my eyes. This is strange. Charlie bothers me. Perhaps I shouldn't have been quick making friends with her. The mirror clouds over and I wipe off the condensation with my sleeve as the housekeeper strides up to me.

'I've brought you a glass of water. Charlotte is lying down in her bedroom. Rest here and when you're ready, I'll drive you home.'

'I'm OK now,' I say, and gulp down the cold water. She opens the front door and ushers me into her car. On the way home, the housekeeper concentrates on the road, but all I can think of is the image of the woman with a thick rope coiled around her neck.

When I arrive home, Dad is pacing up and down, his face reddening by the minute. Mum is biting her nails. Charlotte's dad has been in contact, and I wait for the outburst. Bella is swinging her legs over the arm of the chair and beaming at me. Even though I'm relieved she's there, the meaning of the vision worries me.

'It wasn't my fault,' I say before he can tell me off.

'What those girls did was inexcusable, and I've spoken to the principal who reassures me it won't happen again. Your mother wants you to leave. However, I think you should stick it out. The school has an excellent reputation for exam results and pupils entering Oxbridge.'

Mum shakes her head and says, 'Try not to get into trouble. Ignore them and they'll get bored.'

Dad runs his hand through his hair. 'Then having Charlie's father phone us with some bizarre tale about spells is the last straw. I'm not happy that you're messing with magic. Revising for your exams and getting on with other girls at school should be your priority. Aren't you too old for that larking around? What's next, believing in unicorns?'

Bella laughs and walks into the kitchen.

I storm off to my room. Even though I'm having second thoughts about Charlie, *they're* not allowed to. She doesn't answer her phone, which is worrying. I sink into a hot bath to ease my aching muscles and think about how nasty those girls were to me.

I dream of Octavio kicking me while faceless figures in gowns chant my name over and over.

***

In the morning, I wake up with a tightness in my chest. I'm apprehensive, sensing trouble ahead.

For a change, I'm dressed first and stuff a piece of toast in my mouth before leaving for school. I'm desperate to check on my friend. At the entrance to the gates is a noticeboard informing all year groups there will be a whole school assembly in the hall. Nervousness creeps over me. I search for my friend amongst the crowd milling in the cloakroom, but the hall is packed. The staff stride onto the stage; a few younger teachers are wiping their eyes. I still can't spot Charlie. We sing a hymn and Father Ignatius leads us in prayer. When he stops, he scans the assembly hall and his gaze settles on me.

After the service, the principal informs us that counsellors are available. I twist around and spot her a couple of rows behind me, and notice girls bawling and holding onto each other.

'Why?' I mouth. She shakes her head.

The principal explains how Octavia slipped on the stairs at home and cracked her skull on the hall floor. She died instantly.

The room is hushed apart from her friends weeping.

I glimpse at Charlie. She has a grin on her face.

The bullying has ended.

CHAPTER 4

One week later …

We're late leaving school, and the throng of pupils has dispersed. It's one of those humid days causing sweat to gather at the nape of your neck. I want to lie in the cool grass and forget about school and Octavia. Many of the girls took up the offer of the counsellor. I didn't, just in case I blurted out our secret. Charlie doesn't mention Octavia; it's almost as if she didn't exist.

Perspiration drips from my face, and I swat at a bumblebee droning in my ear. Gazing upwards, I admire the brilliance of the blue sky and place my hands over my eyes to shield them from the glare. We stroll deep into the woods and open the bar on the wooden gate. The apple blossoms are in bloom as we wander through a tunnel of trees. In the distance, figures of pupils dressed in our red school uniform vanish around the corner and out of view. The grass by the side of the path is a vivid shade of green; dandelions grow wild, their seeds dispersing in the air as I brush pass them. Monkton House materialises through the gaps in the trees. This is a short way home and we usually follow the other pupils. However, today we lag behind.

The air is still with anticipation. I stand and concentrate. Nothing. The crowd has disappeared around a bend in the path. The flowery scent of the hawthorn bush drifts in my nose. Charlie is dashing on ahead and it's tough trying to keep up with her. I've not been able to sleep since we carried out the banishing spell, even though Charlie pretends not to hear whenever I question her about it.

The path is becoming narrower and overgrown with nettles. They sting my bare legs, and red spots erupt as I scratch them, while bubbles of blood ooze out. We take a detour from the others, and thick woody hedges block our view. Amongst the gaps is the broken frame of an old wooden jetty, and the stench of fetid water wafts towards me. Dragonflies with their fragile, jade green shimmering wings flutter near my face as I brush them away.

I sense it first. A breeze wafting through my hair. A pressure on my shoulder. The heavy and potent aroma of the wallflowers bewitching me. The afternoon sun is warm on my face. Words clog my mouth as if I've swallowed thick cotton wool and I try to shout at Charlie to wait. Silence is in the air, till the crack of a branch sends a pheasant squawking into the sky.

I twist around and encounter a hazy figure.

Pale grey, ghostly mist.

The fluid form of a young girl swaying and undulating.

I run.

'Wait a minute!' I yell. 'I've seen… I've seen…'

'What?'

I turn and look.

'Someone was standing over there.' I tug on her shirtsleeve and point to the clearing.

'Who was it?' She whips around and frowns in disbelief. 'There's nothing there. Do you want to carry on?' she says, gesturing to the stile.

She climbs over it with the ease of a gazelle while I stumble on the first step. My stubby legs can't lift over the high wooden plank. After several tries, I haul my body over the stile and collapse in a heap. Charlie watches me, her hand clasped over her mouth trying not to laugh.

'Hurry up,' I say. The stile leads us through a path into an open space. The shrieks and laughter of the other pupils tail off, as a dangerous feeling creeps over me amid this peaceful area.

'Wait a minute, Charlie. Should we do this? I mean, so soon after what happened to Octavia?' I stare into the distance, trying to remove the image of a girl falling down the stairs.

'Don't worry, that was an accident. Anyway, this is your idea. You're the one who's always moaning about her sister.' She narrows her eyes and glares at me.

This hostile side to her personality bothers me, and I study her as we pass the field of yellow rapeseed flowers. The trees merge into a mass of twisted branches.

'How much further?' she says.

'It's over here.' I gesture to my right.

A circle of beech trees with their overhanging branches covers a perfect circle of red soil. Charlie stops, swivels on her heel and grabs my arm at the sound of cracking above us. For once, her confident air vanishes, and her eyes widen as she looks around. This is my secret place.

It's silent here, apart from the faint trickle of water and the squirrels scuttling up the branches. The drumming of the green woodpecker pecking for insects makes me flinch. Tension grows in my stomach. I sense the oppressive atmosphere and glance upwards; the tree's branches merge at the top, shading any remnant of light.

Opening my rucksack, I remove a plastic sandwich bag. Inside, is a twist of greaseproof paper enclosing a handful of salt, a garlic clove, and a pack of playing cards.

'What did you bring?' I ask.

'This.' She pulls out a bottle of water from her bag. 'Where's the witch's ball?'

I shake my head. 'Couldn't get it. It's a glass decoration. Mum would be mad if I broke it. But why do we need it?'

I watch her unscrew the bottle cap.

'Centuries ago, villagers bound suspected witches with rope and threw them into lakes. If they survived, people believed it proved they were witches, and sentenced them to death. Strangely, though, they dangled glass balls in cottage windows to ward off evil. That's your lesson on witchcraft for the day. I thought you knew that. Haven't you been working on our project?' She scowls at me.

I ignore her last remark. 'Have you blessed the water?'

'No, do it now.'

We wave our hands over the plastic bottle and together say, 'Water of life. Protect us from evil.'

'Sit in the middle,' she commands, pointing to the ground. I sit cross-legged as she creates a salt circle around us and pours the water over it.

'Are we ready?' she asks.

I stare at the feverish glow in her eyes.

Taking my pack of cards, I shuffle them, cut them, and shuffle again.

'Pick three cards and I'll predict the future.'

Facing my friend, I fan the cards in a semi-circle. Charlie picks hers and places them down in front of her. I do the same.

'OK; one, two, three, flip them over now, together.'

We twist our first one. Charlie has the Joker.

'Oh no,' she says.

'What?'

'This card means we're in danger. What about you?'

'No way. Let's go. This is a daft idea. What was I thinking?' I say, glancing around me. The air is still and the trees loom in front of me. Charlie has her back to the cloud that's moving closer. I examine my card: nine of spades.

'I've forgotten what that means,' she says, pointing to the card.

'Never mind.' I gather up the pack. 'This is a silly game, let's go.'

She hasn't forgotten; she taught me the meaning behind the deck and knows that nine of spades means nightmares, anxiety and depression.

'Let's begin, scaredy cat,' she says, smoothing a crumpled-up page from a magazine and passing it to me.

'A spell to destroy annoying people,' I read. 'I'm not sure now. What if it works, and she's in danger?'

'Oh, for god's sake, Sienna, you're the one who's always complaining about your sister. The spell didn't kill Octavia; she tripped over her two enormous feet.'

'Charlie, don't say that.' I make a snorting noise, in between a laugh and a cry. From my pocket I bring out a tiny jay's feather – bright azure blue, striated with black lines – which I found in our garden; a few hairs from Bella's comb; a hen's egg; and, the pièce de résistance, Bella's gel nail clippings from her wastebasket, and place them in front of us.

'Have you been carrying an egg in your pocket since this morning?'

'No, silly,' I say. 'I sneaked into the school kitchen at home time and pinched it from the fridge.'

'Ooh, rebel,' laughs Charlie as my face flushes with embarrassment.

'They won't miss it.' I'm annoyed with myself for blushing and look down so she can't see my burning cheeks. 'Let's get it over with.'

She draws a circle in the red soil with arrows extending outwards.

'Do we read a line from the spell and place the object in the circle?' I ask. She nods and in our spookiest voice we read a sentence each:

'A feather as dark as the deepest ocean.

Bristles plucked from a wild boar.

A shattered raven's egg fallen from a nest of twigs,

Nail clippings from the chosen one.

A handful of bedbugs swollen with putrid blood.

Place in a large silver bowl, stir over the heat, and wait for the flame to erupt.'

We stare at each other as she clicks the wheel at the top of a disposable lighter and it sparks onto the heaped objects. The feather catches the flame first. It melts and shrivels, emitting a pungent stink which catches at the back of my throat.

'Quick, crack the egg over it.' As I follow her instruction, she stirs the molten mixture using a pencil. The grey smoke is rising steadily, making me cough. I stand up and pour the water over the mess.

'That's it then,' she says. 'Puff, your sister evaporates.' She laughs and snaps her fingers at me, trying to imitate a magician. I stare at the ground. What if I've harmed Bella, and it's my fault for suggesting this?

'Or at least stops pestering you. Now, where are those bed bugs?' she grins and punches my upper arm. 'Lighten up. You wanted to do this.'

'Yes, but that was before you-know-what happened.'

'Are you still worried about Octavia? We had nothing to do with her and I keep telling you it was an accident. These spells are fun but if you don't want to hang out with me…'

'It's time to go,' I say as we pick up our things. 'We'll take the other way home. There's no way I'm climbing over the stile again.'

Charlie steps out of the circle. I kick the salty water mixture into the red soil to hide the evidence. I don't turn around because someone is watching as the gentle wind spirals over me.

She's there.

Watching and whispering.

I'm relieved the spell is over. I only mentioned that my sister annoyed me, and Charlie jumped straight in with the idea of getting rid of her. In the recesses of my brain, the thought of being manipulated by my friend pops into my mind.

'Come on, time to go,' I say.

'Tell me again why you don't like your sister?'

'Where do I start? Bella annoys me because she's everyone's darling. My parents idolise her, and even the grumpy newsagent shares jokes with her. Unlike me, she's a keep-fit fiend and is always on the go. My sister has loads of friends and takes part in all the after-school clubs. Nan loves her and not me.'

Charlie raises her eyebrows.

'Come on, last one out is a loser,' she shouts and runs through the tall grass on to the worn path. I watch as she disappears around the corner and I'm alone. Running is not my strength, so I amble along the stony track until I reach a metal gate, opening into a large play area behind it. Sitting on a bench is Charlie, studying her nails.

'You took your time,' she says. I glare at her and we continue towards my house in silence. I'm sweating and my fingers slip when I stick the key in the door. Bella opens it, carrying a plastic bowl of ham salad in her free hand.

'Told you the spell was a load of bull,' murmurs Charlie.

'What are you two whispering about?' asks Bella.

'Nothing,' I say. 'Just checking you're still here.'

'Why shouldn't I be?'

'We found a spell to get rid of you and want to see if it works,' laughs Charlie.

I grab her arm. 'Why did you say that? Now she'll blab to my parents.'

'Relax, she won't.'

'Weirdos,' hisses Bella, moving away from us as we enter my room.

We lie on the bed and I open my laptop to research Cotswold hauntings. There's a knock and Mum comes in.

'Hello, Charlotte. How's your family?'

'They're fine, Mrs Stevens. Dad said he'll phone you with details about the trip to Ireland.'

'That's great. I'll talk to your parents later today. But right now, I could do with your help,' she says, walking out of my room.

'What do you want?' I jump off my bed and follow her.

'Come out here and hold this steady for me while I go into the loft,' She pulls down the ladder and climbs the steps.

'Whatcha doing up there?' I yell.

'Yes, I've found it.'

'Get down, I'm leaving soon,' says Bella, gripping onto the ladder.

I help Mum manoeuvre the last step and grab hold of the box from her.

'I'm off now. I'll text you the arrangements,' Charlie says, running downstairs and letting herself out the front door. I stand at the top of the stairs and watch her go. The place is quiet without her.

'Mum, what's in here?' I ask, pointing to a box containing two squashed black plastic bags.

'Clothes I brought back from the charity shop ages ago. They're too tight for me and I'll return them. Where did you say you were off to, Isabella?' She turns to my sister.

'The usual – training at the stadium and meeting up with my mates. I'll grab a burger at the sports café. Rob and Matthew's mum is taking us there and back. Rob has joined my sports team,' she says, cuddling up to my mother. My sister has glossy black hair tied in braids, her skin smooth and free of spots; no wonder people stare at her. We're totally different. I'm sixteen, short and chunky, with a face that looks miserable even when I'm not. I'm fed up with people telling me to, 'Cheer up, love, it may never happen.'

'You train too often, Isabella. Give it a rest and concentrate on your studies, like your sister. Don't be late or your dad will be annoyed if you arrive home after him,' says Mum.

'Bye,' yells Bella, sprinting to the door.

My sister is a whirlwind of activity, but the athletic gene has bypassed me. Even though she's a pest, I'm relieved the spell we performed didn't harm her. Tonight it's just Mum and me eating dinner. My dad is a financial advisor for Capital Trust, a large investment company in Oxford. Tonight, he is celebrating a financial deal with his colleagues at the local restaurant. After helping Mum tidy the kitchen, I retreat to my room and curl up on my bed and reflect on the spell we chanted today. I scroll through my phone to check if Charlie messaged me. My eyes are closing when I hear the opening squeak of the fridge. Tiptoeing downstairs, I discover Dad slumped in the armchair with a glass of whisky in his hand, his suit crumpled, his tie lying on the floor, and his work papers scattered around him. The bottle is half-empty and his face is flushed. I enter the room and he opens his eyes.

'Hi love, how are you? What have you been up to?'

'Nothing much. Charlie was here.'

'What was all that about, Sienna?' He peers at me over the rim of his glass.

'What?'

'That dream you had about Monkton House. Tell me what

happened.'

As I'm talking, his eyelids close and the whisky glass slips through his fingers.

'Perhaps you need to talk to someone about it,' he slurs.

'Dad, it's time for bed,' I say. 'Mum and Bella are already asleep.'

He stumbles out of the chair, staggers up the stairs, and falls into the bedroom. I follow him. The central heating is off and even though it's summer, I'm cold. My feet are blue, and I rub my arms for warmth.

I climb into bed and pull the duvet over me, but can't relax. Why did I let Charlie talk me into performing a stupid spell? As I shut my eyes, I sense it. A prickle, similar to a nettle sting, starts at the base of my spine and travels up towards my head. My body feels as if it's on fire. I'm floating into a bottomless hole as darkness washes over me.

CHAPTER 5

The week passes quickly; the class is excited about May half term. Groups of friends are discussing Lake District holidays while others argue about the best villas in France. I brood over my weekend away with Charlie. The prospect of staying in Ireland worries me because of her mood changes. Sometimes she seems happy when I'm around, but other times I'm ignored and I've even caught her chatting to Octavia's friends. Being the cool girl in our class, everyone wants her attention and I wonder why I'm the chosen one.

Mum drives me to the airport where I meet her and her dad, and we board our plane. I'm sitting in the middle of them and try to chat, but she angles her body away and stares out of the window. I hope she's not regretting inviting me. It's not long before the emerald green fields of Ireland emerge through the blanket of clouds.

Brendan picks up the hire car and we're on our way. Charlie stops sulking and even laughs at her dad's attempts at jokes. The journey from the airport is picturesque. Ireland is abundant with lush green fields, rolling hills, and there's hardly any traffic on the roads. We stop at the ancient town of Cashel and stretch our legs. Brendan strolls over to a café while we explore the town. We're busy chatting and I don't notice the ancient granite stone church till it's in front of us.

Charlie pushes open the heavy oak doors to St John the Baptist

Church. 'Quick, inside before we're soaked,' she says as a fine rain hits my face.

An aura of tranquillity meets me. I watch my friend drop a handful of coins in the collection box and light a candle, but a primeval force draws me towards the altar. The bitter stench of dying flowers fills the air: vases of camellias, their once lustrous white petals decaying. Without warning, my throat constricts and I'm unable to breathe; my ears clog up, and the earthy stink of muddy water filters into my nose. Religious statues loom over me. My head aches and pinpricks of light dance behind my eyes. There's a whisper in my ear. *'I saw it. She led the group into the dank cellar, and they sang the song of the dead while she stirred the bowl of bloody liquid. Something else was there. By her side. Watching. She used locks of my hair and feathers from a dead bird.'*

I open my eyes. What was that? I stumble into the pew and retch, my mouth full of acid saliva. My hands are trembling. I sit underneath a figure of St Michael slaying the devil. Charlie is next to me and points upwards. Craning my neck, I see a plume of grey smoke coiling above me.

'What's wrong? You were mumbling about feathers.' She studies me and rubs my back.

From the side door, a priest slinks out and blesses himself. Charlie clutches my arm and we dash out of the church. I look upwards. Perched on top of the roof are stone gargoyles covered in lichen, their eyes bulging and their mouths open in maniacal screams. The rain clouds burst and a dense shower drenches our summer clothes.

'What was that about?' she asks.

'I'm not sure. I have these visions and hear someone whispering. The images are bleary and I pass out for a couple of minutes.'

Her dad comes towards us carrying bottles of water.

'Hush,' I say, pretending to zip my lips.

'Tell me later. Honestly, I can't take you anywhere,' she laughs, linking arms with me. 'Here, get under this umbrella.'

The rain gushes down and we jump into the car. The images have scared me, and I'm unaware I'm biting my nails and don't notice drops of salty blood on my lips.

'Stop it,' whispers Charlie. She dabs at my fingers as spots of red stain the white tissue.

We arrive in Killarney but are stuck behind a group of men and horses trotting along the road, taking people for rides. Two men are sitting high in the carriage, their faces reddened from the wind, holding a set of reins in their hands. People in the waggon squeal as the horse pulls the large wheels over the bumpy road.

'How quaint. What are they?' I ask.

'They're jaunting cars. Queen Victoria rode in them when she stayed in our town,' replies Brendan. 'They're popular with tourists who love riding around Killarney.'

'We're coming to our property now,' he says, gesturing to a house in the distance. A long road snakes through a vast estate filled with trees, their boughs stretching up to the sky.

'What's over there?' I ask, pointing to an expanse of dull grey water.

'It's Lough Leane, otherwise known as the Lake of Learning.' Brendan gestures to the driveway.' Welcome to our humble abode.'

Fields of green lie on either side of their drive; cows and sheep roam on the grass, and horses gallop in the distance. As we approach, the size of their house surprises me: it's a mansion. Guarding the entrance to their property are two ornamental terracotta lion sculptures. Brendan leans over and taps in a code on the keypad and the high electric gates open gradually. Tall marble columns shelter the front door, and a double garage is attached to the side of the house.

The outside walls are a brilliant powder blue, enhanced by baskets of variegated flowers contrasting against the greyness of the lake. The window frames are shiny white, glittering in the afternoon sun. The rain has stopped and a rainbow arches over their land, ending in the lake.

'That means good luck,' says Charlie, as we climb out of the car and I admire the views.

'Here we are,' says Brendan.

She drags me away while her dad carries the cases out of the boot. Two people emerge from the door as a black and white cocker spaniel hurtles up to Charlie, wagging its tail.

'Good boy, Alfie,' she says, rubbing the dog's ears.

'Who are they?' I ask.

'Maureen, the housekeeper, and Sean, her husband. They live in the cottage at the entrance to the drive. Time to feed the horses,' she says, pulling me over to the paddocks.

As I'm stroking the glossy chestnut mane of Amber, her horse, I pause.

'Charlie. That conversation we had outside the church. Why me? Why do I have spooky visions?'

She picks up a brush and untangles her horse's mane while studying me.

'My family originates from a long line of Irish mystics, which is why I also see things,' she says, puffing out her chest.

'This is the first time you've told me.' I inspect her face for the trace of a lie.

She looks away. 'Do you remember when we chanted that spell to end the bullying? After you repeated the last word, I saw murky shapes swirling around you and hands reaching out.' She shudders. 'It was terrifying, and I'm wondering with our school project about hauntings whether we're more attuned to the supernatural than others. The other day, for a laugh, I carried out an online witch identification quiz,' she grins. 'What a joke. The results claim I'm a green witch, love the earth and want to protect it. It's a sham. I hate being out in the fresh air, apart from riding my horses. You should do the quiz, too,' she says, oblivious to my frustration at being ignored. 'Oh, and I want you to meet my grandma, Rose; you're both similar, both hypersensitive. Gran natters to the trees and says flowers possess a soul. She imagines fairies live at the bottom of the garden, looking after her roses. If you tell her about your hallucinations, I'm sure she'll help you make sense of their meaning. Alfie, here boy,' she yells, as her cocker spaniel scampers away. We bolt the stable door and chase after him. The grounds stretch on forever. A path curves through the garden, leading to stone steps. The dog bounds to the outskirts of the lake and rolls in the grass.

'Are your parents worried when you tell them about the images?'

I lower my head and sniff.

'Hey, hey, don't cry. What does your mum say?' she asks, wrapping her arms around me.

'Nothing. They're too involved in their own problems.' I snivel again. 'It's difficult at the moment. They argue about money and I'm worried they might separate.' My nose is dripping as Charlie passes me a tissue.

'No way. I mean, my parents, yes, that's possible, seeing as they don't have much contact with each other. Dad travels the world with his job while my mother occupies herself lunching with the ladies, beauty treatments and Pilates at the gym.'

'Is she here?'

'No, Mum's visiting a "friend" in Paris this weekend.' She makes air quotes with her fingers. There's the hint of a tear in her eye.

'I didn't realise you have problems,' I say, stroking her arm.

'My family is mixed up. Dad's job has given him more responsibility, but he wanted us with him, which means we follow him around and I have to change schools. Also, Mum found Ireland too quiet, and she missed England. The constant upheaval means I don't make friends easily.'

'But you appear so confident.'

'Why do you think I dress this way?' She gestures to herself. 'It's to keep people away so I don't get hurt.'

Standing in front of me is a tall, slim girl with black, short, spikey hair, dark eye make-up, silver nose ring and silver bracelets jingling up her arms. She's wearing a short black skirt and grey t-shirt with the symbol of a skull embossed in sequins printed on it. If I had the nerve, I would copy her. Today, I'm in my usual ripped jeans, trainers and sweatshirt and look underdressed compared to her. She continues.

'I'm glad we met and bonded over our supernatural interest, but this obsession isn't helping me study for my exams. However, those ancient stories of the Cotswolds hauntings intrigue me.'

'I'm still worried we caused Octavia's death,' I whisper. 'It was an accident, wasn't it?'

'Yea, I hope so. Anyway, let's sit over here,' she says. Linking arms and moving over to the stone bench, we study the expanse of water in the distance. Peacefulness and a sense of contentment washes over me. I yawn and stretch my arms above my head.

'They should bottle this feeling,' I say.

'What, and label it 'Contentment £5 a jar?' We could sell it to those jumped-up divas. I've been comparing the school with others I've attended, and it's no wonder you can't stand it. Those girls are snobby and the boys are ignorant. I've learnt one thing though,' she says, leaning towards me.

'What?'

'Matthew has the hots for you.'

'Come off it,' I laugh, pushing her off the bench.

'I'm starving. Time for dinner.' She jumps up and grabs my arm.

We dash towards the house and head into the kitchen. I'm hot and sticky, but Charlie hasn't raised a sweat. She unscrews a bottle of sparkling Perrier water and takes me up to the guest room.

'Here's your room. Make yourself at home. Dinner will be at seven o'clock. Will you be OK on your own? Have a bath or shower and rest. There are a couple of fashion mags for you to read. Or have a snooze. See you later.'

I open the door. My room is better than a hotel: the cream carpet soft and sumptuous as I tiptoe on it. A basket of red apples, peaches, bananas and grapes is on the bedside locker. A tray with a kettle, a variety of teas, coffees, and bottles of water is by the side. A large cream-coloured double wardrobe with a matching cream dressing table faces the window and a pink velvet chair is tucked underneath. Crisp, white fluffy towels and various expensive facial creams are arranged neatly on the shelf. I breathe out. This is bliss. The bathroom is just as luxurious, with white units and a rainfall power shower. My toes touch the underfloor heated black granite tiles, and I pull off a white towel from the heated rail. I gawp at the name of the designer foam bath and shower cream. I didn't know Charlie was rich, which puts me at a disadvantage. What must she think when she visits our small house full of second-hand furniture? As the shower gushes over me, I reflect on what Charlie said about Matt. Shivers course over my skin thinking about him. I jump out, wrap myself in a warm towel and after a short doze, I wake and get dressed.

Strolling down the winding staircase, I approach the dining room and gaze in astonishment. The highly polished table is arranged with silver cutlery and matching crockery. This is different to our mismatched chipped plates and paper napkins. Maureen, the housekeeper, carries in our food: smoked salmon starter in tiny glass bowls with the hint of crème fresh and strands of dill. That vanishes in a mouthful and she carries in a rack of lamb with petit pois, Chantenay carrots and tiny Jersey new potatoes which glisten with melted butter. This food is delicious and I'm drowsy, half-listening as Charlie's father boasts how he's the only one from the O' Toole family to attend university. He is describing how he achieved the position of chief executive and Charlie raises her eyebrows as if she has heard it before. She stifles a yawn, and I gaze out the large window to the lake in the distance. It lures me with its gloomy, mysterious haze over the still water. Then I see her. She's floating towards me, hand outstretched. Her long gown drenched, weighing her down, slowing her movements. Green fronds of weed are wrapped around her hair. The stench of stagnant water invades my nose as she whispers, 'Find her, find her.'

'Sienna, am I boring you?' asks Brendan, staring at me.

I rub my eyes and turn to Charlie. 'What happened?'

'God, it was creepy. My dad was talking about work. Your eyes closed, and you twisted your head to one side as if you were listening. It was over in a couple of minutes.' She waves her hand in front of her face. 'It's hot in here – let's finish eating and wander around the grounds.'

'Yes, I need some fresh air,' I say, confused by the image.

With our plates removed, bowls of cherry chocolate torte and Chantilly cream are placed in front of us. We devour our dessert in silence, giving me the opportunity to stare again at the silvery expanse of the lake.

After finishing our meal, Charlie links my arm, and we wander into the garden. It's a balmy evening, and the fragrant perfume from the lilac flowers drifts towards me as the wind blows through the branches of the trees above us.

Back in my room, I sink into the downy feather duvet and watch as moonlight sparkles through the gap in the curtains. Glittery silver threads as fine as gossamer lace light up the room. Peacefulness sweeps over me until I hear the continuous whisper of, 'Watch out for the lilies.'

CHAPTER 6

A rough tongue licks my face.

'Yuck,' I say, wiping the foamy spittle from my cheek.

'Down, Alfie,' orders Charlie, as her energetic mutt tries unsuccessfully to leap on the bed, his legs scrabbling to get a grip on the silky sheets.

'You're dressed. Let me put some clothes on,' I say, walking into the bathroom. When I come out, the sun is shining in the room, bouncing off the enormous ornate gold-rimmed mirror. Charlie is standing there, with a bunch of sweet-smelling yellow roses for me.

'These are from the garden to say sorry for worrying you with those spells. I wish I could help you figure out the message behind the visions, and I blame myself for showing you those witchcraft magazines,' she says, thrusting the blooms into my hands. A flush of colour sweeps along her cheeks.

I bury my nose in the bouquet. 'Oh, they're gorgeous.'

The scent is heady and makes me lethargic. Charlie's voice is faint, muttering how the rose is a carrier of secrets and how the term 'sub rosa' originates from the Roman tradition of hanging wild flowers above meeting places. She's droning on about Aphrodite, the Greek goddess of beauty, wearing a circlet of these flowers around her head when it happens again: the rush of air and the tingling along my spine; the voice in my ear, whispering:

My wish came true, and they selected me to wear the long pearly white satin dress. The handmaidens carried bunches of sweet peas and lilies of the valley. The woody aroma of incense flooded my nostrils and my eyes stung from the candle smoke. My hands trembled when the shrill notes of the organ started. The distinct voices of the girls resonated throughout the high ceiling as we marched across the lawn. I closed my eyes and waited for the ring of flowers to be placed on my head. Instead, the sharpness of the thorns when that horrid girl pressed them on my scalp made me cry out. The crowd of girls screamed and placed a short red cape on my shoulders to cover the blood dripping from my head. They banished her to another room and she will hate me even more now. Her meanness is unforgivable. She smiled her wicked smile and passed a piece of paper to me. When I returned to the dormitory, I smoothed it free of creases. It was a section ripped out of the bible which read: 'Yea, they sacrificed their sons and their daughters unto devils.' Psalm 106:37.'

'Sienna, wake up.'

Someone is shaking me. I'm lying on the floor. Charlie is on her knees, her hand on my forehead, while her dad stands behind her. Through narrowed eyes, I see the hazy outline of a young girl. I blink, and the image evaporates, leaving behind droplets of clear, sparkling water.

'What's wrong?' she asks, raising a glass of water to my parched lips.

'The same thing happened to you when we chanted the spell,' I whisper.

'Yes,' says Brendan, joining in. 'We found out Charlotte is anaemic and you could be too. She took iron tablets and soon improved. Isn't that right?' He turns to Charlie.

'Mmm… How are you now?' Her cool hand strokes my forehead. 'What did you see?'

'A crowning of thorns,' I murmur and sit up.

Charlie stares at me. 'No way. Do you mean Jesus on the cross? This is too much. My gran is religious and might help. Come on. Let's see her.' She pulls me up.

Brendan smacks his hand on his head.

'Hang on, we've not had breakfast yet – I bet your blood sugar is low.'

'I'm fine, thank you.'

We enter the conservatory and Maureen carries in plates of bacon, fried eggs, sausages, beans, vine tomatoes, and soda bread. The food piled on the plate makes me queasy, and Charlie watches me as I nibble at the bacon. When she reaches over for more bread, I sneak the greasy meat to her dog, who is nuzzling my hand under the table. After the meal is over, her dad opens the patio doors and we make our way out.

The glint of morning sunlight shines on the water, highlighting a grassy area of land sitting in the middle. Brendan points towards it.

'Our special lake has an island which contains the ruins of Inisfallen Abbey. A group of monks lived there years ago, and they scribed the chronicle of events in medieval Ireland. One man began writing in 1090, and the other monks added to it. It recounts the story of St Patrick arriving here and is called the *Annals of Inisfallen.*'

'Dad, Sienna doesn't want you lecturing her about dreary old history.' Charlie yawns.

'No, it's fine. The lake of learning – sounds fascinating.'

'The Bodleian in Oxford holds the manuscript. Have you ever been?' asks Brendan.

'Not there, but Dad works in Oxford so we could travel in with him one day.'

'No way, boring. That's not my idea of fun. Now look what you've done, Dad, giving Sienna ideas. We're not history buffs like you,' she laughs and cuffs him playfully on his arm.

'Dear daughter, if you spent more time studying instead of doing your makeup and chatting up lads online, perhaps you might learn something.'

I gaze at the monastery ruins over on the island. The waves are lapping onto the shingle beach; the water looks bottomless and unwelcoming. A dark fogginess surrounds the mountains, making them appear fierce and hostile.

'Brr...' I shiver.

'Someone's treading on your grave,' giggles Charlie.

'Ooh, don't say that.' I rub my arms as tremors creep over my skin.

'Sorry, Sienna.'

'Did you know it's an old saying from centuries ago?' says Brendan.

'Here we go again with the history lesson.' Charlie looks at me and rolls her eyes.

I stare at the water in the distance and contemplate the lives of the monks – isolated from civilisation, living on the island in the lake. Men dressed in long brown tunics appear. They march in single file, hands clasped in prayer, and the chanting of voices rising melodiously echoes in my head.

Charlie and her dad are sauntering away from me, talking to each other, and haven't noticed the shimmering figures of monks. I follow my friend down the steps, away from the house and into a wooded area at the bottom of the garden.

The path leads us through the trees; fragrances of the garden surround me with hypnotic perfume of honeysuckle and the heady aroma of gardenia. Clumps of rhododendron bushes, their white petals drifting to the floor, as we brush against them are reminiscent of angel feathers. The chattering of the birds reminds me of children in the playground. I'm floating through paradise, while Common Blue butterflies and bees hover over the rose bushes. A path, edged with seashells and bleached rocks, leads us to a whitewashed cottage. Masses of roses, a variety of colours and perfumes mingling with each other, surround the garden. The fragrance from the various flowers is intoxicating.

'It's a fairy tale cottage,' I murmur.

'This is where my gran lives,' says Charlie.

As we approach, the tinkling of the wind chimes alerts Charlie's gran to our arrival. A diminutive lady strolls out with her eyes shaded by tinted glasses; she ambles towards us.

'Is she blind?' I whisper.

'No; migraine problems,' she whispers back. 'Hi, Gran. My friend from England is here and I've brought her to chat about magic with you.' She laughs and rushes over to kiss her.

I approach her gran. Rose is petite, her faded brown hair tied up in a bun, grey strands trailing over her face. Her skin is as white as milk; she's wearing a pair of cotton gardening gloves and removes them to shake my hand.

She grasps my hand and a jolt of electricity fizzes across my body. 'You possess it, too, my dear,' she exclaims. The crackle of blazing flames and the glow from the flash make me woozy. Acrid smoke permeates my nose and the stench of scorched flesh sickens me.

'We share the same gift,' she whispers, holding onto my arm as we enter her cottage.

Her living room is cosy with vases of colourful flowers dotted on the table and sideboard. Charlie and her dad carry on walking in front of us.

Pulling me back and taking my hand, Rose whispers to me.

'Use your gift of vision for selfless deeds and be vigilant. You suffer the torture of lost souls, but your sensitivity will be your salvation and your downfall. Beware of the evil encasing you, and protect yourself, my dear. Charlotte told me you were coming. She chatters endlessly about spells and your antics in school.' I smile across at my friend. 'Now describe the images and I'll try to help you with them.'

'Hush, Gran.' Charlie places her finger on her lips and gestures towards the kitchen. Luckily, her dad is making tea and the sound of boiling water drowns out my voice. While he's busy, we sit down and I recount my visions and the whisperings.

She studies me, her head on one side.

'Have you ever considered you could be a conduit, dear?'

This comment puzzles me, but before I can ask what she means, Brendan enters carrying a pot of tea and a plate of biscuits.

'Here's your favourite drink, Mam. I'll contact you after I've completed my paperwork. You'll be okay here, Sienna. You didn't eat your breakfast, so make sure you have a homemade shortbread biscuit.'

I relax back in the chintzy two-seater settee with Charlie by my side. Rose pours out the tea and hands me a cup.

'What's this?' I ask.

'Chamomile tea to settle the nerves. Sienna, a conduit, is a messenger possessing psychic energies. When a conduit enters a trance, it can appear frightening and look like they are having a mental or physical breakdown. You encounter light and dark but it is a lonely existence which needs channelling, so take care.' She closes her eyes and holds my hand.

'Carry out the search, but be careful of non-believers,' a voice whispers.

A fierce wind gushes in and a photo frame smashes on the floor.

Charlie cries out. 'What the heck was that? Gran, are you OK?'

she asks.

'Oh, my dear, yes, I'm fine. I saw a haze encircling Sienna. It drifted over her head. But now my energy is leaving me. It's no fun growing old.' She sinks back into the chair.

'Gran, you're only sixty-four.'

'Well, dear, sometimes I find it difficult to move about. Arthritis, the doctor said, but I told him my mind is younger than my body.' She laughs and looks at me. 'Sienna, will you return tomorrow?'

'Is that alright with you?' I look across at my friend.

'Yes, no problem.'

Rose takes a sip of tea and waves goodbye to us as we walk towards the door.

'Did you enjoy meeting my gran?' asks Charlie. 'I know we weren't there very long, but she seems exhausted after meeting you. What did you do to her?' She glares at me.

I study my friend as we walk up the path. There's a tightness in her eyes.

'Nothing! She's sweet and a lot younger than my grandmother. My nan is eighty and has Alzheimer's, and it's tiring when she repeats herself. The head nurse told my parents that it's worsening,' I say as we head back.

'What does she keep saying?'

'She gabbles on about school and my exam grades. She's paying the fees, which causes loads of problems between my parents.'

Charlie's mouth pulls down.

'Mmm, tricky.'

'The strangest thing, though, was showing her an old book and she screamed about lilies.'

'What?'

'Yeah, creepy, isn't it? Ever since she entered that care home, an eerie sensation floods over me when I'm there. It's like I'm being choked and can't breathe.'

'I bet your dad was mad when her eyes started bleeding. Wow, that's straight out of a horror film,' she laughs.

I'm annoyed she thinks it's funny.

'Yes, it was freaky at the time but it's a side effect of her medication,' I say, frowning at her.

We amble back and she chats about the lads at school, while I consider the idea that I'm a conduit. I have a sneaky suspicion Charlie isn't happy her grandmother paid me so much attention, but I hope I'm wrong.

'We'll go into the town centre to take your mind off things. My gran is a dear, but she blathers on and I sometimes wonder if she's losing it. She's always been interested in witches and fairies, which influenced me. I mean I love her to bits but it's a shame she doesn't see many people.'

'She must be lonely in the cottage when you're not here.'

'Rose hasn't been the same since my grandad died, but she attends a spiritualist church group which helps her. Anyway, there's no time for gloomy talk. We have the local town procession today and I wouldn't miss it for the world,' she says, with a sarcastic grin. 'Race you.'

After much puffing and panting, we arrive back in time to pick up our purses and bags. The path to Killarney town centre cuts through the park, but I can't concentrate while she's chatting away. I'm aware she's trying to distract me, which isn't working as thoughts of Rose dominate my mind.

We pass shops displaying Irish shawls, linen, and souvenirs. Music is blaring out from one of the many pubs. A one-legged man with a tin whistle is sitting on a wheelchair in the doorway, playing a jaunty tune. A crowd gathers as a parade of Irish dancers pass by. They're wearing colourful short dresses, white socks, black soft shoes, and they dance in unison, raising their legs higher to the beat of the music. The girls have masses of curly hair, black, blonde, and shades of red tied up with multi-coloured ribbons that bounce when they dance along the road.

'The design on their dresses and the shawls are amazing,' I say.

'Yes, they're patterns from *The Book of Kells.*'

'What's that?'

'It's a 9th-century manuscript and includes the four gospels about the life of Jesus Christ. The monks from Britain and Ireland wrote it in Latin and inscribed Celtic knots, animal figures and mystical creatures to illustrate the stories. Sienna, haven't you read up about Irish culture?' she says with a grin.

'Wow, have you been searching Wikipedia? Don't forget, this is the first time I've been to Ireland,' I reply.

'We studied Irish history at school when I lived here,' she says, linking arms with me.

We enter Skelly's coffee shop and find a seat at the back. Devouring chocolate chip muffins, drinking cappuccino, and chatting with my best friend is the ideal way to spend an afternoon. After stuffing ourselves and people watching, we amble back home.

'What's it like living in a tourist area?' I ask, passing traders selling postcards of the lake and piskie key rings.

'Dad was born here and only comes back to visit Gran, but soon loses interest. Same for me,' she says.

'Oh, I don't agree. This is a magical place.'

When we arrive home, nobody is in and her dad has left a message on the kitchen board about him going out.

'Hmm, as usual,' she says, opening the kitchen door. 'We won't bother eating in the dining room.'

'What do you mean, 'as usual'?' I ask.

'He's never around.'

'Same here. My dad's always working too and gets home late.'

She doesn't reply but sighs and walks over to the fridge.

'How did you end up in our village?' I ask.

'Mainly Dad's job and Gran had a premonition. Now, what have we got to eat? Oh no, Dad is on his health kick again and we've salads or more salads. I'm glad we ate those muffins,' she says, rummaging around in the large freezer and pulling out a cardboard box. 'Found a pizza and chips. Great. I'm starving. Shouldn't be long,' she says, opening the plastic wrapper and sticking the chips in the microwave.

'Charlie.'

'What?'

'Can Rose predict the future?'

'Told you she was special, didn't I?'

'Did she tell your dad to send you to my school?'

'Sort of. Dad's new job is in the centre of London, but he wanted us to live outside. We looked at Maidenhead, Henley-on-Thames, and Windsor. Gran suggested travelling further into the Cotswolds and told him to track down a body of water near a school. Said I would be happy there, and that's true since I've found you.' She laughs. 'We arrived at Lakeview, saw the lake in the distance, and that was it. Dad told me to try school out for the day and meeting you proves Gran was right.' The microwave pings and she opens the door.

'Charlie, that's amazing.'

I'm surprised at the coincidence and remember a black and white film I saw with Mum one rainy day called *Casablanca*. What were those words?

'Of all the gin joints in all the town in all the world she walks into mine,' I say.

'What was that?' Charlie asks, dishing up the food onto plates.

'It's from a film,' I say, cutting my pizza up in small pieces. 'Isn't it unusual we met? You could have attended a school anywhere.'

'Now you mention it, yes, it seems a coincidence. Don't you want that?' she asks, studying my plate. 'Hurry up eating those chips, coz I need my fix of ice-cream.'

We eat in silence. When we're done, Charlie loads the dishwasher and removes the ice-cream tub from the fridge while I ponder about Rose and our connection.

The landing creaks.

'Charlie, are we here on our own?'

'No. Maureen is probably tidying upstairs. Right, what do you want – strawberry or caramel crunch?'

'Crunch for me, please,' I say, nibbling at the crispy pizza crust lying on the plate.

'When you've finished, we'll chill in the television room and check out *Supernatural.* Who do you fancy, Sam or Dean? I bet it's Sam Winchester; he's the spitting image of Matt.'

'Charlie,' I giggle, slapping her arm.

'He's gorgeous, though – watch it,' she says, licking the ice-cream off her spoon.

'Why?'

'Another girl might nab him while you're busy playing with your spells.'

I stare at her.

'Only joking,' she shrieks, throwing the cushion at me as we settle down to view my favourite programme. 'He's the fit nerdy kind, not my type,' she says, grinning at me.

We settle down to the episode when Sam faces a vampire on his own, armed only with a garlic clove and crucifix. Charlie is texting, but I'm involved with the scene and waiting for the jump factor when she grabs the remote and ends the programme. I glare at her.

'I've had enough of this – I want to meet up with a few mates.'

'We haven't finished. It was just coming up to the scary part,' I say.

'You can watch it anytime on Catch-up.'

'What about your dad? Won't he be worried if we go out?'

'God, Sienna. Live a little.'

'I haven't anything decent to wear.' I look down at my ripped jeans.

'There's loads of stuff in my wardrobe you can borrow. Now, let's see what I'll wear. Yes, my black shorts, long socks, black corset and I'll finish it with my lacy long cardigan. Oh, my silver chains and I've got a great pair of black patent Louboutins.'

I haven't the foggiest idea what she's talking about and glance at the television.

'Christ, don't tell me you don't know what Louboutins are? You know the ones with the red heels?' She waves her hands at me as if in dismissal.

My eyes sting from her sarcasm. 'I – er – didn't realise we would go out at night.'

'I'm bored staying in and changed my mind. What size are you?' she asks, weighing me up and down.

'Never mind, I'll wear my black jeans. Can I borrow your skull T-shirt?' I ask.

'I guess,' she says as I traipse upstairs after her.

We pass a wall full of photographs, and I stop.

'Look at your gran on her wedding day. She's beautiful,' I say, admiring her large bouquet of white lilies and roses.

'Of course she is. Come on.' She brushes past it and dislodges the frame.

I put my hand out to straighten the photograph and as I touch it, a wave of sorrow overcomes me. The delicate stroke of fingertips grazes against my cheek and wipes away a tear.

'What's up now?' says Charlie, turning around to stare at me.

'Nothing. I'm not sure.' I shake my head to rid myself of the sensation of someone next to me. 'Just being silly. I – 'er – felt sad when I saw Rose's photo.'

'Well, don't tell her that, will you? She hasn't got over my grandad's death.'

As I trail after Charlie, the whispering follows me.

'Find her.'

CHAPTER 7

It's dark by the time we've showered and dressed. Charlie has ordered a taxi and the notification pops up on her phone as we are finishing our make-up.

'He's waiting outside. Here, drink this.' She passes me a shot glass of colourless fluid.

'What is it?'

'God's sake, neck it. It's no wonder you're always alone.'

'What did you say?' I take a sip and grimace at the sharpness of the liquid.

'Nothing.' She sneers at me. 'Your sweatshirt suits you.' In one gulp, her drink disappears, and I watch the dribble snaking down her chin. The taxi driver is beeping his horn as we dash downstairs.

'Where to, love?' he asks Charlie.

'Drop us in the centre,' she says, climbing into the car.

'What about getting back?' I ask, following her.

'Yeah, pick us up at midnight please.'

'Or you'll change into a pumpkin,' he says and laughs.

I slide into the seat, taking care not to cough at the amount of musky perfume radiating from Charlie. She's wearing her black outfit; sprayed blue dye on the ends of her dark hair, gelling it into sharp spikes. Smoky grey shadow coats her eyelids and dark plum lipstick smears her lips. Around her throat is a spiky silver necklace. Her arms jangle with bracelets and the silver nose ring is back in. I'm wearing my black jeans and a navy blue sweatshirt bought from our local market. She told me that her skull T-shirt needed washing and there was nothing else in my size. Every so often, I hear a huffing and a tutting coming from her.

'What's up? Do I annoy you?' I ask quietly, but she's not heard, or is ignoring me.

'Here you are. Have a good night, ladies,' he says, winking at Charlie.

'How much?' I ask, reaching for my purse.

'Sienna, it's OK. Dad has an account with this company.

'See ya later,' she says as he waves his hand and drives away.

'Where to now?' I ask.

'Nowhere. We'll hang around the town centre till something happens in this dead hole.'

'Oh, I thought we were going…'

'Going where?' she asks, stomping over towards the shops.

'Maybe a club or hang out with your friends?'

'A club. In those clothes? You look about twelve. Did your mum get them from the charity shop?'

I stare at her, but she laughs and grabs my arm.

'Joking. You should see your face,' she says.

We stroll towards the shops, which are closing their shutters, and flop on the park benches. Charlie reaches into her bag and pulls out a bottle of vodka.

'Here drink this; it will keep you warm.'

As she passes it over, a lad saunters towards us wearing dark trousers and a dark shirt with a lit cigarette in his hand.

'Hiya, Chas. Didn't notice you skulking back there,' he laughs. 'How long are you home for this time?'

'Not long. Give us a puff.' She snatches the cigarette off him. Takes a long draw and blows out a cloud of smoke.

'England OK?'

'Yeah. Oh, this is Sienna,' She coughs and points at me.

'Pleased to meet you,' he says, mimicking a posh accent.

I sip the cold liquid and stare at Charlie as ash drops from the end of the cigarette.

'What's going down?' she asks.

'Nothin' much. Same old. I'm on the door at the theatre,' he says, checking me out. 'Come in tonight. There's a geezer on telling the future or something.' He twists Charlie's wrist over to check her watch. 'Is that the time? Must dash. Catch you there?' he says and stubs the cigarette on the floor.

'Might do,' she says as he rushes off.

'Who was that?' I ask.

'Jack. He's the doorman at the Kenny Theatre and can sneak us in. It'll be a laugh.' She turns around, surveying the empty shopping centre. 'Yeah, we'll do that. Sometimes they have decent acts on.'

We stand up and follow Jack towards a small, red brick provincial theatre. Charlie pulls me down the side of the wall by the fire exit and we wait outside while she texts him.

'Right, in five minutes he'll open the fire door and we rush in before it shuts.' She swigs back the vodka and passes it over to me. I take a large gulp. This one hits the back of my throat and burns my stomach.

'Get ready. Now.' The heavy door opens and we hurtle into the darkness, stumbling over each other while a scaly finger touches my face.

'Ah! Get it off me,' I shout.

'Jeez, Sienna, it's only a cardboard cut-out. Careful of the boxes piled high with leaflets. This way.' She grabs my arm, steering me up a flight of steps leading to another door. 'This is the side entrance, so keep your head down and don't draw attention to yourself.' I look at her outfit and wonder if she's being sarcastic.

'It's nearly starting and there are loads of empty seats.' She points towards the back by the aisle. 'Grab those two, before anyone catches us.'

I glance around. 'Where is everyone?'

The lights dim as we stumble into the seats by the aisle steps. A woman in front of us tuts as we plonk ourselves down. She opens a family bag of chocolate limes with her teeth, making more noise than us.

'This is exciting,' says Charlie.

She grabs my arm. A hush sweeps over the audience. The lights dim and shadows swirl around the room. The music is faint and as the tempo increases, vapours of dry ice swirls from the back of the stage. A figure glides out. The haze evaporates and, as the music reaches its climax, the stage lights up and I recognise him: famous for his television programmes on haunted properties. His followers travel around the country to listen to his messages.

Antonio De Silva wears a sequin jacket that sparkles under the stage lights. His thick white hair is brushed off his tanned face, and his gleaming teeth stand out when he grins. He reminds me of a presenter from a television game show. Antonio greets us and recounts his story from rags-to-riches. He talks about his failed marriages, gambling addiction and his conversion to religion. I'm bored by his disclosures and wonder what will happen next.

'This is dull,' I whisper to Charlie.

'You're joking, aren't you? He's cool for an old guy. If there are questions at the end, tell him we're researching hauntings. He might pay us a visit.'

The woman in front turns around. 'Hush,' she mutters.

He describes when praying for guidance a presence in the form of wind swept over him. It was his spirit guide. When he mentions the word 'presence', I'm aware of his stare.

'The name of my spirit is Phoenix,' he proclaims, standing up and opening his arms wide.

'That means renewal,' I whisper to Charlie.

'Well, yeah, everyone knows that,' she says.

A screen lights up on the stage and a PowerPoint shows clips of celebrities discussing their spiritual encounters with him. I recognise several of them and am surprised at the admiration they have for the man. The music starts up again; the heavy velvet curtains swish shut, and the audience stands up.

'Is that it? I expected more to happen.'

'No, looks like the interval.'

'It can't be.'

'Why not?' Charlie laughs and points to the clock above the stage door.

An hour has passed while I've been concentrating on his backstory. We stagger into the foyer, blinded by the lights as people collect their drinks and discuss the show. There's a group huddled around the bar and I catch snatches of their conversation.

'I bet he won't turn up.'

'If he does, I'll be a believer for ever,' says another girl.

I grab hold of Charlie.

'Can we walk out? This show is making me uncomfortable,' I say.

'Isn't this your hobby – witches, spells, hauntings, whooo… whooo…?' she waves her hands and tries to imitate a menacing face. 'I'm off to the loo. See you in a minute,' she laughs and strides away.

The older women are having a cup of tea while a few younger

people are drinking and giggling at the bar. Someone touches my shoulder and I spin around expecting Charlie, but a young man clutches my arm. He's wearing a long, old-fashioned black velvet coat, the kind they wore in Victorian times. I imagine he's part of the show, selling programmes, but he stands next to me and grabs hold of my hand.

'I'm a fan of Antonio. If you read his website, you'll discover more about him and the charities he supports. However, he won't help you because his skills are for entertainment only. He gives people what they want. Your problem is too intense for him. If you want advice on the various levels of spirit worlds, I'm Paddy – at your service,' he says, bowing.

I pull away, but he drags me to one side. With his deep-set eyes analysing me, he says, 'Martha needs your help.'

'What?' I shout as he vanishes into the crowd. Charlie arrives back from the toilet and grabs my arm.

'Stop shouting, or they'll throw us out and I want to know what happens next.'

'I've met someone…'

'Shush,' she says, grabbing me as we rush back.

The lights dim and I check the crowd, hoping to catch Paddy. I can't concentrate on this show and want to ask about Martha, but the music plays and I slump in my seat.

'What's with the creepy music?' I nudge Charlie.

'Ssh. It's Dies Irae from Verdi. It's obvious you don't pay attention to classical music during school assembly.' She sniggers and pops a mint in her mouth. I try to think of a sarcastic reply, but then she holds out the packet.

'Peace offering?'

I smile at her, but she's staring at the stage and fiddling with her watch strap. As the music increases in tempo, I lick my dry lips, and my stomach tightens. She nudges me as a figure emerges from behind and stands in our row, staring at us. He carries on and marches up the few steps leading onto the stage, his long cape billowing behind him. With a dramatic flourish, he sweeps it off and in a booming voice, cries, *"Intra spiritus."* Antonio has changed out of his showtime silver jacket into black trousers and a polo neck jumper.

'It's Latin,' the person next to me mumbles to his partner.

'What does it mean?' I ask, swivelling around to face him.

'It means 'Enter, spirit' – he announces it each session,' the man whispers.

Next minute, Antonio's voice bellows out, echoing throughout the theatre.

'A male figure is by my side; searching for his sister. Yes, he's coming through.' Antonio peers into the audience. 'He wants me over here.' The medium points his finger and walks to the right of the theatre. The glaring lights shine over a group of young women.

'Does the name Lee or Leo mean anything to anyone?'

'It's my brother, Leroy,' a voice in the audience shouts.

'A quick sharp sting as darkness came and a dazzling glow encircled him,' he says, rubbing under his ribs. 'Yes, I'll tell her,' he whispers. 'At the end you held on to him when he passed and you sang his favourite song.'

I stare across at a tall girl, surrounded by her tearful friends.

'I played *Where is the love* by Black-Eyed Peas. My baby brother was fifteen.' Her voice is soft yet commanding and she holds a microphone the floor manager hands her.

'Yes, yes, I'm listening.' Antonio taps his ear as if someone is communicating with him. 'He's grateful for the care and support you gave. Wait. He recognises who stabbed him.' The medium peers across the audience at her. I prod Charlie.

'Shush,' she says.

'He's fading, but it was an accident. The lad didn't mean to do it, and Leroy doesn't blame him. Your grandparents are here now to take your brother.' Her friends huddle around, comforting her.

'One more thing. He says fix the latch on the back door. That's it, dear, his love is with you.'

Antonio mops the sweat glistening on his brow.

'What did he mean?' I ask Charlie.

She stares at me.

'I've read that one way of encouraging people to trust in a psychic reading is to mention something personal, like a dodgy latch. This strengthens the medium's credibility. There was a TV programme about debunking clairvoyants and their claims.'

'Is he fake?' I ask.

'Hush. He's coming back on.'

'Do we have an Edna in the audience today?' Several hands shoot up. 'I'm over here, yes, you love,' he says, gesturing towards my side of the theatre. 'An elderly gentleman is holding onto me.' Antonio coughs and grasps his side. 'Fluid is developing in his lungs and he can't breathe.'

The people in front of me twist around. I do the same and observe an old woman with short, grey, permed hair, wearing a beige jumper and brown skirt, and around her neck is a set of pearls. Her hand reaches up to the necklace and she strokes the pearls as the medium continues.

Edna is leaning forward and waiting for the message.

'He was glad you stayed with him at the end and pleased with the memorial arrangements, apart from the choice of music. He had left instructions in the pocket of his best suit for his favourite hymns.

Unfortunately you sent it to the dry cleaners.'

A couple of people snigger as the young man next to Edna tries to comfort her, but she pushes him away.

'Hang on, Jim. You're coming through.'

Edna stands up and dabs her eyes with a tissue. 'My husband's name is not Jim.'

Antonio cups his hand round his ear. 'Yes, I'll tell her.'

'Edna, love, his name was Robert James, but in the spirit world, he's called Jim,' he says, smiling at her. 'He's departing from us now, his strength is fading, but he has a message for you.' Antonio pauses. 'Your pearl bracelet is trapped between the runners in the chest of drawers.'

The medium's face has turned an unhealthy shade of grey. This show terrifies me. Even though I'm interested in the supernatural, this is chilling.

Charlie reaches for my hand as the medium strides towards us. The woman in front twists around and stares at me.

'I'm coming over,' he says, his hand cupping his ear.

I glance around in case one of his helpers is sending him messages through his earpiece. I wonder if he's choosing vulnerable people. I slump lower. There's a nervous tension in the air and I'm desperate to dash outside.

'I sense an affinity with water over here. Yes, you love,' Antonio says, pointing at Charlie.

Icy sparks of fear strike me as his position changes and his intense blue eyes hypnotise me.

'No, you.' He points at me.

My hand is shaking and I grab Charlie's.

'He means you,' Edna says, tapping me on the shoulder.

'A wide expanse of water is beckoning,' he announces.

An overweight woman in front stands up and blocks my view of Antonio.

'That's us. We've booked a cruise, haven't we, Bert?' she says, elbowing the man next to her and pulling him to his feet. He rubs his chin and glances at the exit.

'Right, love, yes,' says Antonio. 'It's your wedding anniversary and I'm being told you're suffering with health problems.'

The woman holds her husband's hand, and Antonio continues.

'Mavis is here with me, a bossy character; she has been trying to contact an Annie for ages. Is that you? She's adamant you need to…' He stops. 'I can't say that,' he says, twisting to his right-hand side.

'Carry on,' says Annie. 'If it's our Mavis, I don't mind. We say it like it is in our family.'

The woman laughs while the medium continues.

'Apologies, love, she's telling me you need to watch your weight.' He wipes his brow and studies her.

'That's my gran, alright,' squeals Annie.

'She doesn't want you to suffer from the same health issues that she had. I can see a table laden with food. Mavis is fading now and sends you this message. *Don't overeat on that cruise.*'

The woman wheezes as she plonks herself back down. A man at the side of the stage stands by the curtain touching his earpiece. He's staring at me and nods to Antonio.

'Ladies and gentlemen, thank you for your attendance at my show. We need silence while another spirit tries to contact me.' The audience quietens and the stage lights flicker.

'A young girl is standing by my side. She passed over many years ago and the connection is faint. Yes, I'll tell her,' he says as he turns towards me.

A sharp flash of red flame blinds me, stinging my eyes as a golden aura emanates from him. His features fade into an unrecognisable blur. Charlie grips my arm. My body floods with heat as Antonio points at me and in a girl's voice, he whispers.

'Why did she do it?'

I stare at him, eager to know more. Behind me, Edna pokes my back.

'Stand up,' she orders.

His voice continues.

'Listen to the flapping of ravens' wings beating against the windows. The sap from the lilies blinded her eyes.'

'What the hell is he saying?' Charlie whispers.

'No idea,' I reply, gripping her hand and standing up. 'Although Nan Ria has mentioned weird things about lilies.'

In a normal voice, he says, 'The spirit is holding out a rose and wants you to find her, but she's fading.'

Antonio grips his left arm, rubs his chest and drops to the floor, screaming, 'Too hot, too hot, it's burning me!'

The next minute, the curtains crash together. People nudge each other and laugh, believing it's part of the act. The manager stands on the stage and announces Antonio has collapsed and the show is over. The audience is muttering about refunds.

'Quick, we need to move now or they'll be on to us.'

'What happened?' I ask.

Charlie drags me out of the seat, and I stand up and follow her towards the exit. People are milling around and pushing me in their rush to get out. My head whirs with images of ravens and lilies, reminding me of Monkton House.

CHAPTER 8

The crowds surround us, and one woman jabs her elbow into my ribs, her face twisted with fury.

'You've ruined it now. I've been waiting for my Nigel to materialise!' she screams and prods her finger in my chest.

'It's not my fault,' I whimper.

'What the hell, Paddy? What are you doing here?' Charlie whips around to face him.

'This way.' He grabs my hand and pushes me through the fire doors.

'I could ask the same question. What brings *you* here?' He grins at Charlie. 'And you're dressed for the occasion. How come you're together?' he asks, staring at me.

'Sienna, meet Paddy Flanagan.' She gestures towards him. 'Paddy. This is Sienna from England.'

He stands with one hand on his hip, scrutinising me.

Charlie watches us. 'Enough of the intros. Let's go before the crowd follows us. God, that was a laugh, wasn't it?'

'This way,' he says, pulling us away from the theatre.

'Where are we going?' I ask him.

'A party. Haven't you guessed by the way she's dressed?' He nods his head towards Charlie.

She's sipping from the vodka bottle and grins at me.

'Are you coming?' he asks.

'Only if you explain what you meant when you warned me about Martha needing my help.'

'Later,' he murmurs.

'Sienna, Paddy boasts he's the seventh son of a seventh son, making him psychic. Am I right?'

'Of course,' he says, and with a sweeping movement, removes his black velvet top hat and bows.

'But don't believe that nonsense. He hangs out at theatres. Which is why he's wearing that ridiculous outfit,' she says, pointing to him. He's removed his black velvet coat to reveal dark trousers, tucked into black army boots, a white frilly shirt and a black frock jacket with silver buttons. Underneath the jacket is an embossed satin waistcoat and tucked into his pocket is a silver fob watch and chain. This gothic punk outfit suits him with his skinny body and pale face.

'Last year he went through a phase of dressing similar to what's his name, the English gent?' she says to me.

'Er, I'm not sure.'

'*You* can talk, my dear Charlotte. It's important to keep up one's appearance and get noticed by my fellow thespians. The character was from Downton Abbey. I wore a three-piece tweed suit, with a waistcoat, watch, spats and straw boater and the obligatory silver-topped walking cane. I buy my clothes from the vintage clothes shop off Davern Alley in Dublin. Ever been there?' he asks me.

'No, this is the first time I've been to Ireland.'

'I hope you enjoy your time here,' he says, and turning to Charlie, asks, 'You know the way?'

He gestures towards a side street where a hint of desperation surrounds the rundown area. Scaffolding covers the ramshackle terraced houses. The whiff of cat's piss and fried onions pollutes the air. Heaps of black plastic bags pile up in the corner from which half-eaten burgers and chips spill out. Empty cans of lager stand in rows, and shards of broken wine bottles litter the pavement. Petrol fumes and the heat of rubber tyres mix with cooking oil from the cafes.

'Where are we?' I whisper to Charlie.

'Right, nearly there,' says Paddy, disappearing into an open front door.

'Stop worrying. This is where the kids hang out,' she says and scowls at me. 'You'll ruin everything.'

The drumming of music booms out. A couple of young lads are outside, leaning against the wall with bottles of lager in their hands.

'Chaz! Hiya, babe. When did you fly back?'

'Hiya, Alex. How's school?'

'Same old, same old,' he says, studying me. 'And who's this?'

'This is Sienna from England. She goes to my school.'

Goes to her school. What a cheek – I was there first and I'm surprised she didn't introduce me as her best friend.

'Come on, time for a drink,' Charlie says pushing through the open door.

The linoleum sticks to my shoes as we ascend the creaky stairs. There's an oily, woody aroma coming from a group of boys who are leaning against the banister and smoking.

'Hiya, Chaz,' says a girl, strolling out of a room off the landing. 'Come with me, did you hear about…'

Charlie grabs her arm and walks off with her while I'm left on my own. The room is lit by candles in jam jars dotted around the place and a table at the side is loaded with bottles of lager and wine. As I'm wondering what to drink, Paddy strolls towards me.

'You need to avenge her,' he murmurs and places his hand on my arm.

I yank my arm away from him but my heart is pounding and as I lick my dry lips, her voice sighs in my ear, *'Stay.'*

Paddy holds my hand and leads me through a dingy narrow passageway covered with faded carpet. We pass an alcove containing a mop and bucket and cleaning fluids which leads into the kitchen. Over the sink and attached to the wall is an old-fashioned water heater with soggy tea bags strewn on the draining board, and more bottles of lager. This place is a mess. I stare at his gaunt face. Greasy hair tied back in a straggly ponytail, bushy eyebrows, and colourless eyes that seem translucent, set against alabaster skin. He places his hand on the small of my back and pushes me through the tiny kitchen into an empty room.

'Ow, stop that. Where the hell am I?' I ask.

'Here, Sienna,' he says, pointing to a cracked leather settee. As I sit, the springs dig into my back and I move around to get comfy.

Paddy straddles a chair opposite me, and grasping my hand, caresses my palm. His face is pale and the black eyeliner around the bottom eyelid has smudged. His nails are varnished a dark plum colour. When he closes his eyes, I try to extract my hand, but he holds on tighter. This is dangerous and I want to escape, yet I'm trapped. A sense of nervousness creeps over me and I scour the room for an escape route.

'Sienna, pay attention. The flames of destruction surround you while the perfume of a hundred roses suffocate and poison your aura. The thorns pierce your throat. Martha is trying to communicate, but your resistance is strong. Will you undertake your quest?'

I gasp. 'What the hell are you saying?'

'Martha won't rest until you find the girl who destroyed her.'

Paddy collapses forward onto me. His hand catches on my arm and his sharp nails scratch my skin. I push him away and close my eyes as a montage of scenes flash in front of me, pictures of a winding, gloomy tunnel and figures gliding to their fate, crying babies wrenched from their mothers. I'm part of the scene; suffocating with grief as desolation clutches at my heart. The images are blurry. The sorrow of lost souls drifts into my mind; the aura of misery surrounds me. Incense and candle fumes waft around the room. I'm spellbound by the syrupy perfume of lilies as girls sit on the stone floor, chanting invocations, while a cloud of ash floats towards them. The ravens caw and smash at windows with their sharp beaks.

Paddy breathes out a high-pitched wail. Hammering in my ears wakens me.

I gasp and open my eyes. 'What the hell are you saying?'

'Martha won't rest until you find the girl who destroyed her.'

'Sienna, it's me. Open the door,' screams Charlie, bursting into the room.

I open my eyes. Paddy slumps in his chair. Beads of sweat coat his face and he sits up straight. He stares at me.

'You possess the gift of sight,' he says, 'but you must protect yourself from those who mean you harm. You need to buy white sage, burn it, and waft the smoke into the corners of your room.'

I look across at the doorway. Charlie is leaning against the door with her mouth open.

'Run a cool salt bath, scrub your body and dress in freshly washed white clothes,' he says.

'God sakes, Paddy, what are you on this time?' she asks.

'You should guard yourself against evil by introducing these gems into your home.' He pulls out a plastic bag from his pocket and unties it. 'Place these red jasper stones under your pillow and you will gain strength and spiritual grounding from their properties.' He holds me tight.

'Get off her!' yells Charlie.

'A terrible deed took place there. Martha has chosen you,' he whispers.

'Who is Martha?' I ask. 'Is she the one from my visions?'

'You need to reflect on the message and walk the path of understanding.'

'What should I do about these images? Nobody believes me.'

Paddy bends down and whispers in my ear. 'Find her and they will.'

The nagging doubt deep in my stomach is making me uneasy. Why me?

'Jeez, Paddy, which play are you rehearsing this time? Macbeth?' laughs Charlie. 'Ignore him. My friend Patrick Flanagan, or Paddy to his friends, is a drama student hoping to make a career as an actor. It's fun trying to second guess which character he'll be next. Try someone else, Paddy. Your acting didn't fool Sienna. Time to grab a drink. Come on,' she says, pulling me by the arm out of the room.

Charlie is the centre of attention. The crowd swarm up to her, enabling me to study her behaviour around these friends. The girls are patting her hair, admiring her clothes, giggling and studying me. At one point, she replies to a comment with a shrill laugh, glares at me, and grabs the arm of the girl next to her. Jack, the guy from the theatre, slumps next to me, holding a bottle of lager.

'Here, take a sip of this.'

'Thanks,' I say, taking it off him.

'What did you think of the performance? Glad you sneaked in?'

'I'm not sure but it's incredible he communicates with spirits.'

'Yes, he's famous around this part of the world. Is this your first time at a medium show?'

I nod at him, unsure why he's asking me.

'Have you ever seen a ghost?' he continues.

'Well, I…'

'I guessed you were on the same wavelength with them lot in the show,' he says, staring at me. 'It's odd how you're not like Charlie's usual friends, though.'

'What do you mean?' I ask, standing my bottle on the floor.

'Oh, whenever Charlie goes to a different school, she makes a new friend and invites her back here. You're different. What's the word I'm looking for?' He scratches his head, gulps his drink and burps. 'Sorry,' he laughs, wiping his mouth. 'Could be introvert or introspective. Have to get the dictionary down from the attic.' He laughs again and coughs.

I stand up, but he drags me down.

'Yes, you're quieter than the others. She's usually attracted to the outgoing type, similar to her,' he says. 'Our Charlie is getting a reputation here for running wild, so you might be what she needs. Her parents can't control her and I wouldn't want a nice girl like you following in her footsteps,' he says, brushing a curl off my face. I bat his hand away, exposing my birthmark.

'God, Jack, leave her alone. Sienna, get up.'

I stand up, but topple down again. Jack's face is blurry, the noise is deafening; Charlie is coming over towards me and shouting. I try to stand again and slump against her.

'What did you give me?' I ask him.

'A little something to help you chill.'

'Clear off. She doesn't do that, you fool. Sienna, we're going outside.' Heaving me up, she places an arm around my shoulders and drags me down the stairs and out of the door. When the fresh air hits me, I stumble and collapse on the concrete.

'Go away, I want to sleep.'

'Get up, the taxi is coming.' She hauls me up and hisses, 'Keep your mouth shut to Dad about this or he'll stop me going out.'

The car arrives, and I tumble into it. Charlie is chatting with the driver but my head is whizzing – the sky is black and the stars are cascading onto me.

'I feel, I feel…'

'Hold it in, we're nearly there,' says the driver. 'It'll be an extra charge if you're sick in my cab.'

'Drop us at the side gate,' says Charlie.

As soon as we stop, I tumble out onto the grass verge. I rest my head against the dampness of the grass and lie still. Then a wave surges up from my stomach and I'm sick everywhere.

Charlie stands over me. When I've finished, she places her arm around me and we enter the side door.

'Lucky for you, Dad is still out,' she says, dragging me into the kitchen.

'What did Jack give me?' I ask as she pours me a glass of water.

'Could be anything, but it's my fault. You're not a party girl and I should have told you to get your own drinks. Go to bed and try to sleep,' she says, pushing me up the stairs to the bedroom.

I flop on the bed, fully clothed. My head is spinning. Now I know who is pursuing me.

Martha.

CHAPTER 9

The light shining through the thin muslin curtain exacerbates my headache. The dog bounds into the room, his tail wagging, and his tongue dribbling with saliva, ready to lick me. Charlie is following behind him and yells, 'Wake up, sleepy head – breakfast first, then Gran wants to see us.'

I yawn and put my hands over my eyes. 'Stop shouting. I feel sick and my mouth is dry. How are you?'

'Me? I'm fine. Why?'

'Did Jack spike my drink?'

'What are you talking about? You had too much vodka and lager and shouldn't mix your drinks.' She stands over me, blocking out the light.

'I don't normally drink and my head is pounding.'

'That's the problem. You're not used to it. Here, have this. You'll be better soon.' She passes me a glass of water.

I sit up and blink at the brilliant light dazzling through the window. 'Staying here is so…'

'Boring?'

'No, peaceful and spiritual. Look at the lake.' I gesture to the window. 'The rolling of the waves is hypnotic.'

'Get a move on, dreamy head; breakfast is waiting downstairs.'

She walks out with Alfie at her heel.

I throw back the covers, but that makes me dizzy, so I open the window and breathe in the sweet air. Then a voice whispers, '*Watch out for the lilies.*'

Nan's face, with her bloody tears rolling down her cheeks, comes to mind. I'm about to check up on her when Charlie shouts.

'Hurry up, Sienna, I'm starving.'

My head is killing me and my throat is raw but I manage to stagger downstairs. Once again, there's a massive spread on the table and the prospect of eating gooey yellow egg yolks makes me retch. I turn away, wipe my mouth with a tissue and using my fork spread the food around on my plate to make it appear I've eaten. Where's her dog when I need him?

Charlie hasn't noticed what I'm doing and is chatting about Rose. She's eager to meet her again, and I want to learn more about the gift of sight; of seeing dead people.

'Can't believe the weekend is over. Thanks for inviting me, Charlie. Otherwise, I'd be mooching around with my sister, annoying me.'

'It was only a quick break but I'm glad you came coz you're my sister now,' she says, linking arms. 'Let's go. Gran is waiting for us.'

We stroll down the path. With the blazing sun heating the air, the perfume from the flowers is stronger than yesterday. The colours are more intense. The sky is a dazzling aquamarine blue. The intensity of the sun stings my eyes. Rose is resting on a garden chair, wearing a pale green cotton dress belted at the waist with a purple cord. She stands up and brushes dust off her clothes. Her large straw sombrero has tassels that swing when she fans herself with a piece of paper.

'Gran, you've kept the hat we bought you from Majorca,' laughs Charlie.

'This weather doesn't suit me. I bet you're the same with your complexion, aren't you, Sienna?'

I study her. She possesses a calmness and an inner light as if I've known her for years.

'I've been busy since yesterday,' she says as we follow her into the cottage. The contrast is immediate; the room is darker and cooler. Yesterday, I hadn't noticed the number of documents and paper piled on the floor, waiting for me to trip over them. The shelves bow from their weight, ready to collapse.

'I'm writing a book,' she says, pointing to a pile of pages scattered on the floor. 'I'm in the middle of research about Irish folklore. Here, pull up a pew, I've made gallons of fresh lemon water.' On the round table is a jug of ice-cold water filled with ice cubes and slices of lemon. A sense of anticipation creeps over me. She pours us a drink, opens the side window, and shuts the curtains.

'That nice weather forecaster off the telly says it will be hotter this afternoon and you're leaving later, aren't you, dear?' she asks me.

'Gran, what's this?' Charlie examines the top of the sideboard. Yesterday it held a few photograph frames, vases of roses and a bowl of fruit. They've gone and different-sized boxes are piled on top of each other. I stand up and wander over to them.

'No, don't move them, my dear,' she says to me. 'My power is sending me a message.' I glance at Charlie, who raises her eyebrows, and picks off her black nail varnish. 'Stop that, you'll ruin your nails.' Rose turns to me. 'After you left yesterday, Sienna, a force struck me and I needed to lie down.'

'Gran.' Charlie reaches out towards her.

'I'm fine, dear, don't worry, but a voice told me to search everywhere. Hunting through cupboards exhausted me, so I crawled into bed and dreamt of tipping boxes up and rummaging through them. It came to me in my dream. Why did I overlook it? It was a message.'

'Gran, what do you mean?' asks Charlie putting her arms around her.

'Don't you worry about me, dear. I found it,' she says, waving her hands at the boxes on top of the sideboard. 'I was filthy and changed into this old dress,' she says, brushing her hands over the cotton fabric.

'You didn't climb into the attic, did you? Dad will be mad.'

'We won't say a word will we, dear? Lips shut,' she says, making a zipping gesture over her mouth. 'Right, it's here somewhere.'

'What is, Gran?' asks Charlie.

'I'll help if I know what we're searching for,' I say.

'In my dream a young girl came to me and told me to find the answer.'

'What's the question?' I ask.

'Will she?' says Rose.

Charlie stares from me, then to her gran. 'I'm going to get Dad.'

'No, you don't need to involve him. The message was, *Will she?*'

'It makes no sense, Gran. Will she *what?*'

'The girl said, "Will she help me?" then I woke up.'

Charlie raises her eyebrows at me.

'I saw that, young lady. Now, let's discover what's in these boxes.'

'What are they?' I ask.

'School books, papers and clothes, from my childhood. My parents stuck them away in their loft and when they died, I ended up with them. I forgot about them until now. I'll make us a cup of chamomile tea and we'll start.'

'We'll do it,' says Charlie.

We struggle to lift the first box off the sideboard and dump it on the floor. How she managed to carry the heavy boxes from the attic surprises me. Sitting on the floor, we open the cardboard flaps and pull out an old folder overflowing with paper.

'Here are your report cards. Ha ha, read this.'

'St Peter's Catholic school. Rose O'Toole has the potential to excel when she pays attention.'

'I remember that teacher. She didn't possess an exciting bone in her body. Mind you, I *was* a daydreamer. Let's have a gander. What else is there?' she asks.

'Old teenage magazines.'

'Wow, the *Jackie Annual*,' laughs Rose. 'And the *Bunty*. My collection of *Enid Blyton, Malory Towers* – you must read them. I'm surprised my mother saved those.' She unfolds a large piece of paper. 'It's my poster from my bedroom wall.'

'Who's that?' I ask, examining a picture of a young man with shiny black hair.

'Aw, look at that quiff. You don't recognise old swivel hips? It's Elvis, my heartthrob.'

'Are these posters worth anything? We could sell them on eBay.'

'You're joking. I'm not giving these away. Memories of my youth.' She rummages through the box. 'That's a shame. It's not in here.'

'What are you searching for?' I ask.

'Something I had forgotten about for years.'

'What's in this box?' Charlie reaches out and drags the next one onto the floor.

The second box is full of clothes. Rose examines a child's white satin dress and strokes the fabric rosebuds sewed onto the collar. 'My mother made it for my First Holy Communion. It's yellowed with age. Fancy saving it.'

'What's this?' I pick up a green and black dress adorned with Celtic symbols.

'It's my Irish dancing costume. When I was younger, I entered dancing competitions and won loads of medals.' Rose peers into the box. 'Oh, great, they're still there.'

I stroke the raised embroidery on the dress and turn to Charlie.

'Those girls in the procession wore similar ones.' She grabs it and holds the dress up against her. The colour suits her with her pale skin and dark hair. 'Don't you dance?' I ask.

'That's a sore subject,' she says, putting it back before her gran notices. 'My mum isn't Irish and didn't want me to learn.'

Rose hasn't heard us and pulls out another dress. 'Do you like this? It's a mini dress from my teenage years.'

The colours are vivid, psychedelic greens and oranges with circles and swirling patterns, making my hangover worse.

'Did girls really wear these fluorescent colours in your day?' I stare down at my uniform of jeans and sweatshirt.

'I wore it to the youth club where I met Charlotte's granddad.' She sniffs and pats Charlie's hand. 'I want you to keep it, for the fancy-dress 60s night you told me about.'

'I've forgotten about the end-of-school dance.' I look at Rose. 'What should I wear?'

'Anything bright, or black and white. Can your mum sew?'

'You're joking, aren't you?' I laugh. 'Mind you, she volunteers at the charity shop and can keep an eye out for me. Don't think I'll find an original one like this though,' I say, stroking the silky material.

Rose removes a flat box packed with white tissue paper and holds up a christening gown.

'I wondered where this was and searched throughout the cottage, but forgot it was in the attic. You should have worn this for your baptism, Charlotte, instead of paying an exorbitant amount of money for the exclusive gown from Dublin.'

'Hey, what do you mean? I've photos of me looking cute in the expensive one. Anyway, this is a bit…' She turns towards me, holding her nose.

I'm not sure her gran saw that gesture, but I'm aware of tension increasing between them.

'Look, there's a photo album in the box.' I pull it out and show them. We pore over the pages and discover a photo of her lying on a sheepskin rug.

'Aww, Gran, you were adorable. What happened?'

'Cheeky. Less of that, young lady,' laughs Rose.

There are more childhood photos gathered with an elastic band.

'Here's one wearing your Irish dress and dancing in a competition. I'm surprised these photos aren't on your shelves,' I say.

'There's enough scattered around the room gathering dust.'

I touch a flat object, wrapped in a shabby baby blanket, at the same time as Rose, and hear a cry.

'Ow, it hurts. Help me. The pain burns like a knife slicing through my skin. I can't bear it anymore. My baby is coming. Pull it out.'

We yank our hands away.

'What did you see, child? Tell me.' Rose stares at me, her forehead wrinkling in a frown.

'Oh my god, it was painful. Someone having a baby,' I cry, clutching at my stomach as the rhythmic pangs decrease.

'Gran, should we carry on with this? I mean, check out Sienna's face.'

'I'm fine now. It was just a shock,' I say, rubbing my stomach.

'You experienced that from handling an old blanket?' asks Charlie.

'Do you want to continue, dear?' Rose asks me. 'Is this too upsetting for you?'

'I'm okay now.' The discomfort has passed.

Rose opens the blanket to reveal an old tatty leather book, jammed full of paper. 'Found it. I'm glad they didn't throw it away.'

'What is it?' asks Charlie.

The book has ornate brass fastenings with hinges attached to the side, and is bound by two narrow leather straps and rusted buckles. The faded cover is inscribed with a decorative border of lilies and feathers, but water damage has curled and gummed the pages stuck. The handwriting is large, scrawling and difficult to read.

'Come over to the kitchen table and we'll figure out what it says.' Rose opens the pages, taking care not to rip the delicate paper.

'This looks interesting,' I say to Charlie.

'I wasn't aware my mother was saving these.' She waves her hand at the boxes. 'But I remember glancing at this book once. Didn't think to ask her what it was. It's only since you came into my life, Sienna, that the urge to find it became stronger.'

Charlie is glaring at me and I wish her gran would say something positive to her instead of addressing me.

'I want you and Sienna to take it.'

'Why, Gran? What's the real reason you want us to keep it?' asks Charlie.

'One of you needs to investigate who left it amongst my keepsakes.'

'Surely it belonged to your parents?' asks Charlie.

'No, it's not their handwriting.'

'Did you ever ask them about it?'

'Yes, but we couldn't open the pages and gave up.'

'What are you nattering on about, Gran? Do you want a lie down?'

'Charlotte O' Toole, there's no need to use that tone. I'm not senile,' she says, wagging a finger at her. 'Before I married, my parents wanted me to keep this book. However, being busy with my wedding preparations, it went out of my head. It's since meeting Sienna and having the dream I've realised it's important,' she says, smiling at me. 'My parents never spoke of it again, but this could be a clue.' She points to a dried flower.

'What, Gran?'

'The flower on the front page,' says Rose. She opens the cover and carefully separates the first page.

A piece of dried tape holds a withered flower down on the paper, its petals disintegrating.

'When I first saw this book, I looked in the family encyclopaedia, but there was nothing about the flower. I gave up, and it went clear out of my mind,' says Rose.

'Sienna, Google it on your phone and I bet it will pop up straight away.'

I pull out my mobile from my jeans pocket and search for white flowers. Loads appear as we scan through the websites.

'Maybe it's a weed, Gran,' says Charlie.

'Rose, I've compared the flower to the ones on the website and it says it's cow parsley which is often mistaken for poisonous hemlock.'

'Are you sure? Here, let me see,' she says, putting on her glasses.

'Mmm… it says the hemlock plant cause blisters and long-term blindness if the sap gets into a person's eyes. Best be on the safe side and not handle them.'

'There are loads of them growing wild, near our school, and in the woods,' I say. 'They're common,' I whisper to Charlie.

'I heard that, Sienna – are you saying there's nothing special about it?'

'Gran, it's not as unique as you thought. It's impossible to discover the owner of the book by tracing the origins of the flower. It could grow anywhere in the United Kingdom.'

'Oh,' says Rose.

I pity her as she slumps into the chair.

'Why did I even consider I could find it?' she says.

'Why are you so upset about it? You've never mentioned it before. You keep it, Gran, it might disintegrate if we open it.'

'I don't want it here, Charlotte. You take it. Discover where the flowers grow and I'll know who gave it to my parents,' she says, handing her the book. 'They might still be alive and reveal stories about their childhood and growing up. I'm interested in those kinds of things.'

'They would be ancient now,' says Charlie.

'Cheeky.' Her gran laughs.

'Did you ever question your parents?' I ask.

'To be honest, Sienna, no. My parents were older than my friends' parents. I'm ashamed to say I didn't ask them anything about their life and it's horrible to admit this, but they embarrassed me. They were lovely, but old-fashioned, and it took them ages to modernise. You see the 60s mini dress? Even though my mum made it for me, Dad thought it too revealing, so I only wore it once at the youth club. Mind you, your grandad whistled when he saw me in it. Bless his soul. I thought my old school things had been thrown away.'

I want to examine it further, but Charlie sticks it in her bag. Rose slumps on the kitchen table with her head in her hands.

'Do you want a cup of tea?' I ask her.

'No, I'm fine, darling. It's a shock finding out it could be a weed. Can you investigate why the book is amongst my things?' she asks.

'Gran, Sienna needs to catch the afternoon plane so I'm not going to have time to help you tidy up here.'

'What are you doing after that?' she asks.

'Remember, Dad and I are meeting Mum in Paris,' says Charlie, biting her nails. 'Are you going to be alright here on your own? Don't climb in the attic again and wait for Dad to put the boxes back.'

'Ah, I'll be fine, you enjoy yourself.' Rose stands up. 'Sienna, I'm so happy you came. We'll meet again and discuss potions and spells.' She laughs as she squeezes me and Charlie.

'I'd love that,' I say, holding her close.

I open the front door.

'You'll need your sunglasses, Charlie, it's boiling out here,' I say as the warmth seeps through my body after the coolness of the cottage. 'Hey, I want to adopt Rose as my own,' I laugh, twisting back to wave at her gran standing in the doorway.

'That was a surprise. Gran has never talked to me about her life before you came,' says Charlie, scowling.

'Well, I suppose opening the boxes brought back memories.'

'Hurry up. We've been ages.' She storms off and we rush back. Brendan is waiting with his jacket on and picks up his car keys.

'You're late. Are you ready?'

We jump into the hire car and retrace our journey. This time, we have a quick stop for petrol and drive through the town of Cashel. I shudder as the church looms over the town, remembering the vision. As Brendan is paying at the petrol station, Charlie opens her bag and removes her gran's book.

'You keep this, Sienna,' she says, handing it to me.

'Why me? Surely it's yours?'

'You want it more than me, don't you?' she replies, and grins.

'Are you positive? Thank you. I'll take care of it. Listen, are we cool?' I ask, holding her arm. 'I get the impression you aren't happy with me being friendly with your gran?'

'Nah, don't be silly. It's my problem. I'm the jealous kind,' she says, reaching out and twisting a curl away from my eyes.

It's late afternoon by the time we arrive at Dublin airport. Their flight to Paris is two hours after mine, so after saying goodbye, I board the plane. I reflect on my time in Ireland, with the medium show and Paddy. Charlie's changing moods bother me. I rest my head against the headrest and close my eyes, thinking about Rose and our shared psychic ability.

The important task now is to discover who gave her a tatty ancient leather book wrapped in a baby's blanket.

CHAPTER 10

My parents pick me up from the airport. As we travel back, they bombard me with questions about Ireland and Charlie's family. I make out it was fun but don't go into detail about the medium show or what happened after.

'You look peaky, love. I hope you've been eating?' asks Mum.

'Yes,' I reply and settle down to enjoy the view.

Two hours later, we approach Lakeview. It reminds me of a Constable landscape with cows lying in the fields and the river meandering through the forest. A sense of happiness washes over me when I spot the distinctive church steeple rising in the distance. Seeing the familiar landmarks of vast country estates, houses and cottages of my village relaxes me. When we arrive home, Mum enters the kitchen and I go to my room.

'Hiya, Sienna,' shouts my sister over the pounding of the treadmill in her bedroom.

It's a relief to be home. I hadn't realised how intense Charlie could be. Meeting Rose was fun but I'm wondering what my friend is playing at. Whenever her gran spoke to me, she sighed or tutted and I'm not happy about her ignoring me at the party.

I go to my room, all the time thinking about Rose and Charlie. To take my mind off them, I pull some books out of the shelves. One of them is the book which triggered Nan's anxiety, *The History of Lakeview Village* written by Anne Duncan. The cover shows a black-and-white photograph of a group of girls standing on a lawn with the shadow of a house in the background. Older women, dressed in black, stand behind the girls, their hands on their shoulders, their stern faces staring at the camera. Heading the group is a tall, imposing woman, and, in her hands, she's clasping a large folder with a set of keys tied around her waist. One girl in the middle is wearing a circlet of flowers on her head, the whiteness of her dress contrasting with the sombre colours.

As I'm reading, the room temperature drops, and prickles trace a path from my feet through my legs, inching up my body. There's a cold breeze wafting in through the window so I stand on my bed to shut it.

'Sienna, be careful!' cries Mum, entering the room with a mug of tea and a cheese and pickle sandwich.

Her cry startles me and I topple backwards, knocking my books off the bed. Stooping to pick them up, a blinding pain shoots across my head.

'Mum, Mum!' I scream.

'What's going on? Are you all right, Sienna?' asks Dad, following Mum. Next minute, Bella storms in.

'Shut up. I'm trying to read. It's been quiet while you've been away.'

'My head hurts,' I cry and flop on the bed.

'I'll fetch you a paracetamol from the bathroom; it's probably jet lag,' says Mum.

'Jet lag!' laughs Dad. 'Where have you been again – Australia or living it up in Ireland?'

I shoot a grateful glance at my mother as they walk out. She returns, hands me a paracetamol and a glass of water, and I lie down.

As I examine the front cover of *The History of Lakeview Village*, the pounding in my head shifts to my eyes. Pinpricks of light dance in front of me, and the dense perfume of lilies with its sweet, cloying aroma surrounds me. I'm stunned by a melancholic atmosphere. My head still aches. The darkness is overpowering. I'm in an ominous place. A ribbon of scents burst into my subconscious, and my limbs are sluggish. Hidden impressions from the past, whispers of smoke fill the room, and I cough. The smog creeps into my eyes and stings. A girl wearing a long white dress walks forwards, holding masses and masses of flowers, their colours merging into each other. I rub my eyes, and the haze evaporates.

'Mum!' I shout, dashing downstairs and colliding with my father.

'Steady on. Where's the fire?' he asks, sticking his hand out to catch me.

'Weird pictures are shooting through my head.'

'What kind of pictures?' asks Mum.

'I see a girl in a white dress with a ring of flowers on her head.'

'Maybe it's from a picture in a magazine or...'

'No, she was real.' I turn away and sniff, then hold my hand up to my nose. 'What's that stench?'

'I can't smell anything. Can you, James?' asks Mum, glancing at him.

'It reminds me of decaying lilies.'

'What's the obsession with those flowers? Have you been listening to your nan?' he asks, twisting around as Bella bounds into the room. She's wearing her tennis outfit: shorts and a T-shirt. Two years younger and already taller than me. Her shiny hair is scrunched into a ponytail, and her sunglasses perch on top of her head.

'I'm heading out for a game of tennis. Guess who'll be there? Matt and Rob,' she laughs.

'Shut up,' I say, throwing a cushion at her.

'Sienna, why don't you play a game with them?' He looks at me then turns to my sister and hands her the racket.

'Are you alright? You look pale, love. Not overdoing it, are you?'

I stomp upstairs. My anger is increasing. Why do they ignore me and the images that burst into my head? They are real to *me*. Staring at the front cover of the *Lakeview Village* book, my eyes become heavy with weariness. Through a chink in the curtain, a mysterious red dust sweeps over the black sky. The sound of scratching in the corner of my room alerts me. The brassy cry of pealing bells; the heady scent of decaying flowers; the smoke from the candle; and the throbbing of blood pulsating through my birthmark, invade my senses. A pressure sweeps over me as a nebulous shape catches my eye. It doesn't belong here. I shout into the oppressive air.

'What do you want? Go away.'

Someone is humming in my room.

The wind whips around me and the figure of a young girl materialises.

No one answers.

'Mum,' I call. She opens the door, filling the room with light.

'Hush, Sienna. What's wrong?'

'Mum, images are crowding my head and I don't understand them,' I cry.

'Oh, love. Why don't you stop reading those paranormal books? Try to rest.'

I stare at her as she turns her back on me and walks away. Why doesn't she pay attention to me? My mind is full of thoughts. I can't sleep and pad over to the bathroom. Mum and Dad are bickering downstairs and I turn on the tap to drown out their noise. When I look in the mirror, the wraithlike figure is behind me, projecting a sense of calm. Walking to my room, I settle back into bed and dream about thick weeds covering my body and pulling me down.

When I awake, puddles of dank water trace a path from the door to my bed.

CHAPTER 11

It's the day before we return to school. I've been revising, trying to keep my mind off Paddy, when the urge to read Rose's book overwhelms me. Taking it out of the plastic bag, I carefully open the front cover. After examining the first page, I spot another flower fixed behind the dried one. These petals are white with a distinctive middle. The next page holds a withered bunch of foliage stuck down with a piece of old, yellowing tape. Written underneath in large sloping distinctive style are the following details:

Henbane causes hallucinations, lethargy, and delirium. Otherwise known as the witch's drug.

A witch's drug? What's that? A dark shadow passes over me and my stomach clenches with nausea. Why is this information in Rose's book? The leaves crinkle in my fingers, leaving behind a mass of dried flakes. I flip over to the next page, unsure of what I'll read next. There's another bunch of dried fronds with the following sentences written in the same handwriting:

Thyme. This herb will increase strength and courage and help you keep an optimistic attitude. Use in spells to communicate with the underworld.

The underworld is where people go after death. Coldness slithers over my body. This book fascinates me so I carry on.

This next plant, once green, is now brown and flaky with a faint earthy odour:

Wild nettles. Pick and steep in boiling water, and drink as a tea. This will grant you courage, protection, and deter any evil.

I've never heard of this so I Google nettle tea and learn that the nettle leaf has barbs which contain harmful chemicals.

The contents of Rose's book worry me. I'm about to turn to the next page when voices drift upstairs.

'Hi, Charlie, when did you arrive back?' I hear my sister ask.

'I flew in last night. What've you been up to?'

'Nothing much,' she says. 'Apart from trying to keep away from Sienna.'

The raucous laugh of my friend booms out. Bella hollers at me from the bottom of the stairs. 'Come down, sis. Charlie is here.'

I rush downstairs to see her standing at the door. 'Hiya. I've missed you. Was Paris exciting? I've been waiting to show you Rose's book. There are pages with bunches of dried-up leaves stuck on them.' I babble on, excited at seeing her again.

'Forget about that. I've brought a surprise with me,' she says. 'I phoned you-know-who and persuaded him to join us.'

'You-know-who? Join us and to do what? Don't keep me in suspense.'

'Get moving.' She shoves me out of the door.

'Charlie, why? Where are we off to? You've not been in contact since Ireland and dash in as if you've discovered the meaning of life and want me to drop what I'm doing and follow you,' I laugh, swirling her around to face me. 'Slow down, what's the rush?' I ask. 'By the way, how's your gran?'

'Gran, yeah, she's fine.'

'What about Paris?'

'It rained most of the time but you'll never guess what I picked up from the flea market there.' She holds up a creased brown paper bag.

'What?'

'You'll see when we arrive. Hurry up, they're waiting for us.'

She grabs my arm and we stride along the pavement, past the housing estate and along the path, through the play area with the children's swings and on towards the woods into the picnic area. I'm busy chatting to Charlie about Rose's book when we enter the forest. Monkton House lies in the distance which reminds me of Nan and her obsession with lilies. Matt and Rob are reclining on a bench, guzzling from cans of cider. Heat swamps my body and I shake my hair over my face to hide my birthmark and burning cheeks. We saunter over to them and Matt nods at me as I sit down.

'Hiya Charlie, wassup?' says Rob, flicking back his hair and trying to act cool.

Charlie reaches into the bag and removes a flat piece of wood.

'Right, we need to keep quiet.'

I study the ancient wooden board which is inscribed with numbers and the alphabet in faded black gothic writing. In each corner is the image of a skull and the words YES and NO. Engraved at the top of the board is a moon and stars. The board has letters of the alphabet on two lines in a semicircle, with numbers starting with 1 and ending with 0. At the bottom is the word *Goodbye*. Engraved along four sides are tiny flowers with ivy curling around them.

'Place your fingers on the planchette and ask it a question,' demands Charlie.

'What are we doing and what the hell is a planchette? Have you tried this before, Sienna?' asks Matt, staring at me.

He's waiting for an answer. A lock of brown hair flops over his eyebrows and he brushes it to one side, exposing the wide forehead, fair skin, and emerald green eyes. I stare at his full lips and lick mine, imagining the sensation of being kissed.

'It's French which means 'little plank,' and it's a heart-shaped piece of wood used to spell out names or messages. These Ouija boards were popular in Victorian times to conjure up spirits in séances. Funny enough, Ouija means 'good luck',' I say.

As I finish talking, Matt crinkles up his nose and a vertical frown line emerges between his eyes.

'We haven't got all day,' says Charlie.

Rob leans over and, resting his finger on the board, asks, 'Is anybody there?'

Silence.

Charlie prods my ribs.

'Ouch, Charlie.' I copy Rob and whisper, 'Is anyone there?'

The wooden planchette glides towards the YES sign.

'Did you tap it?' Charlie glares at me. My chest tightens as the sky changes to a dirty grey.

'Charlie, you're next,' says Rob.

I stare at the board. Nothing is happening.

'What's your name?'

It slides to the letter M.

'Rob, this is silly, let's go,' Matt says, staring at me.

I glance over at them.

'I bet it's Gran,' Rob says. 'She died last year. Is that you, Margaret? Her nickname is Mags.'

Our fingers are still on the planchette as it slides to the letter A.

'Granny, are you there?' he asks, gripping Charlie with one hand and resting his finger on the board.

It glides towards the letter R.

Then T.

We gaze at each other; it's not Margaret unless they can't spell. I'm certain one of them is moving it, either Rob or Charlie. They're always fooling around with each other.

After a jolt, it pushes towards the letter H.

Heavy rain clouds cover the sky. The silence of the park unnerves me.

'Show yourself,' I demand.

The skies burst open, and the rain pelts down in large drops. The wooden planchette spins out of control and ends up pointing to the letter A again.

'What does it spell?' questions Matt.

M-A-R-T-H-A

I stand up quickly. Too quickly. My legs weaken, my hands shake, there's a heaviness in my stomach and a tingling slithering up my spine. Fear strokes the back of my neck. Martha's familiar voice whispers in my ear, '*Find her.*'

'Go!' I scream.

'Stop it, Sienna. You're scaring me,' cries Charlie.

I grab her hand and run. She yells at me, but her voice is muffled against the sound of heavy rain. Hazy fog drifts towards us while the rain blinds and disorientates me. We scramble on the path leading to the spinney, skidding on loose rocks and twisted roots. The hoot of an owl in the distance pierces the silence. '*Find her. Find her.*' The voice echoes. Charlie trips onto the prickly spikes of the gorse bush and grazes her forehead. I try to pick her up but struggle to grip her.

Matt and Rob are behind us, their voices muffled by the noise of the rain. The water is lashing down, soaking us. The ground is boggy. Charlie trips again and drags me with her. Mud and ferns saturate the floor. We lie there, holding each other and struggling to breathe.

'Get up,' says Matt. 'We're drenched.'

The earth is sucking us under and thick mud coats my feet. I've lost my bearings. Yanking Charlie up, we trudge past the eerie, ominous shapes of beech trees. Past the blackthorn bushes waving their wiry branches trying to scratch us. We've been plodding for what seems ages and I'm exhausted. Sloshing through the thick sludge, we arrive at the local bog. When younger, my classmates frightened me with tales of The Tree Creature: a tall thing, roots swirling around him. Thin, spindly twigs for arms and rough bark that would scrape off your skin, leaving you bleeding to death. This creature would snare unsuspecting children with his prickly branches and enfold them into his world, never to be seen again.

The Tree Creature is in my view. The outline is hazy. It's closer, closer. A beam of light flickers from side to side, searching. As I wipe the rain from my eyes, a figure approaches. It's Dad. Thank God. He's standing in a clearing where the path awaits. We've run full circle back to the picnic area and the table is still there, with the Ouija board lying underneath it. Charlie has noticed it too and slips it back in her bag. Matt and Rob are behind us.

'Why are you in the woods? Whose idea was it?' Dad asks, glaring at us. We bend our heads, study the wet grass, and Matt speaks first.

'Sorry, Mr Stevens, it's my fault,' he says.

I stare at him. Why is he taking the blame when it was Charlie's idea to play the stupid board?

'We'll be on our way, Sienna; catch you at school tomorrow,' he says, smiling at me.

Charlie sidles up to us and squeezes my arm.

'I've got it,' she whispers, patting her bag.

'Charlotte, I'll give you a lift home,' says Dad. 'You're dripping wet. What about you two boys?'

'Are you sure, Mr Stevens? Thanks. We're soaked,' laughs Matt, shaking water droplets off his hair.

'No problem. Can't have you catching a chill, can we now?' says Dad.

'Thank you.'

The car is waiting at the entrance to the park and we climb into it.

I turn to Dad. 'I'm glad you're here, but why are you out in this weather?'

'Not now, I'm trying to concentrate on the road.'

The rain is gushing down and the windscreen wipers swish furiously. Charlie is dropped off first and twists the key in her door but nobody is there to welcome her. I sit in my wet clothes and reflect on the message from the Ouija board. Ten minutes later, Dad stops the car and the boys jump out. We carry on in silence. The rain is lashing against the windows.

At home, I head upstairs and switch on the shower. I'm shaking and as the boiling water gushes over me, I reflect on the evening. The rivulets of water trail down the shower wall and I wipe the condensation away. I drape the warm towel around my body, dry myself, and throw on my pyjamas. I want to ring Charlie, but it's late and I don't want to wake her. The spinney with its spooky history about tree creatures worries me because it's too close to Nan's care home. I scan through my magazines for an article I've read about Lakeview village hauntings. I find a passage that tells how people saw a young girl wandering the woods at night, crying out for revenge and taking shortcuts through the forest towards Monkton House. Questions are buzzing in my head. The Ouija board spelled out

Martha, the spirit of a young girl pursuing me.

Who is Martha?

CHAPTER 12

First day back at school after the May holidays and I find Charlie in the toilets surrounded by a group of girls. They're studying the way she shades feathery strokes to her already full brows with her eyebrow pencil. Next, she sweeps black kohl liner into a flick over her eyelids. She's not aware I'm there, or the admiring glances the girls send her, and when I cough, they spin around and edge away.

'Witches,' one whispers as she pushes past me with the others following.

During our study time, we carry on researching ghostly manifestations around our village. The creepiness of last night's Ouija session constantly pops into my mind and I try talking to Charlie, but she dismisses my worries with a wave of her hand. The day carries on as normal, with the girls chatting about their holidays. No-one asks me what I've been doing and I don't tell them about visiting Ireland.

On arriving home, I notice the mess in the kitchen. Unwashed dishes are still in the sink and pancake mix has congealed in the pan, with blobs of batter stuck to the sides. Toast crumbs and sticky orange marmalade cover the work surface. Mum is slumped at the table with her head in her hands.

'What's wrong?' I ask.

She gazes at me.

'This morning, after you rushed off to school, your sister felt ill and dragged herself back to bed. She felt better so made pancakes, but couldn't eat them. At lunchtime, I phoned the doctor because of her breathlessness. Isabella's never been that pale before and he suggested we took her to hospital.' Mum is staring into the distance and picking at the skin around her fingernails.

'Why, what's caused this?'

'Last night, Isabella followed you to the park and watched that silly game. Your sister tried shouting, but you dashed into the woods so she ran back to get Dad.'

'Oh, that's why he was there. I… I… didn't know.'

'She saw you jumping up and running away. It scared her, and she came home and told us. You're stronger than Isabella. We need to protect her.'

'What do you mean? Bella is fitter than me.'

'It's nothing to do with how physically fit she is. It's a confidence thing.'

'I don't know what you're saying.'

Mum sighs. 'Bella craves approval. She dotes on you, but you couldn't care less about other people.'

'Hold on a minute. That's strong, isn't it? I care about my family.'

'Oh, really? What about that spell to get rid of your sister?'

'That was a joke.' I look down and bite my lips.

'I sometimes wonder how we could have two different girls. I remember when your nan nicknamed you Red because of your hair and temper.'

'What's that got to do with it? Why are you bringing that up now? It's an insult and I hate that nickname, but I guess Bella is better behaved?'

I pick up the breakfast dishes and load them into the dishwasher, slamming the door.

Mum doesn't respond. She's picking at the skin around her cuticles, fascinated by the tiny beads of blood bubbling over her nail bed. The clink of the key in the door heralds Dad and Bella.

'We're back. Had to wait ages for a doctor and they carried out blood tests,' says Dad.

'Have you eaten, love?' Mum puts her arm around her and strokes Bella's hair.

'No, I wasn't hungry in the hospital but could have something now. I'm sorry for scaring you both,' she says.

Dad still hasn't mentioned yesterday's Ouija session and I'm expecting a long lecture. He's helping my sister off with her jacket and says, 'Right, time for a cuppa.'

I fill the kettle and get the mugs out. 'What did they say?' I shout above the noise of the running water.

'High blood pressure because of shock and a low iron count, which means you need to eat more green veg and swallow these, young lady.' He smiles at Bella and shakes a bottle of iron tablets at her.

'Yuk, broccoli is disgusting.' She pulls a face.

'But…' He turns to me. 'No more playing with the Ouija board.'

'It wasn't my fault. Charlie didn't tell me she bought one.'

'It's a risky game you're playing and you should have more sense,' says Dad.

Bella is lying on the settee, smirking at me. The kettle clicks off and I drop in the tea bags as Mum enters the kitchen.

'I remember playing on the Ouija board with my sister, who was about your age. She bought it from a jumble sale and set it up on the living room table. We scared ourselves silly and ended up bolting out of the room. Our mother was mad at us and told us we had introduced the Antichrist into the family,' Mum says as she pours the water into the teapot.

'Tracey, what on earth are you talking about?' asks Dad, staring at her.

'Carry on, Mum,' I say, as she picks up the tea tray and we follow her into the lounge.

'The door slammed shut and the glass vase fell and shattered on the floor. It petrified us, but Mum told us it was the wind. It makes me shiver, even now – it can be dangerous if you experiment with it.'

'For God's sake, Tracey, what are you trying to do? Make a dangerous situation worse?'

'Calm down, James. Kids have always been interested in that creepy board and I'm sure Sienna has learnt her lesson.' Mum smiles at me and I notice the wrinkles around her eyes.

'I'm not happy with the company she's keeping. She's changed since she's met that girl,' says Dad.

'That girl you are referring to is my best friend, Charlie. The one who helped me when you did nothing about the bullying.' I glare at him.

My sister grins at me but her face is pale with a sheen of sweat on her upper lip.

'Goodnight,' I shout, eager to escape. I trudge up to bed and lie awake, mulling over my problems.

***

The next day, Bella is still in bed. I call for her but there's no reply, so I trudge off to school. Charlie's chair is empty and I sense Matt glancing over several times during the day. Another boring day with boring subjects to revise. At lunchtime, I traipse outside and sit on an empty bench to eat. But I'm not hungry and throw most of the food away. I'm alone. I've got no idea where Charlie is and carry on with my topic work on the local hauntings.

When I arrive back home, Bella is lying on the sofa reading her athletic magazine. She ignores me.

'Did you take a sickie?' I ask. She nods and carries on reading.

I escape to my bedroom, change out of my school uniform and lie on my bed. My project needs more details on the hauntings near me so I scan through the books and start typing on my laptop. We've constructed a PowerPoint and also a brochure detailing the various ghosts found in this area. I'm engrossed and miss the first ring of the doorbell. When it happens again, I rush downstairs and notice the figure of a woman behind the glass pane in the front door.

Mum's sister, Aunt Debbie, is standing on the doorstep. I open the door and she bursts in. At nearly six foot, she's taller than my mother, and her presence fills the room. She pulls me into a massive bear hug, leaving behind a trail of her musky perfume. The wine bottles clink against each other in the plastic bag, and she grins at me.

Tonight, she entertains us with stories about her latest boyfriends. They're onto their second bottle of wine when Aunt Debbie pours me a small glass. Mum shakes her head as I swig it down and gets up to fetch a bowl of crisps while I'm left with my aunt.

'So, pet, I'm here to check up on your sister and she's fine now, but what about you and these dreams you're having?' she asks, pouring herself another drink.

'I'm OK,' I say, unsure how much to divulge. 'At the moment, studying and school is too much.'

'What's too much?' interrupts Mum entering the room.

'Nothing. Another, Tracey?' asks Debbie, unscrewing the top of the bottle.

Mum pours the wine and it sloshes over the glass, dripping onto the coffee table. I escape upstairs to my room while they mop up the liquid. I'm not in the mood to talk about my dreams with them while they're drinking; I settle down on my bed and pick up the book about Lakeview village. My eyes grow heavy and a wind flows through the room. A sense of peace drifts over me as a hand rests on my shoulder and the spirit of Martha arrives.

She whispers, *'Sienna, two girls are resting on the wooden benches overlooking the garden. They are distraught. A car drives away and a girl chases after it, but that horrid woman pulls her back. The woman points her finger and screams my name. I am in danger. You must help me.'*

The wind dies down and she disappears.

What was that? Martha is communicating to me and although it seems scary, somehow I'm comforted, as if she trusts me. I'm not sure whether to tell someone about this, but then a grating voice from downstairs screams into my brain. My aunt's voice is increasing in volume.

'Tell her, Tracey.'

Throwing my duvet off, I stand by the door and eavesdrop on their conversation.

'Keep your voice down,' slurs Mum.

It's difficult to work out what they're saying, so I storm downstairs. Mum is lounging on the sofa with my aunt sitting next to her.

'You're making too much noise,' I grumble.

'Sienna, love, your mother told me about these strange visions,' says my aunt, staggering over to me.

'You're both drunk,' I shout.

'We want to help. I could ring a psychiatrist friend, and he'll chat with you over the phone. He deals with teenage problems,' says my aunt.

'No thanks. I don't want to speak to anyone. These dreams began with my paranormal research and we've nearly finished.' I glare at her.

'We believe it started years ago,' says Mum, taking a slurp from her glass. Debbie flops down and pours herself another drink.

'No, it didn't,' I reply.

As they talk, their voices fade away, and a picture flashes into my head. A layer of snow covers the grass like a soft cushion. The weight of the white dust pulls down the boughs of the tree. Animal paw prints ruin the beauty of the sparkling white crystals. The heavy clouds burst open and the swirling icy water strikes Martha's face. She's running, panting into the freezing air. She slips, and the thin layer of ice cracks with a splintering sound which echoes over the still landscape. Into the murky water, Martha sinks to the bottom of the lake.

Their voices drift back to me.

'What's wrong?' Mum asks, staring at me.

"I'm freezing.' I rub the circulation back in my arms. They're both frowning, so I keep quiet. If my aunt is talking about a psychiatrist, that means they think I have mental problems. My heart is pounding as the rancid taste of muddy pond water fills my mouth.

'When you were younger, you would chat on your own. No one else was in the room.'

'I don't remember.'

'We didn't worry about it because children have imaginary friends. Tell you what, I'll talk to your dad and we'll arrange a doctor's appointment. Go to bed and get some sleep.'

I'm not listening and rush upstairs, aware that a force is demanding I read Rose's book. On opening the next page, there's a drawing of a girl with a piece of shrivelled grey material, resembling a dress, glued on top of the figure. A clump of hair is stuck on its head with dried wrinkled black cloves for eyes. The figure clasps a tiny bunch of dried flowers and a musky stench surrounds the page. As I read the description, I shudder.

Atropa Belladonna (deadly nightshade). Psychoactive, unsafe. Found in scrub and woodland, the deadly nightshade lives up to its name and is highly poisonous. Sprinkle seeds in food. Symptoms include blurred vision, headaches, confusion and tremors.

What the hell? Why would anyone write this? I place the book under my pillow and dream of a thick rope winding around me, trapping me in its grasp.

I'm unable to breathe and wake up panting with the earthy stink of rotten wood and sweet-smelling roses drifting up from my bedsheets.

CHAPTER 13

The next morning when I go downstairs, Debbie is leaning against the kitchen work surface drinking a cup of coffee, all traces of their drink-fuelled night cleared away.

'Your mum is still in bed and I need to get off before the traffic builds up.'

She pops a couple of slices of bread into the toaster and removes the butter from the fridge.

'Are you okay, love? I mean, you seem distracted these days. I hope you're studying for your exams and still intend applying to university?'

'Yes, of course, but you sound like Dad and Nan. What's this obsession with university? Mum told me she didn't want to go.'

'You're joking, aren't you? Your mum had to give up her university place when she found out she was pregnant with you.'

'Why couldn't *you* look after me?'

'Me?' She points to herself and laughs. 'I'm not great with kids. But our mother would have loved to have taken care of you. It's sad she died before you were born. I was studying for my law degree and Nan Ria didn't want the responsibility.'

'Why not?'

'Your mum had the chance to study part-time at university, but

Ria wouldn't forsake her career. They even offered her a job-share at her school, which she rejected. It's a control thing,' she says, pouring the remains of her coffee down the sink.

'You don't think much of her, do you?'

'No, I don't because of…'

'What?'

'… the way she treats your mum. Anyway, I'm the eldest sister so I'll sort this family out,' she says, grinning.

'We're fine and don't need your help.' I'm annoyed she wants to control us. Is Mum that weak she needs to involve her sister in our difficulties?

'I've been part of your family's life for years; whenever there's a problem, I'm called for. Your mum is worried about these visions and phones me for advice. You need to talk to her. I'm off now. Tell your mum I'll be in touch.' Debbie holds me tight. 'Don't worry, it will work out,' she says, swirling her voluminous pashmina around her body.

I open the door. She waves to me and climbs in her car, accelerating in a whirlwind of gravel. Mum staggers downstairs. Her eyes are bloodshot and she stinks of stale alcohol.

'I need a coffee and then back to bed for me. Whenever my sister is around, it's always the same. Too much to drink and I've a rotten headache. When will I learn?' She shakes her head and plugs in the coffee machine.

***

It's late evening and we're headed towards our favourite family Greek restaurant to celebrate Dad's success in gaining a new client. It's always busy with laughter and the waiting staff's singing. I want to talk to Dad but can't with Bella chatting on about some latest sports hero. So wrapped up in her athletic world, she hasn't even noticed that he is silent.

As we finish our meal, my sister's voice fades away and instead the persistent humming of a familiar nursery rhyme pops into my ear. I rest my chin on my hand and prop my elbow on the table, watching. Waiting. The candles have blown out, leaving behind a smoky trail. The restaurant darkens. In the haze, a petite figure, her sodden hair plastered to her head, beckons. She glides towards me; the hem of her dress is soaked, leaving behind muddy footprints. She stands behind my father and rests her hand on his shoulder. 'M…Martha,' I stammer, but the stench of putrefying water blocks my throat and she evaporates in a cloud of water vapour.

The waiter ignites our candles again, which only illuminates the film of perspiration on my father's brow and his colourless, clammy skin. Mum stands up, wipes the corners of her mouth and throws the napkin on the table.

'We're leaving, James. You've hardly spoken to me and it's obvious you're exhausted from working too many hours.'

We exit the restaurant and bundle into the car. Mum drives, and Dad rests his head against the door frame. When we arrive home, I go to my bedroom and lie down. I can't think straight. This is incredible. I've finally seen Martha. But why is she showing herself? What should I do?

My hand hovers over my phone, ready to text Charlie, but then I stop, unsure of her reaction. The appearance of the spirit girl might make her jealous. The thought that she could demand I return gran's book makes me want to finish reading it. On opening the book, a torn piece of delicate paper from a prayer book is stuck on the brown, water-damaged pages with the following words written on it: *Meet me by the lake.* I'm baffled. What does it mean and who wrote it? While moving around in bed, the book drops to the floor and reveals another entry. A squashed petal sticks in between the page, but the orange pollen has burst out of the flower and dried over the writing, obscuring the words. Scraping the particles off with my fingernail, puffs of dust gather on the paper. It says:

Calla lilies – represent death. Similar to other plants in the Araceae family, they contain insoluble calcium oxalate crystals. Though poisoning is rare, eating and swallowing any part of the calla lily plant causes vomiting and dizzy spells. I will crush it and tell her it is a special potion to seduce him, but she has to drink the syrupy nectar. Then, when it is over, I will place the funeral bouquet on her headstone and weep empty tears.

As I turn the page, the hazy shadow of Martha appears, holding a bunch of lilies. Attached to the flowers is a folded piece of paper. I watch her throw the posy away. Is this it? Is Martha connected to Rose's spell book? The information in this book bothers me and I need to tell Mum. She's lying on the sofa with another glass of wine perched on the coffee table. Bella and Dad are not with her.

'Where are they?' I ask.

'Isabella's in bed and your dad is out. He said…' She hesitates.

'What, Mum?'

'…he felt peculiar in the restaurant.'

'What do you mean?'

Mum stands up and knocks the wineglass over, stumbles and reaches out for me. I grasp her arm to prevent her from falling.

'I don't know what to do. Every day, all we do is argue about these visions of yours.' She's slurring her words. 'Your dad wants to call in the local vicar but I think it might be…'

I don't know what Mum thinks it is because Bella slams open the door, dashes over and hugs her.

'Mum, don't upset yourself.'

A tickle starts behind my eyes and I hold it back. With Bella by her side, Mum is calmer and wipes her hand over her brow.

'Listen, love. I'm sorry for my outburst; we want to sort this out. Your dad doesn't understand why you're having these dreams and hasn't stopped worrying since you took part in the Ouija board session. He wants to contact Father Ignatius.'

'No way.'

'We'll discuss this tomorrow; it's time for bed.' Mum yawns, leaning on Bella and leaves the room.

The prospect of discussing my visions to the school priest is daunting. He'll tell the principal and I'm sure the governors won't want a pupil visualising ghosts. Dad bothers me. Did he sense Martha standing behind him in the restaurant? I text Charlie and ask her to meet me in the library tomorrow. I want these dreams to go and hopefully we can figure how to get rid of them. I'm drifting off when the key twisting in the front door disturbs me, so I get up and go downstairs.

'Hiya, love. Are you still up?' asks Dad.

'Yes, I'm not tired. Are you alright?'

'Me? I'm fine,' he says, rubbing his hand over his forehead. 'I felt strange in the restaurant but nothing to worry about. Had a jog around the block to get some fresh air.'

'Dad?'

'Yes?'

'I'm concerned about Mum's drinking. Is there anything else apart from me worrying her?'

'Nah, your mum's okay, but this supernatural business freaks her out and it's about time you finished that project. I'm surprised the school gave you that topic.'

'They didn't.'

'Oh, who did?'

'The staff don't know what we're researching.'

'If the teachers didn't choose your topic, who did?'

'Charlie,' I say, and escape to bed.

CHAPTER 14

At lunchtime, I stroll outside to the old red brick library. Most of the pupils study inside the school where there is an array of computers. Placing my revision guides on the table, I copy facts onto flash cards, but my mind drifts to my parents arguing about me. I can't concentrate while waiting for Charlie and keep reading the same page over and over. A few girls sprawl over the table, gazing at their text books, but when they spot me, they scurry out. After a while, the emptiness of the room unnerves me, and I pack my folders away. She's late, but someone else is in the room; the voice in my head is telling me to, '*Find her. I need to know.*' The breeze wafts through the window, and the beating of the blind's cord against the glass echoes throughout the quietness of the room.

I've brought Rose's book with me and remove it from my bag, but every time I touch it, my heart beats faster. I try to separate the pages but they're stuck together with a dried, reddish brown stain, and to my horror a shrivelled black feather is tucked amongst the pages with the words:

Blackbird Crow, a member of the Corvus family. Messenger of death. Pluck out the feathers of the blackbird and hide under the pillow of your enemy.
Chant these words:

'Dark soul, black soul.
Devil of the night.
Take flight.'

I throw the book back into my bag. Charlie can collect it and solve the mystery herself. I've enough problems without adding to it. Standing up from the table, my legs wobble. Holding on to the back of the chair, I take deep breaths but psychedelic colours of red and orange flash across my eyes. Martha murmurs in my ear like the breeze of the wind, her voice low and gentle, reeking of woody fern and muddy soil. *Joe has jet black, wavy hair and chocolate brown eyes; he stands tall and strong, confident and steady. He possesses a tanned ruggedness that excites me. Joe tends to the borders of lavender while bumblebees hover around the purple flowers. Soil from his labours stains his nails. My sweet love picks me bunches of the honey-sweet blossoms and the exquisite perfumed oil drips from the petals onto my fingers. He sings me songs about becoming his queen. One day we will be together again, but you need to help me find her.'*

Where is Charlie? I want to discuss these visions and whisperings with her. I tiptoe away. It's not late, but the room has dimmed since I arrived and a sense of gloom permeates me. On reaching the stairs, I stand still, sensing the air moving behind me.

'Charlie, you're too late. I'm leaving now,' I shout.

Placing one foot in front of the other, the panting of my breath reverberates throughout the stillness. The motion sensor lights switch on and off, blinding me. A stench of dank water and acrid smoke fills my nostrils. Thankfully, the front door is ahead and I grip the handle, desperate to escape. I sense a figure behind me.

'Why? Why? Why me?' she cries out.

Tearing out of the double doors, I bump into Matt heading along the path towards the Science block. He sticks out his hand and catches me.

'Whoa, steady on, Sienna. Where's the ghost?' he laughs.

'Oh Matt, I... I'm scared.'

'Hey, what's wrong?' he asks. The sunshine is powerful after the dimness of the library, and I shield my eyes against the brightness. A few girls are lying on the lawn and snigger when we pass.

'Here, sit down and tell me what's up,' he says, ushering me towards a bench.

Perching on the end of the wooden slats, I place my bag on the ground and blurt out my worries, but stop when I realise he might blab to his mates about me.

'Did the Ouija board session cause this?' he asks. 'Charlie didn't tell me she would bring it to the park.'

'What do you mean?'

'I had a video call from her when she stayed in Paris. The Louvre was in the background. Impressive, eh? Ever been to France?'

I clench my teeth and place my hands in my pockets. I'm annoyed Charlie spoke to him and not me. She's supposed to be my best friend. Matt carries on, unaware of the jealousy that overwhelms me.

'As well as the dreams. I'm also having problems with my parents,' I blurt out.

'Sienna, your parents arguing could just be a rough patch. I'd keep out of their way for a while.'

'What are you, a marriage counsellor, now?' I laugh. He fidgets with the wooden arm of the bench.

'Changing the subject, I've been meaning to ask you a question,' he says, glancing up at me.

I'm unsure what's coming next. The girls sprawling on the lawn have left so I stand up, ready to go, but he grabs my hand and pulls me down.

'I've been volunteering at the care home at the weekends for a few months now and they're desperate for more helpers. Do you want to work with me during the holidays?' he asks.

'Volunteer at the same place where my nan lives? You're joking, aren't you? I don't like that place. Creepy... ooh,' I say and shudder.

His forehead puckers into a frown and he stares into the distance.

'Can I think about it?' I ask.

'Yeah, sure, no worries. See you around, Sienna.'

He stands up and joins the other students ambling towards the science lab, then swivels around and beams at me. Working with Matt might be a great idea. Get to know him after all and be in Nan's good books. Sorted.

My days at school are winding down with study periods and a few teaching sessions. Most pupils bunk off. Charlie and Matt aren't around so I'm on my own, with no one to discuss the library incident.

I rub my hand over my eyes. A heaviness builds in my head when I realise Charlie hasn't been around. Is she trying to avoid me? She hasn't been in school much either. As I'm pondering over this, she texts me with the news that Rose is ill, and they're in Ireland caring for her. I immediately reply, asking for more details. She mentions severe migraine attack, lasting days. I'm not sure if Charlie is being too casual about her gran's illness and text again asking if it's serious. 'No' is her curt reply. What's with the attitude? Surely she's not annoyed about my concern for her gran?

My sister has recovered from the park incident, but keeps away from me. I miss her bantering; it's too quiet. Now that study leave has officially started, I'm at home alone with my thoughts, and being a worrier is the worse place to be. I open the front page of *The History of Lakeview Village* and read the dedication to lost souls. I'm a lost soul. Nobody loves me; my parents argue about me, and my sister keeps away. I'm mixed up about Matt and unsure whether he fancies me or Charlie with her dyed, black hair. An idea hits me. Why don't I change my appearance?

Slipping the front door keys in my pocket, I nip to the local chemist and buy a temporary dye to cover my ginger hair. There's a section near the health foods which displays slimming tablets. The assistant behind the counter tuts as I hand them over, and I glare at her. Back at home, I examine myself in the bathroom cabinet mirror. Mmm… I'm not too ugly, I suppose. Pale skin, freckles dotted around my nose with a red splodge of a birthmark. On further inspection, there are a couple of lines on my forehead and a spot developing on my chin. And what is that? A golden hair sprouting on my upper lip, which I tweeze out.

The hair dye stings my scalp. Thirty minutes later, after washing it out, I examine myself in the mirror. What a disappointment. Nothing has changed apart from patches of brown interspersed amongst the ginger. A bleak idea flashes in my head that people will be glad if I'm not around. No more arguments and no more worrying about me. A pair of nail scissors on the bathroom shelf glint and I pick them up. A radiant light floods the room, shining on the metal. I drop them as my eyes close and the sound of girls laughing echoes in my ears. Martha is beside me and whispers, '*She pulled my head back and jabbed at my scalp, making it bleed. Why did she cut my hair? Why does she want to hurt me?*'

The pressure of her hand is over my head and my eyes open. I brush my hand against my scalp and touch the jagged edges of my hair. I'm exhausted and baffled. What happened? Did I do this? I wrap a towel around my wet hair and head for my room. This contact has left me exhausted, so I lie on the bed and rest. After a while, the door opens and my mother enters, holding clumps of sodden red curls in her hand.

'What's this?' she asks, sitting on my bed and fiddling with my duvet cover.

'It's obvious, isn't it?' I snap at her and fold my arms across my chest, scared of what I've done.

'This needs to end now before you hurt yourself or others. I'm worried about you,' she says, holding my hand.

'Oh, Sienna. I'm sorry you're suffering. What can I do to help you?'

'I don't know.' I sob and turn to her. She wraps her arms around me and rocks me until I stop crying.

'Come on, love, it's a gorgeous day. Why don't you go outside and relax? I've got to go to the shops,' she says.

I need time to reflect on the meaning of that vision so I change into my shorts and T-shirt and go downstairs to the back garden. Hauling the sunbed out of the shed, I set my study books on the table. The sun is blazing down on my body and I swallow two of the slimming tablets. The sky is such an intense azure blue it hurts my eyes and I rest for a moment and think about Martha. The creaking of the side gate wakes me as Bella bursts into the garden, shattering my peace.

'It's alright for some, lounging around in the sunshine. By the way, you've burnt your face. Gosh, sis, I don't want to be the bearer of bad news but that hair colour doesn't suit you,' she sniggers and flings her school bag on the grass.

'We can't all be a knockout, can we?' I shout, standing up and going inside. I pass the hall mirror and take a peek. This will show the truth. Has it been worth it? Do I resemble Charlie? No. I'm still ugly. My skin is burnt red from the sun. My hair is patchy, shorter, and uneven. Why did I do this? My face is chubbier than ever. Mum has returned from her shopping trip and is banging cupboard doors, putting the food away. She's talking to someone on the phone.

'Yes, you heard me; she's cut off her curls and dyed her hair.

What? I couldn't. I've been working and wasn't here. Stop shouting at me, James. Why do you keep wanting to involve the church? She needs medical help.'

I storm upstairs, but something makes me stop outside my room. A muffled sound of banging, crashing and a low moaning is coming from inside. I push open the door and stare at the chaos. My books and photo frames are lying on the floor. The duvet is hanging over the headboard. Drawers are open, exposing my underwear, while something has flung the rest of my clothes over the wardrobe door.

'Bella, what the hell have you done?' I turn around and scream at her.

'What's this commotion?' asks Mum, running up the stairs. 'What's this?' she asks, picking the cracked photo frame up from the floor.

My anger is like a burning stone lodged in my chest and I grab my sister's arm.

'Isabella, did you do this?'

She wriggles out of my grasp and hides behind Mum.

'I wouldn't go anywhere near your smelly things,' she squeaks.

The fury blazing inside me wants to hurt her.

'Get lost,' I snarl, elbowing her out of my way.

'That's enough. You're scaring your sister. The wind blew the photo frames over when you left your window open.' Bella bursts into tears and turns to Mum, who manoeuvres her away from me. They walk out of my room, Bella sobbing on Mum's shoulder.

'What's happening? Go away. Why me?' I shout into the still room.

The whispering cuts through the silence, '*I'm waiting. Waiting for you*,' it says.

The lack of air in my room crushes me, and I can't breathe. The need to escape propels me into action and, in a daze, I creep downstairs and open the front door. I have no idea where I'm heading. My heart is pounding as I continue past the housing estate and the park. The school is in front of me and I spot a couple of lads reclining on the bench, the light from their cigarettes illuminating their faces. I'm furious and stamp over the grass as tears stream down my cheeks. Who wrecked my room? Was it my sister? Martha? It certainly wasn't me.

Where the hell am I? I survey the area and sink to the ground. In the distance is a high wooden fence surrounding an old granite stone building. The sparkle of the moon shimmering over the cool, dark lake is inviting. The hoot of a barn owl and the rustle of branches startle me. I keep still and place my hand over my mouth to stop wheezing. This is the back of Monkton House. A disused wooden shed, an old-fashioned lawnmower and rusty tools lie amongst the grass. The greenhouse with shattered glass stands desolate; broken earthenware plant pots are strewn along the grass. The fence has sizeable gaps of rotted wood, and it would be easy for an intruder to lever the planks aside and sneak into the grounds. Nan lives here, so I need to tell Dad about this broken fence.

One by one, the lights go off. A nurse rushes out towards the car park and as she gets closer, I twist around and run away. The sign for Lakeview Park is ahead, but the squeal of a car and dazzling headlights stop me from carrying on. Raising my hand to my eyes to shield against the light, the door opens to reveal my mother.

'Get in now, Sienna.'

'I'm sorry, Mum,' I say.

'I've been driving around for ages. This is the last straw. We had no idea where you went; you're frightening your sister and scaring me witless. Your behaviour and the way you disrespect us is out of order.' Bella is in the back seat and we drive home in silence. My sister still isn't speaking to me, even though I try to placate her.

'Bella, help me. I'm mixed up – one minute I'm fine, then I'm not. It happens without me realising. Can we please be friends?' I ask, but she turns away and stares out the window.

Mum pulls up into our driveway and Bella storms out of the car. We follow her and I wait for the lecture, but Mum stares at me.

'Sienna. What was that about? When I left you, I thought you were resting and then you accuse your sister of trashing your room. You need to stop picking on her.'

'Oh great, so you're taking her side again? I know she's the favourite. I keep telling you I'm fine; just been studying too much.'

'You're not fine. The anger you showed to your sister is wrong. You've had arguments before, but this was different,' she says.

I turn away and walk into my room. What possessed me to head towards Monkton House? As I'm wondering about that, the soft plodding of her footsteps comes closer.

'Mum,' I shout.

'Yes,' she says, opening the bedroom door.

'Can I ask you a question?'

'Of course – what?' she asks, yawning.

'Do you hate me?'

Her eyes widen as she pauses for a second. 'What kind of question is that? You're my little girl and I'm going to make sure you get help.' She bends forward, hugs me, and smooths the duvet.

I close my eyes and the image of Monkton House comes into view, but there's something wrong with the picture. What do I need to tell Dad?

CHAPTER 15

Next morning, I catch a glimpse of myself in the dressing table mirror. I'm greeted by a mess of spiky hair and mauve shadows under my eyes. I'm not sure whether Bella will speak to me but she's gone to school by the time I walk downstairs.

'I've arranged an appointment today,' Mum says, smiling at me. 'This is your opportunity to tell the doctor about your visions and anything else bothering you.'

Dad drives to the medical centre but doesn't come in with us, and I slump on the hard plastic chairs in the waiting room. Mum is fidgeting and keeps getting up and fetching an old magazine from the coffee table. My name is called and we enter into a brilliant white room. Clinical. Doctor Miller looks up and gestures towards the chairs. Perching my hands in my lap, I pick at the skin around my chipped nails.

Toast crumbs have lodged in the corners of his mouth. He grabs hold of my hand and places two fingers against my wrist and, with the hint of coffee on his breath, he leans over me.

'Sienna, how can I help you?'

'I see dead people and smell strange odours.'

'Carry on.' He releases my hand and leans back into his leather chair. I close my eyes and tell him about my visions.

'Her name is Martha. She whispers to me and appears when I'm not expecting her. She shows me images of her life.'

'Sienna,' interrupts Doctor Miller. I open my eyes. Mum is by my side and I reach out to her. They must believe me. The ringing of his phone shatters the silence, but he doesn't answer it.

'You don't need to carry on, love,' Mum says, crinkling her brow and studying me.

'No, I'm fine.' I wipe a hand over my forehead. I'm sweating, this room is too warm. My eyes close, and I continue.

'There's one scene when she's watching a group of girls sitting in a circle, chanting. They wear a uniform. The air is dense. Footsteps descending along a spiral staircase. Water dripping from the moss-covered walls.'

The doctor is scribbling on a pad of loose-leaf paper. I reach for the glass of water and gulp it down, washing away the dust clogging my throat.

'Do you recognise the girl from a film or a book you've read?'

'No,' I say, resting my hand on my trembling leg.

'What goes through your mind when these visions occur?' he asks, clicking his pen up and down.

'What do you think?' I snap. 'This isn't new. I've always felt different. On a school trip years ago, I saw a ghost. It was a little boy dressed in scruffy rags, a cloth cap on his head, and short trousers. His face covered in dirt. He told me he was cleaning the chimney in the stately home and became stuck. He was buried alive. The owners thought he had absconded. I told one girl and naturally the class thought it was hilarious. I've learnt to keep quiet until now.'

Mum tuts and places her hand on my arm.

'Sienna, that's enough.'

I catch him glancing at the clock above the door.

'Have you been studying hard for exams? It's a challenging stage of your life,' he says, and winks at Mum as if they were best friends.

'Yes.' I look away because I haven't been revising.

'What are you working on at the moment?' he asks, closing his laptop.

'It's topic week at school and we study what interests us.'

Mum and the doctor look at each other.

'That's different to our day, isn't it, Mrs Stevens?' he says, picking up a mug of coffee. 'What's your topic, Sienna?'

'Cotswolds Hauntings.'

'What an unusual subject. What made you decide on that?' he asks, coughing and wiping his mouth. Drops of brown liquid stain his white shirt. 'Were you aware of this, Mrs Stevens?'

She looks away and doesn't answer.

He gazes down, crosses his leg and smoothes a crease in his trousers. When he looks up, a frown lines his forehead.

'This could be anxiety over your forthcoming examinations. Many teenagers are experiencing this at the moment. My suggestion is you cease reading paranormal books and concentrate on your studies. These images result from an overexcited mind. Are you sleeping?' he asks.

'No,' I say.

'Drink a glass of warm milk before bed and have an early night. There are sleeping tablets you can buy over the counter. I recommend you get some of those. Keep a dream diary and write down your visions. That way we can spot a pattern.'

'What do you mean?' asks Mum. 'A pattern?'

'Well, to see if something traumatic has happened that day to trigger those kinds of responses. Make an appointment with the receptionist for a couple of weeks from now,' he says, turning back to his computer screen. 'Thank you for coming, and no more reading scary stories,' he laughs, wagging his finger at me as if I'm a child. He stands up and walks over to the door.

'Doctor?' I turn to face him.

'What?' he snaps, a tinge of irritation in his voice.

'Why me?'

He doesn't answer, but looks at his watch and walks back to the desk. Mum storms out and I follow.

'That was a waste of time,' she grunts.

'What did you expect? He didn't take me seriously, just coz I've had a couple of nightmares.'

Mum isn't listening and marches over to the reception desk to make another appointment.

'We'll be late. Your dad is waiting outside.'

The double doors hiss open and we climb into the car. Mum whispers to Dad, 'Pointless.'

I spend the journey to school reflecting on the doctor's remarks. Luckily, my first exam is this afternoon so I head straight into the library and revise. My mind is a whirl of herbs, poisons, and ravens, and I can't concentrate on the periodic table or the industrial revolution. I've allowed my obsession with the supernatural to dominate my life.

The exam hall is packed. Pupils are taking out pens from pencil cases and placing lucky mascots like teddy bears or ornaments on the desk. Charlie's designated seat is about ten rows behind me. When she spots me, she does a thumbs up and grins, but I don't respond and settle into my chair. The room is silent apart from the ticking of the clock on the wood-panelled wall. I open my paper. This will be the first of many tests and each day will follow the same pattern. I write my name and hope inspiration hits me.

**

The week passes in a blur of exams and last-minute cramming. On the final day, the girls in my class stand outside on the lawn and discuss prospective A levels. We tidy out desks and lockers, have a final assembly where the chosen few are allowed to present their topic work. Charlie and I look at each other when we realise our names are not being chosen. I'm unsure whether to stay on at this school and need to discuss the options with Dad. He's from an educational background and studied at Oxford University, as Nan always reminds me.

Last exam finished, I trudge home alone, flopping down on the bed. My phone vibrates and it's Charlie texting me to discuss the exams. When she gives me the answers, it's obvious I've not answered them in enough detail and will only scrape through. I want to forget about exam results and look forward to tonight's end of year 60s party instead.

After a quick shower, I open the wardrobe door and admire the outfit hanging up. Mum has shortened the hem and added a peter pan collar to a black and white dress from the charity shop.

'Wow, love,' she says, as I enter the lounge. 'You remind me of one of those dancers on the old TV programme, *Top of the Pops*. Brush your hair and try this on. Are you applying your makeup at Charlie's?' she asks, passing me a hairband.

'Yes, I'm headed there now. Thanks, Mum, for sorting out my dress.'

'Far out, man.'

'What?'

'Groovy, baby.' She stands in front and wiggles her hips.

'Mum, stop it! You weren't a hippy.'

'I know, but the sixties sound fun. Peace and love.' She spins me around. 'You look gorgeous, but don't stay out late.'

I wave goodbye to Bella lounging on the settee, still wearing her tracksuit.

Charlie doesn't live far away and when I ring the bell, the door opens immediately as if she's been waiting for me.

'Hi, Sienna,' she says, dragging me in and closing the door. 'Wow! That dress suits you.'

A creaking is coming from her bedroom.

'Is anyone at home?' I ask.

'You'll see. Follow me.'

We rush upstairs into her bedroom and stare at Matt dressed in a florescent flowery shirt, wide faded blue jeans, and a headband around his hair. He pretends he's strumming an air guitar.

'Peace man,' he drawls, holding up two fingers in the peace sign.

I clasp my hand up to my mouth, trying to stop myself from laughing, and then realise he's here. With Charlie. In her bedroom. I'm surprised and try to hide my jealousy.

'Hiya Sienna,' he says. 'You look amazing.'

'You too.' Heat floods my face as I speak to him.

'Sienna, sit on the bed and I'll do your makeup. Matt, do us a favour and fetch us a couple of cans from the kitchen.' She waves her hand towards the door. He nods and strolls out. Charlie catches me inspecting her. There must be an odd expression on my face because she sticks up her hand.

'Whoa! This may seem strange to you, but it's cool. When I told him you were going to the disco, he wanted to meet you here.'

'How come he knows his way around your house, then?'

'Hey. Stop that. This is the first time he's been here.'

'Why didn't you tell me?'

'I've been messaging you, but you've not been picking up.'

I study her and check for signs of lying, like fidgeting or looking away.

'Yeah, my phone needed charging. How's your gran?' I ask,

changing the subject.

'She's better now after a severe migraine attack. We flew to Ireland to keep her company and arrange medical help. Which is why I've not been around. My parents are worried about an underlying condition, although she dismissed their concerns. However, the doctor is arranging a brain scan.'

'I hope she's OK.'

'While I was there, Gran asked me about the book. Is there anything exciting in it?' Charlie asks, while applying black eyeliner around my eyes.

'Nothing.' I lie because I haven't finished reading it yet and don't want her to have it. 'Did you meet up with Paddy when you went home?' I try not to blink as she waves the kohl pencil closer towards my eyes.

'Yeah, he's ditched drama school and is backpacking around Europe. I thought he was a convincing actor and foolish to drop out. What's the mystery with Gran's book?'

When I don't answer, she carries on.

'You're not mad that Matt is here, are you?'

'Me? No. Why should I be?' I say, looking away.

'Get moving, you two. We'll be late,' yells Matt from downstairs.

'There,' she says, spreading white eyeshadow on my eyelids. 'Fabuloooous, darling,' she says in an affected voice. I stare at her. She's the one who's fabulous with her short mini dress, white fishnet tights, and plastic boots. Her black hair has grown and is shaped into a bob style. Her large dark eyes are ringed with black eyeliner and white plastic earrings dangle from her ears. 'I've modelled myself on Mary Quant. What do you think?' she asks, twirling to show me.

We're fashion models parading down the stairs, twisting and turning on the steps and hanging onto the banister. My stiletto heels are too high and I try not to slip. Charlie walks down first. Matt grins at her and when he sees me, his face flushes pink.

'Wow, Sienna, you're different with shorter hair and your eyes are…'

'So,' I interrupt, 'I look better dressed from the sixties, do I?'

'No, you suit any style. I'm trying to give you a compliment and, by the looks of things, doing a poor job,' he says.

'Give me a break, you two, enough of the squabbling.' Charlie grabs the cans of cider from Matt and pulls the ring tab. We head towards school as the noise from the disco becomes closer.

'I love 60s music,' says Matt, prancing into the hall.

'Who are you supposed to be?' I ask, watching him stick out his lower lip and wiggle his hips.

'Mick Jagger,' he says and waves his arms about.

'And the nerd can dance,' says Charlie, laughing.

I glare at her but Matt laughs along and for a moment I forget I hate this place. A group of girls rush up to Matt and one links her arms into his, and directs him towards the drinks table. Charlie pulls me to one side.

'Sienna, can't you tell he fancies you?'

'Matt? Nah, it's you, isn't it? You spoke to him in Paris and didn't bother to send me a message. Also, he's been in your house and not mine.'

'OK, park yourself,' she says, gesturing to the corner of the room away from the music.

We sit while the song, '*She loves you.*' blares out. How appropriate for the mood. The teachers stroll around the hall, trying to act cool while jigging to the beat of the music. The girls surround Matt, giggling adoringly at him. Girls with long blonde hair and bubblegum lip gloss. He catches my eye and grins at me with his mischievous smile, creating a dimple in his cheek. He waves and I wave back.

'See,' says Charlie. 'He likes you. He told me.'

'What did you say?'

'You heard. Relax. Sometimes you're too...'

'What?' I ask.

'... serious.'

I stare at her.

'I've not contacted you before the exams because of my er...'

'What did you say?' I shout.

I try to lip read, but it's hard to figure out what she's saying with people screaming over the beat of the music. My dress is too short, annoying me because it keeps riding up and showing off my stubby legs.

'What did you say?'

'OK, I'm being straight with you. I wanted Matt from the moment I saw him, but it was obvious he's interested in you. I'm jealous because you don't notice the way he looks at you when you walk into class. You don't see his cheeks turning pink when you glance over at him.'

'Yeah, sure. It's alright saying that, but I don't stand a chance with all those girls around him.'

'Sienna, don't be naïve. I bought the Ouija board as an excuse to bring you two together. I never expected for one moment we would summon a spirit. Scary or what?'

I don't answer. A boy from our class saunters over to Charlie and asks her to dance. She smiles at me and raises her eyebrows.

'Are you ready for a brilliant night? Forget your spooky thoughts for once.'

Next minute, Matt is behind me, resting his hands on the top of the chair.

'Sienna, are you avoiding me?'

'Me? No. I've been here all the time,' I say, standing up to face him. He grins.

'You can't take a joke, can you? Hey, this is my favourite.' He tilts his head to one side, concentrating on the music.

'What is?' I ask.

'You really got me.'

'Pardon?' I stare at him. His hips are moving to the music, and my body naturally sways in time with him.

You really got me,' he shouts above the noise. 'By the Kinks. Would Madame care for this dance?' he says, bowing and holding out his hand.

I'm not much of a dancer, yet when Matt whisks me on to the gym floor, I'm transformed. Not the plain Jane with the frizzy red hair, but a model from the swinging sixties. Moving to the rhythm with my eyes closed, and with Matt in front of me, is magic. The lights start to strobe, and the room darkens. I hear the distant sound of someone singing an old nursery rhyme. *Lavender blue, dilly dally, lavender green.* A young man is in the garden, tending to the grass. Martha stands next to him. They walk into the greenhouse and he picks handfuls of aromatic lilies and presents them to her. The perfume of the flowers has a hypnotic quality and their bodies touch. Under the long wooden tables covered with plant pots and soil, they lie down and his lips brush hers as their bodies merge. The pain is short and sweet. As she stands to brush off the earth, a figure comes into view. Another girl is lurking behind the shed. She stares at me, puts her finger up to her lips and runs away.

'I saw her! Martha, take care, take care!' I shout.

'Wake up,' says Matt as Charlie shakes me.

'Can't hold her drink,' says a girl dancing behind us.

'Witch,' hisses another, giggling and hanging on to her friend's arm.

'My head hurts,' I say, as a teacher hurries over to us.

'It's fine, sir,' says Matt as the teacher attempts to waft air over me from a rolled-up flyer.

'She suffers from migraines.'

My friends put their arms around me and we stumble outside and flop on a bench in the playground.

'What happened this time?' asks Charlie.

After recounting the vision, we stand up. There's a warmth in the air that cloaks my body as we walk home. Charlie's house is first, and Matt clasps my hand and twists his fingers around mine.

'I'm worried about you. I'm not being mean, but you live in your thoughts and allow your imagination to control you.'

I yank my hand away.

'See, you're being emotional now. To me, life is black or white with no in between. I'm rational, rightly or wrongly. Do you know what I mean?'

'Yes, but why can't I be logical?'

'You're creative and it's great we're different. Do you remember me asking you whether you wanted to work at the care home? You'd be so busy that there'd be no time to worry about your problems. When old people talk about their past life, it makes you realise how lucky we are. Will you do it now that we are on our summer holidays?'

'I'm not sure; I don't get on with old people.'

'You're joking; they're desperate to have a natter and a cup of tea. You're a good listener, or you could play a game of Monopoly or Scrabble with them.'

'OK,' I say. 'We've not booked a summer holiday yet, which means I'll have loads of spare time.'

'Great. I'll text you the details. Bye Sienna,' he says, bending to kiss my cheek.

I stand by the door, my hand against my flushed face.

Matt kissed me.

CHAPTER 16

My first thought on awakening is Matt kissing me. I place my hand up to my cheek and remember the softness of his full lips, but then the vision pops into my mind, spoiling my thoughts. Perhaps Matt is right about having migraines. Opening my laptop, I read up about these types of headaches and discover they cause a loss of vision in part of one or both eyes. The information says that symptoms include seeing zigzag patterns and flashing lights, even hearing or smelling things not there. Prickling, or numbness, and trouble using the correct words. This is what I've been suffering with, and nobody picked it up. What a relief. I'm not insane.

I'm on my own today. Bella has gone to school and Mum is working at the charity shop. I mooch about, unsure what to do with myself. The school didn't want our supernatural project and I have heaps of research papers stuck in a folder. While everyone's out, I fix myself a banana sandwich and walk upstairs to my room, but something stops me.

A feeling. A sensation of warm air breathing on my neck. I turn around but there is nothing there.

'Martha,' I cry. 'Is that you?'

No answer but a cold icy fear creeps behind me. I'm stuck on the stairs holding my banana sandwich. I want to laugh at the ridiculousness of the situation. But something stops me. This feeling isn't Martha. She exudes a warm, friendly aura. This is sinister. Sharp like knives. Eyes pierced by razors. The rattle of a serpent winding around my legs. The pressure of a heavy coil twisting around my throat. I'm being lifted higher and higher till I can no longer see the ground. Grasping my neck to release the pressure, a darkness overcomes me. I look into bottomless black eyes as pinpricks of light fade away.

'Sienna, where are you. I'm home early. Have you made any lunch?'

In the distance, my mother's voice wakes me out of my reverie.

'What are you doing? Get up, you've squashed your sandwich against the banister,' she says, staring at me. 'Did you fall down the stairs?'

'I… I'm not sure,' I say, examining the mess of squashed banana dripping down the painted wooden frame of the stairwell.

'Did you pass out?' Come on, perhaps you need to have a lie down.'

She pulls me to my feet and stops at the top of the stairs.

'There wasn't any alcohol allowed at the disco last night, was there?'

'No, there wasn't. Mum, I think migraines are causing the visions.'

'Migraines? Of course, why didn't we think of that? Have a lie down. I'm going to the station to collect Dad from Oxford later. Do you want to come with me?'

'Yep,' I say, flopping down fully clothed on the bed.

I don't hear her going out because exhaustion overcomes me, and I fall into a dark and dreamless sleep. I'm only woken by the sound of a baby elephant running up the stairs. Bella is home and dashes into my room, followed by Mum.

'Matthew kissed you,' says Bella. I sit up in bed and kick her in the shin.

'Ouch. It's true Mum, he did. They stood outside on the doorstep and I saw them from my window.'

'Why don't you invite him round for tea?' asks Mum.

'He wants me to volunteer with him.'

'Where?'

'At the local care home.'

'You mean where Ria lives?' asks Mum.

'What about those creepy ghosts? Oooh.' Bella screws up her face, waves her hands in front of me and tries to act threatening. I glare at her.

'But that's different, isn't it, if Matthew will be there?' she laughs, walking away.

'We'll discuss this later,' says Mum, opening the front door.

She drives up to the waiting bay as the crowd of passengers swarm out. Dad waves at us and jumps into the car.

'Hi, girls. Everyone okay?'

We nod and Bella chatters on about her latest running time. I haven't said a word about last night's vision or what happened on the stairs. In fact, I don't know how to broach it, because the excuse of studying too much is no longer true.

We spend the rest of the evening relaxing in the garden and enjoying the sunshine. Mum places olives and hummus, bowls of green salad, coleslaw, slices of ham, a platter of salmon, new potatoes, crusty bread and butter, and jugs of Pimms on the table. She hands me a glass and tops it up with strawberries and ice cubes.

'Sienna, now your exams are over, what are your plans?' Dad asks, reclining in the chair with a glass of beer in his hand.

'No idea,' I say, tucking my legs underneath me on the sun lounger.

He peers at me over his glass.

'Choose your A levels carefully and we'll select the best university for you to attend. You're confident you'll pass, aren't you?'

'Yes,' I reply, smiling at him. What he doesn't appreciate is that other things are uppermost in my mind, leaving hardly any time to think about results.

'Don't follow in my footsteps,' mumbles Mum, gulping her third glass of Pinot Grigio.

'I'm not sure whether to stay on at school or try the local sixth form college. Matt is applying there,' I reply, ignoring Mum.

'Why don't we discuss the pros and cons of both?' asks Dad in the pompous way he has when discussing educational matters. He stands up, enters the study, and returns with a large piece of paper. Using a felt-tip pen, he draws two columns. We discuss my future and write the advantages and disadvantages of college and school. Being the centre of attention makes a change, but then Bella finishes eating and huddles next to Dad, spoiling the atmosphere.

'Are we booking a holiday this year, Dad? You're the expert at last-minute deals,' she asks.

'There's plenty of time. I need to request the days off as we usually permit families with young children to choose first,' he says. 'I'll search for availability soon.'

'Isabella has lots of sports meetings to attend during the summer holidays. Sienna, why don't you go with me?' says Mum.

'Or...' Dad interrupts.

'What marvellous idea have you arrived at now?' I laugh.

'Why don't you volunteer and use the experience as evidence for your university supporting statement?' he asks.

'Oh no. I don't want to set foot in a charity shop handling mouldy old clothes.' I look at Bella. 'Mind you, it would be great if I found a box of rare manuscripts.'

'Like what?' asks Bella.

'Oh, I don't know. Perhaps the book *Poems,* by JD. You know who JD is?' She's biting her nails and I want to embarrass her for interrupting my conversation with Dad. Reading is not her strength. 'No? Are you thick, Bella? Too much running frazzled your brain? It's John Donne, stupid.'

'Girls, stop arguing with each other. I'm not talking about that kind of volunteering,' he says.

'And what's the problem with *that kind of volunteering*?' asks Mum, glaring at Dad.

God, now Mum has started.

'Nothing, love, nothing at all.'

'Matt has asked me to help him at the care home,' I pipe up.

'Is he the lad from the night, when…' he whispers and tilts his head towards my sister. Bella doesn't notice the subtle sign he's sending by trying not to mention the Ouija night.

'Yes, he volunteers there, but I'm not sure because I don't want to have to wash old people or give them bedpans. Yuk.'

'Don't worry, they won't ask you to do that. I can see the medical profession isn't for you.' He grins. 'Your Nan was saying to me the other day her diminishing eyesight means she misses her books. You could read to her and the other patients.'

'Did you discuss this with the staff at the home?' demands Mum, narrowing her eyes. She twists her wedding ring around her finger. I study her. The wrinkles around her eyes are deepening. 'Sienna hates going to the care home, don't you?'

The atmosphere is tense, so I try to lift the mood.

'It could be an excellent idea. Spending more time with Nan might improve our relationship. Will they pay me?' I ask, half joking, hoping they might.

'No, the word is *volunteer*, Sienna. This is a charitable scheme for the residents of our village. The neighbourhood is organising it. They'll collect you in their minibus and give you lunch, so you won't starve,' says Dad, swigging down his drink. 'Someone from the council was telling me about it the other day on the train. Why don't you try it for a few days? You might enjoy it. Now, what about snacks, Tracey? We've demolished the buffet,' he says, gesturing at the empty plates.

The idea of reading to the residents excites me and I get up and enter the study in search of classics, Dickens and Thomas Hardy, perhaps. Maybe D. H. Lawrence, and a couple of easy-to-read detective stories. It could be fun to discuss literature with the patients and try to solve the clues. It might not be so dreadful after all. Dad is right – volunteering in a care home will be an impressive addition to my university application.

Bella drifts up to her room and Dad carries on drinking while Mum clears up after us. I should help but there is an urgency to read Rose's book and I escape upstairs to lie down. It's becoming harder to prise open the pages now and difficult to pull apart the fused paper. On the next page is a faded drawing of an object resembling a mushroom. Underneath the picture is the following writing:

Destroying angel (Amanita virosa) – a pure white, deadly poisonous mushroom. Found in mixed woodland, particularly birch trees. Contains deadly amatoxic poisons. Effects seen 8- 24hours after ingestion. Liver and kidney poisoning. Death.

Death cap (Amanita phalloides) – most deadly fungus in England. Found in woods. Cut into chunks, steep and pour into soup. Watch her drink it. Side effects are vomiting, diarrhoea, and stomach pain. Will lead to death.

This is horrible. Who would know this information? An earthy odour drifts off the pages. Destroying me. Hypnotising me. My eyes are heavy so I switch off the lamp and place the book under my pillow. I dream I'm lying on a bed of mushrooms with thick, fleshy roots creeping into my mouth. When I awake, my room is pitch black and a mantle of doom and trepidation swathes me. I sense a presence floating near my bed and close my eyes, too scared to peer out. A gentle touch on my shoulder and Martha emerges in front of me. *'Listen, Sienna, this is what happened,'* she says. *'I crept out of bed and headed towards the door, avoiding the creaky step and tiptoed downstairs. The rusty lock was stiff with age, but I pushed the heavy wooden door, trying to be as quiet as possible. You should have seen it, Sienna'.* Martha reaches out but her fingers are crystal drops of water as an icy chill passes through me. *'The night air was still. I walked forward but my feet sank deeper into the sodden grass. The pearly hue of the moon was aglow and illuminated the way forward. In the distance, the glimmer of the lake beckoned me.'*

I peer out from underneath the covers and rub my eyes as a gust of fetid air swirls towards me from the corner of the room. Closer and closer. Sinking lower into my bed, I wrap the duvet around me. I'm immobile. My eyes widen in terror. The fog envelops me and dampens my sheets. An invisible hand drags the cover off me, the coolness of the air catching my breath. I must be dreaming. This isn't real. The mist evaporates, leaving behind the odour of damp clothes while the heady perfume of lavender lulls me to sleep.

***

In the morning my parents are waiting for me. Sat in the kitchen. Mum fiddling with a cup of tea and Dad pacing up and down. I should have realised that school would phone them about my fainting episode at the disco.

'We've just had the principal on the line,' says Dad. 'Why didn't you tell us you fainted?'

'I'm okay, really. It was a muggy night, and they had a smoke machine in the room.'

'You haven't been eating. I've noticed how those jeans are sliding off your hips.' Dad stares at me.

Mum lifts her coffee cup. 'We've arranged an emergency appointment this afternoon at the medical centre. I promised the charity shop I'll work today, but I can stay home with you instead,' says Mum.

'No, no, I'm fine.' I wave my hand at them. 'I'm tired, that's all. Also, Matt said it could be migraines.'

'So, he's the expert on my daughter now, is he?' asks Dad, picking up his briefcase.

'No, but he reads a lot of medical journals and his uncle is a hospital consultant at St Bart's in London.'

'Fine, fine. But make sure you tell the doctor everything.'

I nod and pick up a piece of toast, making a show of spreading marmalade on it and nibbling around the edges as they both watch me.

'See you later,' they shout as they walk out together.

After they go, I throw the toast in the bin and turn on the television. There's nothing to watch apart from boring programmes about repairing things or buying property. I wander around the house and then remember that the doctor asked me to complete a dream diary which I haven't done. How can I write down my visions and dreams? Nobody would believe me. In fact, I'm starting to doubt them.

By the time Mum comes home at midday, the thought of the impending appointment causes havoc with my nerves. My stomach is clenching too much so I nibble a few crackers while Mum fixes herself a Spanish omelette.

'Sienna, do you want one?' she asks.

'No,' I shake my head. 'I'm not hungry.'

'Dad was right. You're looking peaky and have lost a few pounds.

I hope you eat when I'm at work?'

'Of course I do. Don't worry about me.'

Mum sighs. After lunch, we drive to the medical centre but are early for the appointment. While I wait on the uncomfortable plastic chair, Mum heads over to the reception desk. I stare at the faded pattern on the carpet and ignore the other patients.

A different doctor is sitting at the desk and stands up when we enter the room. This one is younger than Doctor Miller – in his thirties with dark curly hair. His skin is clear with the hint of a dark shadow on his upper lip. He shakes Mum's hand when we enter the room.

'Hello, Mrs Stevens and Sienna. My name is Dr Frank and I'm standing in for your doctor, who's been treating you. I hope that's fine with you both?'

We nod and sit down.

'Sienna, apart from worrying your parents, what else have you been up to?' he says, smiling at me and placing his tanned, smooth fingers over my wrist. His nails are short and clean, and a hint of sandalwood drifts over me. Dr Frank takes my pulse, then wraps the blood pressure cuff around my upper arm.

'There's a slight increase in your blood pressure, otherwise you're healthy. Your mother told me you took a couple of slimming tablets, but that was all. You got rid of them, I hope? Am I correct?' I shrink underneath his stare. 'Those pills are dangerous, with side effects of anxiety and severe headaches. Your case history interests me and I want to investigate these dreams. Tell me about the last one you had,' he says, leaning back in his chair and staring at me.

'Last night, I dreamt Martha strolled to the orchard to collect flowers for the May procession. He was there, standing underneath the cherry blossom tree, waiting for her. She told him about the horrid doll holding a posy that they left on her bed. He warned her about the poisonous flowers growing in the woodland of birch and beech. Then he showed her the abundance of herbs and mushrooms in the garden. When he explained their dangerous properties, the roots moved, swirling over her toes to pull her down.'

'Sienna! This is the first time you've mentioned this,' says Mum, grabbing hold of my arm.

'Mrs Stevens, I want to chat with your daughter on her own. Sienna, do you want your mother with you?'

'No, thanks. Wait outside, Mum. There's a coffee machine in the hall.'

Mum stares at me as the colour rises in her cheeks. 'I'm not happy about this,' she says, storming out the door.

The doctor has been typing on his laptop, then looks up at me.

'Sienna, your dreams bother me. However, I'm concerned there are other problems in your life you're not divulging. What does your family say?'

I disclose my parents' favouritism towards my sister, Mum's drinking, the worry my dad works too hard, and the possible involvement of the priest. He raises his eyebrows.

'How about your mother? How would you describe your relationship with her?'

A picture of Mum lying on the settee drinking wine and not taking me seriously bursts into my mind. I track a wasp crawling up the window, trying to escape, but trapped amongst the slats of the blinds. The thought of Mum dying brings tears to my eyes, and I wipe my hand across my face to remove them.

'What happened, Sienna? You crashed out for a minute. What did you see?' he asks, handing me a tissue.

My eyes are heavy and my mouth is dry, but his voice is as gentle as a soft blanket wafting over me. I drift off and tell him.

'Today in the waiting room, the scent of mown grass came over me. I saw girls skipping amongst fields of wheat. Red Admiral butterflies with colours of red, orange and black flutter by and sprinkle their pollen on the lavender. Martha hurrying to meet him near the climbing vines of the golden honeysuckle. Ripened strawberries have stained her lips red. The tall young man with jet black, crinkly hair and brown eyes holds her hand and they sit down.'

I jerk suddenly as the image darkens, and a sense of danger surges over me.

'Sienna, do you have many friends?' he asks, biting on his lower lip.

I think of Matt and the heat starts from my chest and travels upwards towards my throat, ending up at the birthmark. I place my hand on it to stop the throbbing.

'Let me check what's going on here.'

Wearing a pair of disposable gloves, he holds my chin and twists my face from side to side.

'Mmm, you have a vascular birthmark, otherwise known as a port wine stain. Take your hand away.' He touches the side of my face. 'Has anyone suggested it can be removed?' he asks.

'Is that possible?'

'Sienna, anything is possible. I'll write to a dermatologist colleague and see what she can suggest. In the meantime, make an appointment at our teenage counselling service here at the medical practice with Emma Larkin,' he says, handing me a card.

The vivid yellow card has a drawing of a chrysalis changing into a butterfly with the words, '*Change for good*' *Emma Larkin MSc. MBACP*. How tacky is that? I stick it in my pocket.

'Do you think I'm making up these visions?' I ask.

'They are real to you,' he says. 'However, we'll wait till you chat with Emma and assess your situation from there.'

'Situation?' I shout. 'What does that mean? I haven't got a *situation*. I'm in contact with dead people.'

'Sienna, please don't alarm yourself. We'll uncover the cause of these visions and discuss suitable solutions. In the meantime, try to relax.'

'Relax?' I say, aware that my voice is rising. 'How can I relax when my mind is full of death, destruction, sorrow, flowers, poisonous mushrooms and God knows what.'

He stands up and escorts me to the door. Mum is outside scrolling through her phone and doesn't say a word till we climb into the car.

'Why were you shouting at the doctor? That was really embarrassing. Nan's busybody carer, Mrs Jones, was sitting in the waiting room. What sort of impression does that make? Why didn't you tell me about your dreams? Did you mention migraines?' she asks, accelerating out of the car park.

'No, I forgot to tell him.'

'Oh, well.' She sighs. 'I'll stop at the chemist and pick up some migraine tablets. See if they work.'

'I have to make an appointment with a counsellor and we spoke about my birthmark,' I say.

'What about it?' she asks, her hands clenched on the steering wheel.

'He's contacting a skin professional who specialises in laser treatment for port wine stains.'

'That will be expensive.' She peers out of the window and signals left. 'And with the school bills, I'm not sure we can afford it.'

'You didn't tell me it could be removed. I'll apply for a Saturday job and save up the money.'

'It's not *that* noticeable, and your hair covers it.'

I touch the skin on my cheek. Why does she not realise how much it bothers me? I bet if it was my sister, they would do something about it. When we stop, I yank open the car door and stomp through the hall. Bella is laying the table and arranging the knives and forks. 'I'm starving and didn't know whether to cook,' she says.

'You cook? That will be a first.' I laugh.

'I'm not in the mood for slaving over a hot stove. Let's order a curry,' says Mum, picking up her phone.

While talking to the doctor about herbs and mushrooms, I couldn't stop thinking about Rose's book, so as we wait for the take-away, I sneak upstairs and open it. Prising the sheaves apart, I carry on and inspect the page of writing, careful the withered feather doesn't fall out.

Banishing spell

Herbs to banish people from your life:

Mugwort, Pepper, Rosemary, Sandalwood and St John's wort.

Instructions:

Draw a circle, light a candle, and invite the spirit to join us. Repeat these words.

'Oh blessed one, remove her power.

Give it to me,

Give it to me."

Walk three times around the circle, anticlockwise.

Undertake this at midnight. On the eve of All Hallows draw the inverted pentagram.

This will aid death and destruction.

The contents of this book terrify me, but it draws me in. There's a beat pounding in my temple as I try to understand it. The doorbell rings and soon the house reeks with the aroma of cinnamon, ginger and greasy meat. I'm not hungry and want to stay in my room and carry on reading, but Mum calls me down.

I pick at my Lamb Rogan Josh and Dad turns to me.

'Guess what?'

'What?' I ask, staring at my plate of yellow rice with chunks of brown meat before I mush them together. The stench of spices is strong and stings my eyes.

'The care home management left a voicemail message saying you can volunteer from tomorrow.'

'Mmm, possibly,' I grumble.

I'm having second thoughts. The atmosphere in Monkton House terrifies me and I only agreed because of Matt being there. Environments affect me and I'm not sure I'm the right person for the job. I want to text Charlie but when discussing my visions, I've noticed her attention has wandered as if I'm boring her. Her confession about Matt makes me wonder how secure our friendship is. My mind is overshadowed by her gran's book. It's taking control of me. I'm obsessed with reading it even though the contents are horrific.

'Goodnight,' I say, scraping the curry in the bin and stacking my plate in the dishwasher.

After a quick shower, I head straight to bed, the sound of humming pounding in my brain. I've heard that tune before and try to identify it. Memories of sitting on Nan's knee as she brushed my hair and sang to me. No, that's not possible. I've always thought she didn't want anything to do with me. I must ask Mum about this memory.

An invisible energy draws me to Rose's book so I pull it out. The faded words from the next passage read:

Water hemlock (Oenanthe crocata) – Water hemlock grows in marshy, swampy areas of meadows and along banks of streams, pools and rivers. Accidental poisonings usually occur when water hemlock is confused for edible plants such as artichokes, celery, sweet potatoes, sweet anise or wild parsnip. Water hemlock has poisonous ingredients with many dangerous effects on the body such as muscle weakness, loss of speech and paralysis. This plant is toxic and causes death in 15 minutes.

A draft blows around my head. The floorboards creak and the sweet perfume of lavender enters my nostrils.

'Sienna, Sienna,' she whispers. 'Ask her before her time runs out.'

Martha is in my room.

Resting my head on the pillow, I close my eyes and see her. I reach out as my fingers burst through a bubble of mist. Muddy liquid drips from her hair. Fronds of green weeds twist around Martha's body while water puddles on the floor underneath her feet.

'I can't rest till I forgive that girl,' she whispers.

I toss and turn as the shadows keep me awake.

CHAPTER 17

I must have finally dozed off because it's morning and my father is shaking me.

'The minibus is here ready to take you to do your bit for the elderly of this village,' he laughs, placing a cup of coffee on my bedside table.

'Dad?'

'Yes? I'm in a hurry, Sienna. What's wrong?'

'Nothing – but did I imagine it or did Nan sit me on her knee and sing to me when I was little?'

He smiles. 'Gosh yes, that was when you were a toddler. She would babysit on the rare occasions your mum and I went out. She had a favourite nursery rhyme. Not sure what it was,' he says, turning away.

'Oh, but I thought Nan Ria didn't like me.'

'What makes you think that?' he asks, swivelling around and staring at me.

'Er, just something I feel.'

'No. You're both strong characters. Don't you remember arguing with her when you were younger? Instead of concurring, you would dispute everything she said. Bella on the other hand just agreed for the quiet life. I can't remember half the things you would disagree with. If she said something was black, you would say it was white,' he chuckles.

'Oh yes, I remember now. I think it's because she was a head teacher and thought she knew it all.'

'That's why it's so difficult for her at Monkton House. Anyway, now you're going to work there, you can see her more. Off you go,' he says, dismissing me with a wave of his hand.

I take a quick slurp, but burn my mouth and throw the rest of the coffee away. Get dressed, brush my teeth, scrunch my hair, and grab an energy bar. My stomach is fluttering with nerves. At the end of the drive is the minibus, so I dash out the front door and climb up the steps. It's crowded. People are chattering but stop when I get on. I spot Matt sprawled over a spare seat at the back. His face beams when he spots me and my skin tingles as if I've had an icy shower. Matt is gangly and cannot sit comfortably on the seat. He stretches his long legs in the aisle and I step over them.

'Hey! I'm glad you showed up rather than spending your time scrolling through spooky websites.'

'Nah, you're right. It's time I ventured into the real world and meet other people.' The only person I want to meet is him, so that's a lie. 'What are you reading?' I ask, pointing to a book in his hands.

'It's a physics A level study guide. I'm preparing for next year.'

'You're keen aren't you, studying in the summer holidays? Science is tough with those equations and chemical symbols.'

'If you want help anytime, I'm your man,' he says, smiling at me.

The heat rises from my chest and creeps up to my face. I place my hand over my burning cheeks, trying to hide my embarrassment and stop the throbbing. Matt chats for part of the journey, mainly to do with school and village life. He exudes calmness and I relax in his company while enjoying the pressure of his leg next to mine. The bus negotiates through the rutted roads and overhang of trees till it arrives outside the care home.

'About time your bosses fixed this road,' shouts the driver to no one in particular.

'Aye, you're right there and you can fix the springs in this heap you call a bus,' pipes up Mrs Jones, Nan's carer who's also on the minibus.

We arrive at Monkton House. It's even creepier than ever. The early morning dew has covered the roof and top floor, giving it an eerie, flint-grey haze. I enter with Matt by my side.

'I'll meet you later. Wait in the staff room and a member of the leadership team will have a chat with you. They want me to tidy up the library. Why don't you ask if you can help me?' he says, holding the door open.

The carers disperse, and the friendly banter on the bus fades as they trudge into the home. We enter through the back door and I'm overwhelmed with a sense of melancholy. Luckily, there are no scary statues of Jesus here. Mrs Jones is removing her coat and hanging it on a hook in the staff room whilst studying me.

'I recognise you, my dear,' she says.

'Yes, you care for my nan.'

'Ah, of course, the Stevens girl. Are you volunteering here?' she asks, surveying me with narrowed eyes.

'Yes, today's my first day.'

The head nurse comes in and explains the health and safety rules and we talk about the residents. She suggests I visit Nan first before reading to the others. I head towards a maze of corridors and find Mrs Jones is already there, searching inside the wardrobe for Nan's clothes.

'And who is visiting me this morning? What's your name, dear?' Nan asks, peering at me.

She's lying in her bed, her eyes blinking from the light and her long, crinkly, uncombed grey hair spread on the pillow. No longer looking like the confident woman from my childhood.

'It's me, Sienna.' I'm gripping the door handle.

'Make your mind up. You're letting the heat out,' she barks.

'Hi,' I mutter, leaning over to kiss her cheek. A sharp and pungent aroma of lavender with an underlying layer of dried urine wafts into my nose. Her bony shoulders jut out of the nightdress and she looks thinner.

'Nan, do you want me to feed you?' I look at the half-eaten bowl of congealing porridge on her tray.

'No, I'm not an invalid. Why are you here this early?' she asks, struggling to pull herself up.

'To read you a story. What's your favourite?'.

'Am I a child now? No, don't bother, my helper can do it,' she says, waving her hand dismissively. 'You should revise for your exams. I don't want those expensive school fees wasted.'

'I've finished – it's the summer holidays now.' I try smiling with no reaction. It's obvious I lack my sister's charm.

'Why are you reading to deaf people and those who don't even know what day it is?' Her beady eyes examine me. 'They make me sit with them in rows on those uncomfortable lounge armchairs with that blasted television blaring out. No wonder I prefer staying in my room. Haven't you anything better to occupy your time?'

'What do you want me to read to you, Nan? Romance, thriller, horror, detect–'

'I read classical literature, not trivial rubbish. See those over there?' She points a shaky finger to a few women's magazines lying on the table.

I pick them up and flick through them.

Nan smirks. 'A "kind soul" from the Parish Centre brought them for me. They don't appreciate my intelligence, so I want you to remove them. The half-witted carers can have them.'

Mrs Jones is busy folding Nan's clothes and listening to her remarks.

'Why don't we look at them together?' I bring the chair closer to her and flick through the pile of magazines, but she's scrutinising me with a grin on her face.

'Who are you? What are you doing here?'

'It's me, Nan, I'm here to read to you.'

'My eyes hurt and the words are blurry.'

'Yes, Dad told me.'

'Daddy died years ago and they sent me away to a nasty place.'

'Nan, what do you mean?' I ask.

'Where is he now?'

Mrs Jones raises her eyebrows and beckons me.

'When she gets like this, it's best to change the subject and agree with her, dear,' she says.

'Nan, who are those people in the magazines?' I ask, pointing to a picture of the Royal Family.

'I'm not senile – it's Queen Lillibet, but that dress is frumpy,' she says, pointing a finger at the glossy page. 'I wouldn't say no to those jewels. There was a time when people respected me and called me The Boss behind my back.' She laughs. 'Not now. I'm treated like a child. What's your name and why are you cluttering my room?'

'I'm Sienna and I want to talk to you.' Her face turns ashen grey.

'No,' she cries, gripping my arm with her sharp nails digging into my skin. 'Don't make me tell, it's a secret. She'll kill me.'

'What's wrong? Who'll kill you?' I watch her beady eyes dull to the colour of ditch water.

'Sienna, what a pretty name. It means red, you know. But what have you done to your hair? I used to have a granddaughter with a mane of red curls. Are you my new carer? The other one isn't very good.' She gestures to Mrs Jones, who tuts and walks out.

'No, I'm not, Nan.'

'What did you say? Speak up you're mumbling.'

I sigh and change the subject.

'Nan, why don't we read this magazine; it's the *Gardener's World*.'

'Garden, no. It wasn't me but watch out for the lilies, child,' she says. Her eyelids flicker and she hums under her breath.

'Nan, what did you say? And what's that tune?' I ask.

'What? I'm tired and you ask too many questions. Leave me in peace,' she gestures, waving her hand at me as I stand up from the chair.

'Yes, Nan.'

I feel sorry for what she's become. An elderly woman with her mind and body betraying her. I open the door. The matron is outside and puts her hand on my arm.

'Mrs Jones has spoken to me. Your nan has no recollection and won't remember those harsh words. But she keeps repeating the same phrase, "watch out for the lilies", and we don't know what it means. Will you ask your parents and see if they can shine a light on it? Perhaps that's her favourite type of flower and you could bring her a bunch next time?'

'I'll let my parents know when I go home, but Nan doesn't want me to read to her, so can I work in the library, please?'

'Of course, but at the moment, other residents would appreciate your time. Here's a list for you,' she says, handing me a piece of paper.

The rest of the morning is spent chatting to a variety of people in the home. They're not as forgetful as my nan, and most of them can hold an interesting discussion. I'm exhausted by the time I approach the next resident on my list. I knock on the door.

'Come in, come in. I'm finishing a sentence.'

This room is different to Nan Ria's. There's a simplicity about it compared to Nan's gloomy room stuffed with antique furniture. There are no photographs or ornaments, just a row of book shelves. An old lady sits upright in an office chair. She has her back to me and is writing at a large wooden desk while muttering to herself. Pinned on a cork board are sheets of paper, scribbled with names, dates, and places. I study her; she has a petite frame and is wearing a shapeless dress. A different carer is placing her breakfast dishes on a tray.

'Who are you?' the old lady asks. 'Has she sent you?'

The humming of the nursery rhyme jolts my memory as the sweet scent of lavender wafts over me. She's here again: the flickering shape of Martha stands behind this old lady. Sparkles of light flash in my eyes and my body softens as if I'm without muscles or bones. I grab hold of the top of a chair, overcome by dizziness, and pant for air. A murky grey haze billows around the room. The carer manoeuvres me into a sitting position and I'm handed a paper cup of water.

'I bet you didn't have your Weetabix this morning, did you? You young uns don't eat enough to feed a sparrow. Sit there for a while till you get your breath back,' she says, patting my shoulder. 'My granddaughter is always on the go and the doctor prescribed iron tablets; perhaps you might need them?'

'I'm fine now. Thanks for your help.'

The carer gestures to the button by the side of the bed. 'Anne has an alarm, so press it if you need me. I'll be in the next room,' she says, shutting the door.

The old woman peers at me, her sharp cornflower blue eyes sparkling against the pure white of her hair.

'What on earth are you doing here, child, and why did you faint?'

'My name is Sienna. I'm on my school holidays and I'm here to read to the patients. What did you mean when you asked who sent me?'

'Yes, yes, apologies for being abrupt. You startled me, but how generous to sacrifice your spare time to talk to us oldies.' She examines me as her eyes search my face. 'My mind was elsewhere, daydreaming about someone I knew. However, my dear, I don't need anyone to read to me. I'm a competent reader and in the process of carrying out research. Maybe you will help me collate these?' she asks, pointing to reams of handwritten notes.

'Of course,' I reply.

'That's kind of you, thanks. It's not much fun being in my seventies with these,' she says, showing me her arthritic fingers. 'There's plenty of research still needs carrying out about this old place.'

By her side is a book: *The History of Lakeview Village*.

'Did you write it?' I stare at her. 'Are you Anne Duncan, the author?'

'Yes – not who you're expecting, eh? Have you read it?'

'I've started it,' I say, but don't tell her how it affected Nan and me.

'I'm glad someone has. I'm a member of the local history group and we're researching the Lakeview area, including Monkton House. Do you want to know what I've found out?'

I nod my head and sip the water.

'The office staff let me use the computer and log onto the Internet. Brilliant invention, by the way. You can find anything out. Silly me. You know all about that, don't you?' She smiles at me and holds up her book. 'I discovered various genealogy sites and with the help of colleagues from Oxford University, I've investigated the house's background. My book relates to the Monkton family and their exploits involving countless illegitimate children, connection with the royalty and the church.'

'It sounds interesting. I've been revising for exams but will have more time to finish reading it now.'

'There's more to discover. The library has shelves of books, but it's a mess and I ended up covered in dust. I'm still trying to decipher the writing. After the Monkton family died out, it was sold to a monastery and renamed Monkton Abbey. At the moment, I'm translating various documents relating to its history.'

'I can help you.'

'As you'll see, this is a large rambling building, and the monks neglected the upkeep of it. It was converted into an orphanage, and, finally, this care home. The library contains ancient literature and papers, which will help with my investigation. I'm trying to sift through them, but the task is too immense for me. Enough chatting now,' she says, grasping my hand. Her grip is firm, but the skin is as thin as tissue paper, with mauve blue veins protruding over the bony nodules.

'Sit down, dear, and tell me about yourself,' she says, gesturing to a high-backed armchair covered in a beige blanket.

We chatter on until her lunch tray – a bowl of vegetable soup and a quiche – arrives. I'm supposed to have lunch in the canteen, but the thought of eating on my own worries me so I stay put. She dozes while I read her book. My stomach is rumbling and it's already late afternoon when Anne wakes up.

'I didn't expect to see you still here. Have you eaten anything? You need to keep your strength up. I remember being starving when I was younger. They didn't feed us much, in them days.'

'I'm not hungry. I've been scanning your book to learn more about the local Lakeview hauntings. Have you heard of them?' I ask.

'No, child, you mustn't meddle in dangerous activities. Leave well alone,' she says, fiddling with a small silver cross and chain around her neck.

Her eyes shift away from me and settle on the wall where she has a picture of Jesus.

'Anne, I'm leaving now but I'll be back tomorrow.'

It's late, and I don't want to miss the bus home so I head towards the door, being careful not to trip over the pile of books lying on the floor. Faint sounds of melodic voices are chanting outside. I stop and pivot around to see Anne Duncan staring at the door behind me.

'What's wrong?' I ask.

'Listen to Martha.'

'How do you know Martha? Can you see her too?' I ask, rushing over to her.

'See her? Is she here? Oh no, poor, poor girl,' cries Anne.

'Please, tell me everything about her.'

'Take no notice of me. My mind is in a daze these days. You need to hurry up, and catch your bus.'

'If you remember anything, no matter how trivial you'll tell me, won't you?' I ask, walking away from her. She can't hear me while she's staring in the distance.

As I hurry along the passageway, I sense I'm being followed. Whirling around, I glance behind me. The dim wall lamps and lack of signposts make it difficult to recognise where I'm heading. A large rainbow-coloured stained-glass window shows a dove holding a leaf in its beak, surrounded by figures of men in brown gowns, their faces hidden by their hoods with wooden crosses hanging from their necks. In the dusky rays of evening, the light illuminates vases of flowers perched on the ledges, their blooms dying from the humidity. The portrait of a woman dominates the wall next to the window. Her skin is porcelain white, deep dark eyes that follow me, glossy raven black hair tied up in a mound of waves and thin red lips set in a line. She's wearing a smart two-piece dark suit with a gold chain around her neck and several silver and gold rings on her fingers. In between her hands, she clasps a large brown leather book engraved in gold writing.

A low repetitive noise of a machine in the distance bleeps in my ears. My curiosity is heightened, and I edge towards the source. The sudden pressure of a hand on my shoulder surprises me and I swivel around.

'Oh!' I shout, as a figure creeps up behind me. 'Oh, it's you. Why are you wandering around?' I say to the stooped figure of Anne Duncan.

'Our chat made me restless, and I wanted more information from the library for my investigation. Go home, and I'll meet you tomorrow, dear,' she says, patting my arm.

Anne ambles along the wooden floor, her feet shuffling in her worn slippers. No-one else is around. Fear slinks over my body. The energy encompassing this house is increasing and pressing on my head.

Pushing the double doors open, I see the minibus is waiting, so I climb up the steps into it. Tiredness overwhelms me, and I lean my cheek against the headrest, immune to the banter on the bus. The chat with Anne Duncan bothers me. Next minute, Matt bounds up the steps before the bus drives away.

'Close call,' he laughs, and flops next to me. Heat rushes up from my chest and into my cheeks and I place my hand against my face.

'Why didn't you join us in the canteen? They won't bite,' he says, twisting his head and smiling at the people behind us.

'It's alright for you, Matt, you ooze confidence and can communicate with anybody.'

'You need to forget about yourself and listen to the old folk,' he says.

'OK but the main problem I have at the moment is locating my way around this place. It's a warren of walkways and rooms. Isn't it odd that it was once an orphanage?'

'No! Where did you learn that?'

'One of the residents is the author Anne Duncan; she wrote about its history.'

'That's interesting. I spoke to an old guy who is a hundred. Can you imagine living so long? He's been married for seventy years. His medals are in a frame, next to a picture of his wife.'

'I don't think Nan will live much longer,' I say, looking down at my hands.

'Why do you think that?'

'She didn't recognise me and we had a confusing chat. She was fine for a while, but she relapsed.'

'What did you do the rest of your day?' he asks.

'Had a long talk with Anne Duncan. When she dozed, I read her book, but the peculiar thing was, she told me to listen to Martha.'

'Who's that?'

I don't answer him in case he thinks I'm crazy.

'Oh yes, I remember you shouted out the name Martha during the Ouija session, didn't you?' he says. Mrs Jones, sitting in front, swivels around and glares at me.

'Shush. She's my nan's carer. Did you see the way she looked at me? What have I done? Is it because Nan is always moaning at her?'

I watch Matt bite his lip. 'What?'

He looks down at his hands. 'I've not told you this, but my daft brother pushed the piece of wood around to spell our gran's name. He mentioned it the other day.'

'No way,' I splutter. 'Why didn't you tell me?'

'I'm telling you now,' he says, looking at me.

'So, why did you run and shout after us? You weren't scared, were you?'

'Er, I didn't expect you to get away so fast.'

'What?'

'Yes, you headed the wrong way, and I yelled at you to stop. You ran deeper into the forest and kept on as if something possessed you.'

'Paddy warned me,' I whisper.

'Who's Paddy?' asks Matt.

'Oh, a guy I met in Ireland. He's a drama student.'

'Right then.' He bends down to collect his bag. 'This is my stop. See you tomorrow and I'm sorry my stupid brother messed with the board.'

I give a half-hearted smile, still annoyed with him, but why did I mention Paddy? Was it to make him jealous?

CHAPTER 18

I open the front door and catch my mother in the lounge, reclining on the settee reading her slimming magazine, eating a biscuit while Bella is exercising again. Dad has brought the treadmill down from her bedroom and plugged it in the utility room. The pounding of her feet vibrates throughout the house and Mum places the magazine on the cushion.

'How was your first day? Did you enjoy it?' she asks.

'Yes, it was interesting. Nan didn't want me to read to her so I spent most of my time with another old lady who's an author. But Nan worries me.'

'Why, what's she doing now?'

'The matron told me she keeps repeating the word 'lilies' again.'

'I'll buy her a bunch,' she says, picking up the magazine and flicking through it.

Bella jogs into the living room, wiping her hand across her forehead.

'I've done it,' she yells.

At that moment, the sound of clinking keys dropping into the porcelain bowl by the door announces Dad's arrival.

'Done what?' I ask.

'Broken my step target,' she cries, pointing at her Fitbit. I don't bother asking her the total because it's bound to be high.

After the evening meal, we move to the lounge and I take Rose's book out of my bag. I want to see what my parents think of it.

Bella reads her running magazine, Dad studies the Financial Times and Mum searches through Netflix for a film. When he sees my book, Dad places the newspaper on the table.

'What are you reading?' he says, glancing at the front cover.

'It's an old notebook; Charlie's gran gave it to me.'

'Oh yes, it has a musty old odour about it,' he says, sniffing the air. 'Like sweaty socks.' He laughs and trawls through his phone.

'I want to tell you about it,' I say.

'Put it away,' says Bella holding her hand to her mouth and coughing.

'It's just that there are some weird pages that I don't understand.'

'What do you mean?' asks Mum. 'Weird pages?'

'Well, it doesn't surprise me if it's from that family,' says Dad.

'Why do you criticise my friend and her family? I shout at him.

'OK.' He holds out his hand and starts counting on his fingers. 'Number one – how about being told by her father that you two had made up a spell and his daughter collapsed? Number two – getting another phone call after you returned from Ireland informing me that you were sick over his lawn due to excess of alcohol and possibly drugs.'

'You knew?' I ask.

He nods. My face burns with rage and I look away.

'Number three – playing the Ouija board and causing your sister to become ill. Do you want me to continue?'

I shake my head.

'Sienna, can't you see that your connection with Charlotte is not a healthy one? She's a negative influence on you,' says Mum. 'You need to burn her book if it scares you.'

'Or just give it back,' says Dad, returning to his paper.

I look at the three of them sitting on the settee. Bella didn't utter a word when my dad was telling me off. I look at her and instead of a smirk, find a strange expression, almost one of pity.

'Hummph,' is all I can say and storm up to my room.

I climb into bed, annoyed with Charlie's dad for telling my parents about my drinking. A thought clicks in my head. *Did Charlie tell her dad to get me into trouble?* My mind is working overtime, overthinking every word spoken and every action. Our friendship is coming under scrutiny and I can't figure out if she's genuine or not. I send her a message but she doesn't answer.

The sounds outside keep me awake. The pitiful mewing from a stray cat. The screech of a fox and the revving of a car skidding down our road. I snuggle under the covers to hide from the intensity of the external noises. My mind is a blur, a merging of thoughts weighing me down. I've been taking migraine tablets, but they don't help. After wanting to lose weight for ages, how ironic that I've lost my appetite and food tastes of cardboard. I try to remember the strange conversation I had with Paddy. *What were those things he told me to do?* Sage and something to do with stones.

The temperature is dropping from cold to glacial. My breath catches in my throat. A presence is in my room. Slivers of light shine through the curtains, and I'm about to jump out of bed and shut them when the patter of feet lingers outside my door. Someone is loitering.

I squint at the dim shadows lurking in the corners of my room. It's only a bundle of my clothes draped over the chair. But... but... The indistinct shape of a figure rises.

'Bella, what are you doing?' I whisper.

The door handle tilts down.

'Bella, stop fooling with me.'

It stops.

Someone's humming.

'Lavender's blue, dilly dilly, lavender's green.

I tuck the duvet around me but my ears are alerted to a muffled scratching which increases to a gentle knocking. Peeping out of the covers, drifting towards me is a mass of greyish smoke, twirling, moving faster and faster. The stench of rotting weeds fills my nose and changes to the aromatic scent of fresh grass, of Nan's lavender cologne, and the heady perfume of lilies. I wriggle to the bottom of the bed, trying to hide. Silence. Martha's freezing fingertips touch my hand as she whispers, *'Will you find her? She needs to atone for her sins.'*

I nod my head as she encloses me and coldness spreads through my body. But then she cries:

'Sienna! Take care – your energy is being possessed by a powerful force.'

A sudden burst of noises and clatter of objects being thrown around, coupled with shrill laughter, stuns me. Trapped in my room with no escape, I watch my curtain opening and flooding the room with moonlight. A bedsheet winds around my body. It tightens against my neck and reaching forward, I wrench my hands free and rip the material away from my throat. Heavy footsteps pound towards me. Fluorescent green numbers from the clock pulsate, and an incessant turning on and off from the bedside lamp lights up the darkness. I'm terrified by the actions taking place and can't move. My mirrored wardrobe reflects the lamp's glare. Peering out of the covers, I glance at my image. Black eyes with skin a ghostly pallor. As I try to stand, a heavy presence pushes me down. The bed judders and the ceiling lampshade swings round and round. Someone shouts. My heavy black obsidian stone crashes down, splintering into tiny shards of ebony crystal.

My parents slam their bodies against the door, screaming and shouting my name. The wood splinters and creaks as they enter, and they trip over the furniture that's blocking their way.

'Sienna!' they scream.

I breathe out and the darkness withdraws. Bella sprints into my room and holds me. My parents follow her.

Pulling myself up the bed, I examine the turmoil. Bella is next to me and clasps my hand. 'You must tell them, Sienna. Tell them what happened in Ireland.'

I look at her, unsure of the reaction I'll get, but she smiles, so I reveal my encounter with the medium. Dad rubs the back of his neck and paces up and down while Mum picks at the skin around her nails. The enormity of the problem alarms me as I realise that I've ignored Paddy's advice. I didn't smoke the rooms out with sage or soak in a salt bath. What happened to the red jasper stones that could have saved me?

'I'll help you put an end to this torment,' Bella whispers, and climbs into my bed next to me.

My parent stand outside my room, and I hear them arguing.

'I'm taking her to hospital,' says Dad.

'She's not being sectioned,' says Mum.

'No, they won't. They'll probably give her sedatives. This has been going on for too long. You're here more than me. Why didn't you realise what was happening?'

'Are you saying I'm a bad mother?'

'No. I don't know what I'm saying. I might get in touch with the parish priest and see if he can perform an ex—'

'Christ's sake, James, this is our daughter we're talking about! I'm not having a bloody priest performing an exorcism. What are you thinking?'

'I don't know but let her sleep and I'll phone the medics tomorrow.'

I'm relieved nothing will happen tonight because I'm exhausted. My younger sister holds me tight till I relax and zone out.

CHAPTER 19

The next day, I wake with Bella curled up by my side. I nudge her.

'What are you doing here?'

'Can't you remember? It's too awful to explain. Dad wanted to drive you to hospital straight away but Mum said to wait and phone the doctor in the morning. By the way, you snore.'

'No, I don't remember everything, but thanks for staying with me.'

She yawns and I look at her pale face and swollen eyes. Her hands shake when talking to me and there's a wheezing coming from her chest. While I've been asleep, my room has been tidied and all that's left of last night's scene is the shattered black dust of my obsidian. My memory is hazy, but I remember Martha's voice, warning me.

I walk into the kitchen where I'm handed a piece of toast, which I nibble on. Mum studies me, and I try not to choke on the crumbs. My nose and throat are clogged, and it's an effort to swallow. The doorbell rings and Dad opens the door to Doctor Frank. The morning sun is blazing through the windows but I'm cold, so wrap my pink fluffy dressing gown around me and we sit down.

'You're early,' I say, smiling at him.

'Preferential treatment,' he says. 'Right, Sienna, I'm going to check your blood pressure.'

He leans towards me, and the scent of apples, crisp and verdant, drifts into my nose. He studies me as Mum pulls my arm free from the dressing gown sleeve. Her face is sallow and the dark shadows under her eyes have deepened. She trembles when rolling up my sleeve. He wraps a cuff around my upper arm and it tightens, causing pins and needles in my fingers. My parents sit either side of me as the doctor explains he's arranging an emergency appointment with the counsellor at his practice. They stand up and escort him towards the door and I overhear the words 'schizophrenia' and 'multiple personalities'.

He's wrong. I'm on a mission to investigate Martha. I head into my sister's room.

'Thanks for last night, Bella. What are you doing?'

Her head is bent over the laptop and she looks up.

'Sienna, it was scary. Hearing you scream out petrified me, and when we opened your door, it was a mess. I'm telling you, whatever happened in there was worse than any horror film.'

'What do you mean?'

'God. The noises, the eerie screams, the scratching and banging on the door. And there was something else.'

'What? I don't remember.'

'Hard to describe, but almost like…'

'Go on.'

'Like the sound of a body dropping from above. Like being hung.'

'Crap. You're joking with me?'

'I'm not. Really, I'm not.' Her face is ashen, and she puts her hand over her mouth as she coughs.

I look away and a thought flicks across my brain. A lost memory. I try searching but nothing.

'I'm exploring paranormal websites for advice to stop it.'

'What should I do? They want me to see a counsellor, but what's the point? They'll dose me with medication and lock me away,' I say, staring at her laptop.

'Can you remember when this started?'

I reflect on her question.

'The visions began when Nan went into Monkton House, which coincidentally was the same day I met Charlie. But perhaps my gift, if you can call it that, started earlier because Mum told me when I was younger I had an imaginary friend. Most kids do, don't they?' I ask.

'I didn't,' replied Bella.

'Do you remember me telling you once that I saw dead people?'

'I do, and you teased me when I screamed. Is it similar to that film – Sixth Sense? Do spirits appear to you?'

Should I tell her about Martha? Will she believe me?

'What about the time I frightened you by predicting Mrs Hunt from next door was dead? I dreamt she came into my room wearing a long white nightdress.'

'Yes, but that was a fluke. She was ancient and died in her sleep.'

'I detect atmospheres and smell odd odours, like dirty pond water or flowery perfumes.'

'Everyone does that.'

'When nobody is there?'

'Perhaps you have a heightened sensitivity. Doesn't mean you have to be admitted to hospital. You're not hurt, are you?'

I shake my head.

'OK, what are you detecting now?' asks my sister.

'That Mum and Dad have no idea what to do with me.'

'Spot on, attention seeker, so now we need to investigate further how to stop it,' she says, pointing to a supernatural website. 'The spell you carried out with Charlie might be the answer. Tell me again what you did.'

After an hour, Dad knocks on the door, carrying a tray with two mugs of tea and a plate of toasted cinnamon bagels dripping in butter.

'You picked at your food earlier, Sienna. Thought you might appreciate this. Well, well, both my girls together. Makes a pleasant change. What are you up to?' he asks, leaving the mugs on the bedside locker and moving towards us.

'Thanks, Dad. It's girl's stuff,' Bella replies, as she manoeuvres him out of the room.

'Sienna, an appointment with the counsellor has been arranged for this afternoon,' he says, standing by the door.

'OK, Dad.'

'What will you do today?'

I shrug and look over at my sister.

'Rest, and phone me at work if you need anything.'

I go back to bed for a couple of hours. Mum keeps leaving me cups of tea and plates of sandwiches, but I'm not hungry. At lunchtime, I shower and prepare for my appointment. Dragging the comb through my tangled hair, my hands shake and the knot in my stomach twists tighter. The thought of discussing my problems with a new person worries me.

'Are you ready, pet?' Mum asks. Her eyes are red rimmed. 'Don't worry,' she says, holding my arm as we walk downstairs and out the door.

Mum's face is flushed. She's a nervous driver, and keeps stalling the car at junctions. I text Charlie, but she doesn't answer. Meanwhile, we spot a parking space and squeeze into it. The automatic double door into the Medical Centre hisses as it opens. The receptionist lifts her head and points towards the waiting room, so we sit on the uncomfortable plastic chairs again. I'm reading a tatty out-of-date celebrity magazine when I hear my name.

'Sienna Stevens,'

Mum stands up.

'No, it's fine. I'm OK on my own,' I say, walking towards the door.

Mum's shoulders droop, but I want to talk without interruption. The room is compact and homely, with thank you cards pinned on a corkboard. There are children's toys, plastic bricks, colouring books, crayons, various dolls in stages of undress, and drawings stuck on the wall.

'Hi, Sienna, I'm Emma Larkin, counsellor. We'll use this room today as mine is being painted. This is usually reserved for younger children. Did Doctor Frank explain why he wanted you to see me?' she asks, gesturing for me to sit.

'Because I'm possessed?' I ask, staring at the children's toys.

'It depends on what *you* mean by that. The word possession suggests owning or control. So, what is controlling you?' she asks, opening her laptop lid. Emma Larkin is older than my mum, with wiry grey, short-cropped hair, bushy eyebrows, a tanned, rugged face lacking make up, and gold studs in her ears. She has a tiny hole in her nose where a nose ring has been. Even though it is summer, she's wearing a long-sleeve, brown jumper and baggy multi-coloured patchwork trousers covered in dog hair.

'In your own words, what's bothering you?' She scrutinises me.

'Nothing.' I glare at her and fold my arms. 'I'm wasting time here,' I mutter.

'Beg your pardon, Sienna, what did you say?'

I slump down on a large squashy bean bag and wait for her to start.

She opens a folder and switches on her iPod. Immediately, the room fills with the sound of water. Waves slapping gently against the rocks, and a stream trickling through the woods. I let my head fall back on the cushion and listen to the rhythmic ebb and flow.

'Sienna. I want you to clear your thoughts. Loosen your body from your toes to the top of your head. Relax your face, the muscle in your forehead, in your cheeks, and when you're ready, tell me about your visions,' she says, lowering her voice and taking a piece of paper out from the folder.

The click of a pen. Click. Click. On and off.

The room is warm. The windows and blinds are shut. When did she switch off the lights? There's the aroma of lavender in the air. The mutter of voices and the gentle shuffle of feet outside the room lulls me. I'm tired. She places a thick woolly blanket over me, and I rest my head for a moment on the soft cushion. My eyes close and the icy breath of Martha whispers to me, *I'm running to meet him along the jetty. The pitch-black night surrounds me and I can't see. Has she tricked me? I can hear the patter of footsteps crunching on the snow. Wait, who's that? What are you doing here? Someone grabs my shoulder and I turn around, but my feet slip on the frozen planks. The water is freezing, and the mud coats my gown. Pull me out. The slimy weeds are dragging me in. The chilling noise screeches inside my head. Screaming my name.'*

'Sienna, I'm counting to five and I want you to open your eyes. One, two, three, four and five. Open your eyes slowly.'

The blanket has dropped on the floor and the music has stopped. I rub my hands for warmth. The counsellor passes me a plastic bottle of water and opens the door.

'You've had enough for today. Rest here for a minute. I want a word with the doctor,' she says, leaving me in the room.

I'm alone until Mum enters, followed by Emma Larkin and a man dressed casually in jeans wearing a teddy bear tie tucked inside his shirt.

'Mrs Stevens. Please take a seat,' he says, indicating a chair. 'My name is Peter James, the senior counsellor at the medical centre. Ms

Larkin summoned me during the session when Sienna had her seizure.'

'Seizure – what do you mean?' asks Mum, glancing from me to him and rubbing the back of her neck.

'I've phoned Doctor Frank and relayed the signs and symptoms. We are of the professional opinion Sienna suffered a 'petit mal' seizure during her first counselling session,' he says.

Mum holds my hand to stop me shaking.

'We'll arrange for the relevant blood tests and an electroencephalogram. An EEG is a painless test. It will detect the electrical activity in her brain and translate it into a series of printed patterns, confirming the diagnosis. After discussion with my colleague, I will refer Sienna to the Child and Adolescent Mental Health Department.'

'Petit mal? That's dangerous, isn't it? What do you mean? Child and Adolescent Mental Health? It's hormones and exam stress, isn't it? You're fine, aren't you, Sienna? Go on, tell them,' says Mum, nudging me.

'Mrs Stevens. Please don't worry. Sienna blanked out for a few minutes and Ms Larkin could not rouse her. Has this occurred before?'

'She has these day dreams when she sinks into a trancelike state.'

'Yes, seizures can be interpreted as daydreaming. She may have staring spells or shaking episodes with loss of consciousness and tingling, or smell strange odours. Apologies, Sienna, we're discussing you as if you're not here.' He faces me and places his hand on my arm. 'Does this seem familiar?'

I nod my head. My stomach tightens and I turn to Mum. Two crimson patches of colour have spread over her washed-out face.

'We'll arrange the dates for the blood tests. You'll receive a letter through the post for the other appointments,' says the counsellor. Dr James shakes my hand and smiles at me.

Mum grabs my arm and whisks me out.

'What was that screeching in there? I tried to come in, but the receptionist stood against the door. Nothing could get past her and the patients were gawping at me.'

'Mum, what's a petit mal?'

'It means you pass out. It's a form of epilepsy. What did they say about your visions?'

'I'm not sure what happened. One minute I was relaxing on the bean bag and the next, I woke up freezing and crying.'

'I'm worried. This is the first time the counsellors have seen you and your appearance concerns them.' She grabs my arm and studies me. 'You're becoming thinner and what's happening with your face? It's dry and spotty, and your hair is a mass of frizz. They'll question my parenting skills and say I'm not up to the job.'

'It's your fault. You never listen to me,' I mutter to myself.

'Oh, love, don't say that. We're upset about what's been happening and I'm sure we can work things out,' she cries and pushes open the double doors.

We climb into the car. She leans her head on the dashboard.

'I'm sorry, Mum. It's a battle with the voices in my head, so hopefully the blood tests and this EEG will help. Maybe medication is what I need? I'm a nuisance,' I say, reaching out to her.

'Sienna, I'm sorry too. It's been a struggle for me. Try to imagine being pregnant at seventeen.' She holds my hand. 'I've kept this a secret from you and Bella, but my mother was mentally ill for a long time. It started gradually and worsened. She died in the local psychiatric hospital; my father was heartbroken and died soon after.'

She takes a tissue out of the glove compartment, dabs at her eyes, unscrews a bottle of water, and gulps it down. I stare at her, amazed. This is the first time she has divulged this information to me.

'This is unbelievable. *Now* you tell me this, with my problems? Are you saying I've inherited a mental illness?' I ask.

Mum ignores me and stares out the window.

'I wanted the romantic dream with the thatched cottage in the countryside, university, marriage, and a family. I viewed life through rose-coloured glasses. Nan Ria was always criticising me, and I never felt accepted.'

'What did she criticise you about?' I ask.

'They seem silly now but she told your dad my skirts were too short and my blouses too tight. When she finally invited me for tea, I poured the milk in the tea first. The look on her face was enough to curdle the milk. Me and Debbie lived in a semi-detached house in the 'rougher' areas of Lakeview village. Nan always commented on the crime in my area. There are other examples, but I tolerated her because I fell in love with your dad and became pregnant with you.'

'There's nothing wrong with living there. Is that why she treats me differently?'

'She's old-fashioned and didn't want him to marry me. Thought I was beneath him,' replies Mum, choking back a sob and hunching over the steering wheel. I lean over and rub her back.

'What will I do with you?' she asks, twisting the car key in her hand.

We haven't moved from the car park and people are strolling into the medical centre. A young mum is pushing a pram with one hand on the handle, and the other hand scrolling through her phone. Mum sighs, turns the key in the ignition and indicates left onto the main road leading home. We drive in silence, and I think about the grandmother I've never met. What mental problems did she suffer with? I don't want to bombard Mum with questions, so I recline and stare out the window.

My mother parks the car in the driveway, slams the door and storms out. She throws her jacket over the banister and marches into the kitchen, yanks open the drawer pulling out a knife to start chopping the vegetables.

'Mum?' I say, looking at the food reduced to a pulp. 'I'm sorry for scaring you at the counsellors.'

'I'm being punished for my sins. Why did I ignore the signs? I should have sought help years before, but your dad ignored me,' she mutters to herself.

'What do you mean?'

'At primary school we thought your imaginary friend was a phase, but what if it's never gone away?'

Tears stream down her face as she hacks at the onions.

I need to change the subject. 'Mum, I've learnt that the care home was once a monastery. Fancy you and Dad not realising.' I laugh, trying to ease the situation.

'What's so funny about that?' she asks, rubbing her eyes.

'Isn't Nan an atheist?'

'Yes, I suppose so.'

'Didn't you spot the statues, holy pictures, and the massive crucifix when you first brought her there?'

'A few religious statues are the least of her worries. It was chaotic the day she was admitted. I had left my mobile charging at home, while I enjoyed a facial at Beautiful You in the high street. I didn't know Nan had a stroke. Her neighbour tried to contact your dad, but couldn't get a message through so they phoned for an ambulance. They treated her at the hospital and, after a week's observation, transferred her to Monkton House care home. Her dementia is devastating for someone who held an important position. Do you remember that day?'

I stare at her, but she carries on without waiting for an answer.

'It was manic with the calls and the rushing to the hospital. You're right, she doesn't move out of her room and perhaps hasn't even noticed the religious icons.'

Dad enters the kitchen and watches us. 'What are you girls gossiping about?'

Mum attacks the potatoes with a butter knife while Bella picks an orange from the fruit bowl.

I look at him. 'Did you know that Monkton House was once an orphanage, and before that, a monastery. There are loads of statues and holy pictures still around the place,' I say.

'Does it matter? Nan can't walk very far with her swollen legs, and her eyesight is poor. Don't mention it to her, will you, Sienna? She attended a strict Christian school and has been against religious stuff ever since,' he says, reaching over to take the knife from Mum.

'Hold on – so why has she been adamant we…' I say, pointing to myself and Bella, '… attend a catholic school?'

'It has top ranking on the Sunday Times list of best independent schools. The alternative is the state secondary, and we don't want that for our girls,' he says, wrapping his arms around us.

'Alright, I won't mention anything, but Nan doesn't want me to read to her. Which defeats the object, doesn't it?'

'What do you mean?' asks Mum.

'She's the reason Dad wanted me to volunteer, but there are other jobs to do there, so it doesn't matter.'

He scrolls through his phone while Mum watches him.

'Matt and I are going to tidy up the library,' I say. 'He's volunteering as well and the experience will help with his medical school applications.'

'Matt and Sienna sitting in the tree, k-i-s-s-i-n-g,' chants Bella.

'Don't be childish,' I say, and dip my head before she catches me grinning.

'I'm glad you've made a friend your own age. Although I'm not sure it's the best place for you, being surrounded by death and decay,' says Mum.

'Oooh creepy.' Bella opens her eyes wide and twists her mouth, making a scary expression.

'I'm starving; do you fancy a pizza? There's nothing left of the potatoes, is there Mum?' I say, then turn around and pull an even scarier face at Bella.

'How was the appointment?' Dad asks, lifting his eyes from his phone. Mum raises her eyebrows and explains what the doctor told her.

I let her get on with it while I think about Martha's warning to me.

CHAPTER 20

The next morning, I wake up ready for a new day at the care home. Even though Mum told me about her mother's mental illness, I don't believe I have the same condition. Having a potential medical diagnosis of epilepsy has eased my mind. I rush to catch the bus, glad Matt has saved me a seat. He moves up when I drop next to him.

'Sorry, Sienna, I didn't text you last night.'

'No, it's fine. I had an early night.'

'Are you sure? You're paler than normal.'

'Yes, I'm fine,' I snap. He stares at me, but I'm still mad about his brother messing with the Ouija board.

'You had toast for breakfast,' he says, using his finger to wipe a smudge of butter off my lips.

His nails are short, with a tiny faded scar on the inside of his fingers. The bus lurches forward and I'm pressed up against him. He emits a clean fresh smell of soap. The tautness of his muscles underneath his thin jacket sends shock waves along my body.

'Budge up, you're leaning into me,' he says, holding onto my arm and pushing me upright.

We sit together without the need to speak. Matt is reading a biology text book while I stare out the window and think about yesterday.

'You're quiet. Everything alright?' he asks.

I want to tell him but I see Mrs Jones sitting across the aisle from me.

'Yes,' I say.

The bus pulls up at the care home.

'Catch you later,' he says with a smile as we get off.

This time, I head straight to Anne Duncan's room. She's standing by the patio door, staring at a row of cherry trees lining the driveway. Dried, woody rosebushes and shrubs surround the lawn, all twisted and dying. An old greenhouse is in the background, the panes shattered and lying in pieces on the ground, covered by blades of grass, while ancient trees hide the lake. The constant sensation of premonition starts again, and the urge to unburden to this wise woman is a weight on me.

'Anne, I need your guidance.' I lower my head and shuffle from side to side, reluctant to tell her.

'Why are you anxious? You look as if the cares of the world are pushing down on your young shoulders,' she says. 'What's wrong?'

Such a compassionate voice coming from a kind old lady lulls me into my confession. I tell her about the Ouija board, visions and my awareness of atmospheres. I mention the medium show, meeting Paddy and Rose in Ireland, but omit the spell book and our connection with Octavia. She's stroking the cross around her neck and frowning.

She sticks her hand up to stop me from carrying on.

'You've introduced danger into your life,' she says. 'Sienna, you have a gift of vision and sensitivity, and yet you are irresponsible in your understanding of its power. You play with spells and potions. You dabble in the Ouija board summoning spirits. Involving psychics and mediums disrupts your life-force. Leave me, child, and I will pray for you.' She waves me away. A flush of colour creeps up her cheeks as she picks up her bible and opens the pages.

'No, it's fine – the doctors suspect my condition is physical and can be treated,' I say. 'My friend dragged me to the medium show and I wasn't expecting anything to happen.'

She doesn't answer me but sits reading from the bible. I'm annoyed by her response and storm out of the room. I trusted her with my problems, and now she's brushed me aside. She can find another volunteer to help with typing endless pages of writing. I've had enough of Anne Duncan's demands and this place. I march along the wooden floor, passing numbered oak doors. Nobody is around, and my stomping footsteps are deafening in the quietness.

Large paintings of religious saints dominate the walls, and one labelled *St Bartholomew* catches my eye. As I peer at it, the bile rises in my mouth. I remember studying him at school and how he was punished for converting people to Christianity. They flayed him alive while he watched his entire skin being removed.

Where am I? I'm lost and my anxiety rises and my chest tightens. Twirling around, I retrace my footsteps back to the reception area, up the wooden staircase leading to the staff quarters and dining room on the second floor. The canteen is empty.

'Where are the staff?' I ask the cook who is spooning what resembles brown slop onto plates.

'You're early, dear. Now, do you want steak and kidney pie with chips or vegetarian quiche?'

Large tin dishes displaying today's lunch are drying under the heat lamps. The meat resembles dog food, while the quiche is a mixture of greasy aubergine and mushrooms. The picture of the skinless man is in my head and I'm not hungry, so I pick up an apple and a packet of crisps. The cook shakes her head at me and serves the next person. I sit down and Matt joins me.

'Where have you been?' I ask, relieved to see a familiar face.

'What's wrong?' he asks.

'This place is spooky and I keep getting lost. How many rooms are there?'

'I'm not sure but it takes a few days to get used to the different floors with the winding passageways, and some parts aren't accessible. It's only for a few weeks, to help out while the regular staff are on holiday. I've been observing the head nurse handing out medicine. She's aware I want to attend medical school in a couple of years and lets me shadow her. They've asked me to watch one of the old ladies in the left wing,' he says.

'Can't another helper stay with her?' I ask, nibbling on my apple.

'I'm not sure, but I'll keep her company until the agency nurse arrives.' He pops a chip into his mouth.

'You're a volunteer. What are you expected to do?'

'I'll read to her for a while. When my dad was ill, I cared for him and it made me realise I wanted to become a doctor and help people. Where will you be today?' he asks, wiping his mouth. My stomach flutters as he gazes at me.

'Matt…'

'Yes.'

'I'm sorry for being irritable this morning. I had a rough night last night and the trick your brother played annoyed me.'

He stares at me. 'No worries, Sienna. I'm sorry too. He's a fool and was trying to impress Charlie.'

'Charlie? She's never mentioned him, so don't raise his hopes. By the way, even though your brother pushed the planchette, it ended up spelling the name Martha.' The corner of his mouth curves upwards into a tense smile.

'Forget it. You don't believe me.' I scowl at him. The rest of the staff are tucking into their lunch, but my appetite has gone. 'I'll meet you in the library later on.'

'Yes, check with the matron, but I reckon she'll be pleased if we're both there. I'm in a hurry, catch you later.' He grins, shoving back the metal chair and scraping it against the wooden floor.

Now Matt has left, I finish eating my apple and walk downstairs toward the reception area. While the matron is on the phone, I stand outside, pacing up and down, eager to check out the library.

'Hello, Sienna, is there a problem?'

'Anne Duncan doesn't need me today, so I'd like to help tidy up the library, please?'

She's chewing her pen and staring behind me. 'Good idea but your friend Matthew isn't in there yet.'

'Where is it?'

She points down the corridor. 'It's in the older part of the home, at the end of the hallway. It's been vacant for years and is a mess. Can you arrange the books into order?'

'Yes, no problem. I spend a majority of my time in libraries and love reading.' She's not listening, but staring behind me.

I spin around to see what holds her attention.

Jesus on the cross.

Black mould creeping over his face. A damp patch bubbles through the plaster, making him cry tears.

I walk away. The lamps flicker and fizz. They shine on the pictures and figures on the walls, making weird shapes. The corridor is a freezing, endless dark hole with dim light, and my fingers recoil from the dampness of the brickwork. Slimy green algae cover the crevices, and I wipe the gunge from my fingertips onto my jeans. I keep walking, aware of the dripping of liquid which echoes as if underneath a body of water. This corridor appears to be sloping downwards. I've missed the turning again and pass empty rooms. Uneasiness builds up in me. Scorched, wooden doors lie open, and I peep inside a couple, curious as to why they're vacant. One room contains a burnt camp bed, recognisable by the twisted metal frame. The narrow window lets in a chink of light shining on the ashy remains of a wooden crucifix, and a charred bible. Black dust hangs in the air. I continue passing empty rooms, ending in darkness.

My senses crackle from connecting synapses.

Absolute silence.

The thumping of my pulse corresponds with the beat of a machine. The fine hairs on my neck tingle. Goose bumps on my arms make me tremble and I gasp – starved of oxygen. I need to locate the source of the rhythm, but whirl around when the clumping of heels becomes louder.

'What are you doing here?' demands Mrs Jones, marching towards me.

'Have you lost your way?' asks Matt, following behind her.

'I'm glad to see you. I have no idea where I'm going. I thought you were busy?'

'A nurse is with the old lady now and the matron told me to look for you,' he says.

'Good, coz I keep losing my way and going around in circles.'

'Do you still want to see the library?' he asks.

'Yes.'

'Follow me but watch your step coz this is the oldest part of the home and the lights don't work properly. The authorities need to arrange an electrician,' he says, frowning at Mrs Jones as she shrugs and turns her back on us.

'Matt, listen. Someone is trying to contact me and I need to investigate.'

'Don't be daft. Nobody lives in this part of the house. Who do you think you are? Agatha Christie?' He snorts but stops and looks at me. 'Hey, I'm only joking. What's going on? There's a greenish tinge to your skin.' He rests the back of his hand onto my forehead.

'Mmm, you're not burning up; in fact, the opposite. You're freezing. Here, have this.'

He pulls his sweatshirt up, ruffling his hair, and hands it to me. I glimpse a toned, lean midriff and a spark of longing floods my body. Placing it over my T-shirt, a clean fragrance with a hint of fabric softener wafts into my nose.

Matt takes my arm and twists me around. We go back a different way, but a sense of gloom and misery beckons; nobody has been here for ages. I'm uncertain whether to carry on when we come to an ancient wooden door. The hinges are stiff and the door squeaks when we push it open. This is the library. I gaze around in dismay. A beam of light shines in from the window and illuminates the dust motes floating and landing on the surfaces. My shoes make footprints on the grey ash that covers the reddish parquet floor.

'That's an ichthus,' I say, pointing to figures of fish painted on the walls.

'Yes. We have them at school and I've seen them on car stickers,' says Matt.

'Wasn't it a secret signal in Roman times to show other people you're Christian? It had to be secret, otherwise, you could be persecuted.'

He nods and strides over to a tall wooden bookcase crafted to fit in an alcove. The hint of burnt paper wafts into my nose.

'Look.' I point to ornate crosses with three interlocking circles etched into wood panels.

'The Borromean Rings – they represent the Trinity,' says Matt, studying them.

'Yes, God the Father, the Son and the Holy Spirit,' I reply.

'Someone's been paying attention in assembly,' he laughs.

I look closer. 'Why are the crosses upside down?'

'I don't know.' He frowns and rummages through the papers.

Piled up on the shelves are heaps of torn documents, folders and books ruined by green moulds growing on the leather coverings. Delicate spider webs hang like silky angel hair in the corners of the room. Earthy mildew lingers in the air, making me sneeze. This was once a magnificent library and will take longer to organise than we expected.

'Told you it was messy,' he says, brushing black powder from my shoulder. I tremble from the gentle pressure of his hand, so I look away and study the room.

'If we stay long enough, we might discover rare literature among this lot.' I wave my hands at the shelves. Covered by residue and hidden underneath sheets of paper, I spot a large book coated with grime, so pick it up and show him. But the dust enters my nose and mouth, making me cough again.

'I've noticed this book before on a painting.' I can just about speak from smoky ash clogging my mouth. 'It's inscribed with the title *Monkton Abbey*.'

I hand it over to him. He brushes off the dust, carefully unties the leather straps, and several pieces of singed paper float to the ground.

'What the hell is this?'

I pick up the parchment and study intricate drawings of horned beasts and five-sided pentagrams. Their colours, once a vivid red and yellow, have faded.

Matt holds up a piece of paper and reads out a list of names.

'Ursula Southeil, Agnes Sampson, Merga Bien, Lilias Adie. There's another one that starts with the letter B but it's smudged.'

'They're the names of witches from history,' I whisper. Silence. Blood and stone. Ice-cold crystals pierce my eyes. Someone is watching. Waiting for me.

'This paper needs destroying now,' says Matt, biting his lower lip and watching me. 'How come you recognise these names? What do you think it's doing here?'

'I've read about these witches in the research Charlie and I have been carrying out.'

The minute he passes me the piece of paper, I'm crushed by depravity and wickedness. Tingling passes into my hand, up my arm and into my body as the paper drifts to the floor.

'What's on the others?' I point to them, trying to ignore the fallen page. A frayed cord holds several pieces of faded ivory paper. They emit the suffocating stench of mildew. Gathering the bundle up, Matt unties the string binding them. The sheets are as delicate as tissue paper.

'They're difficult to read; it's written in a foreign language.' I cough again and swig from the water bottle Matt hands me. Then he pulls out his glasses from his pocket and peers at the paper.

'It's Latin.'

'How can you tell?'

'My uncle taught me a few Latin phrases to help with my medical school application. It will show I'm serious about becoming a doctor.'

I gaze at him and wipe my mouth. Whilst I've been fooling around with crazy spells, he's been planning his future.

'Sienna, what's wrong? You're shaking,' he says, grabbing my hand. 'And your hands are freezing.'

'Matt,' I say, taking my hand away and sticking it in my pockets.

'I'm not the same as other girls.' I'm sure he will laugh at me, but instead, he's gathering up the papers. 'I... I... hear voices and see images,' I stutter.

He studies me. 'I know, but there's a wildness in you I admire. You do your own thing and don't follow the crowd. So, pass the book over, will you?'

I'm speechless and keep on glancing at him as we study the papers.

'This style of handwriting is obsolete.' He smooths the flimsy paper. '*Noli intrare* means keep out, but what's this?' he asks, pointing to a list of names. We pore over the script.

'Can you read it?'

'A few phrases and numbers. For instance, this word 'mater' means mother, but the rest is difficult to decipher.'

'Let's give this to Anne for her research, but I've had enough now. Maybe she can make sense of it,' I say, coughing again.

Matt shoves the paper back in the book and holds it under his arm.

'Oh, damn, it's late. Hurry up,' he says.

We slam the library door, rush down to her room, and show her the book.

'Leave it with me,' she says.

We run outside and are just in time to catch the bus.

At home, I don't mention the library, but wonder why the care home has information about witches. My parents are busy discussing Bella's upcoming sports event and ignore me. Nobody sees me scraping my dinner away and escaping to my room.

Rose's book is calling to me. Sitting on my bed, I pull it out from under the pillow and open the next page. The stench of lavender and ditch water is stronger tonight. Closing my eyes, the vision arrives quickly. A flock of ravens, their lustrous wings shining with an indigo brilliance, land on the parched soil. They search amongst the gravel.

The pecking of their beaks smash against the tiny stones. The shriek of anguish as she plucks a wing from his dying body. The pumping of his heartbeat pulsating in my ears. The screams from the flock like the cry of a whistle resonate in my brain. Bright scarlet blood dripping in-between her fingers. I don't recognise this girl. She isn't Martha. She smiles at me. A sweet, sickly grin. Evil surrounds her.

CHAPTER 21

Last night I dreamt of a bird pecking at my eyes, and Nan with blood streaming down her face. The thought of another medical appointment annoys me. It'll be another wasted journey.

I bang my mug of tea down on the table and watch my mother apply a hint of cherry pink lipstick, and mascara on her lashes.

'Going to the doctor is useless. All I do is talk about my visions.'

'We need to check if the results of the blood test are back.'

She picks up her keys, and we leave the house, arriving at the surgery before the car park fills up. The receptionist sends us straight into his room. It's Dr Miller again. He doesn't acknowledge us and continues typing at his keyboard.

Mum coughs and he raises his eyes.

'Good morning. How are things today?' he says, gesturing towards the chairs.

We sit down without answering.

'Sienna, did you purchase the sleeping tablets from the chemist as I recommended? Taking them, I hope?' he asks.

'No, I'm not,' I say, looking at Mum.

Now I have his attention; he swings his body around and stares at me.

'Why not?'

'Taking pills won't stop my nightmares.'

'I also told you to discontinue reading unsuitable material. Have you done that?' he asks, glancing up.

I study my jeans and pick at a piece of loose cotton thread at the knee.

Mum turns to me. 'I'll remove the books. You finished your project and handed it in, didn't you?'

I nod but omit to mention how our choice of topic didn't impress the form teacher.

Dr Miller is checking his phone and laptop. 'Tell me what's happened since last time I saw you.'

'The dreams occur when I sleep, but during the day Martha whispers to me. It happens quickly. My mind becomes fogged with thoughts and wham…' I bang my hand on the table and he flinches. 'For example, Martha told me everyone lied. They promised to care for her, but that didn't happen. She thought it would be a cheerful place, but oh no. Misery has soaked into the skin of the building. It became a prison. The girls are hostile. She tries to speak to them, but they ignore her.'

My mother gasps, placing her hand over her mouth.

'Sienna, do you watch horror films?' he asks.

I ignore him and continue. 'Once, I saw her in a large room. A draft wafting in from a narrow window. Camp beds are placed side by side, covered with coarse sheets. She is without warmth apart from the faint glow radiating from flickering candles. Their footsteps pad past the beds as they creep out of the dormitory. It's a special day and I sense her excitement. They vote to choose the Queen of May. Martha hopes it will be her. Her dream is to wear the crown, proceed into the garden and adorn the statue with garlands of fresh blossom.' I stop. He's writing in a notebook and ignoring me. When he realises

I've finished talking, he looks up.

'That's interesting. You attend Lakeview Catholic Independent School?' he asks, reading his notes.

'Yes,' I say.

'Do you remember taking part in the crowning of Mary? A Catholic tradition when girls wear white and carry flowers?'

'That took place at my primary school, but they didn't choose me,' I say. 'You can't have a fat red-haired Mary as the Queen of the May, can you?'

'Sienna, enough,' says Mum.

The doctor places his pen on the table and studies me. He licks his dry lips.

'I'll write you a prescription for mild sleeping tablets. Did you keep a dream diary?'

I shake my head. 'I don't need to because I can remember them all.'

'The reason to keep a diary is so that we can see if there is a pattern. For example, you may have an argument with a member of your family and then experience a vision. Or you watch a piece of upsetting news and you dream that night. Do you see why I want to investigate the source?' I nod and he carries on. 'Don't eat before bed and remove your mobile, television or iPad from your room, as the light can affect your sleep. Finally, make sure you exercise daily and reduce your input of caffeine,' he says, typing on his computer. Next minute, the whirr of the printer and a prescription shoots out.

'We're still waiting for Dr James' report regarding his diagnosis of epilepsy. My secretary will phone you when we receive them,' he says, opening the door for us.

'Doctor?' Mum faces him. 'I told Doctor James that I'm worried Sienna has inherited my mother's illness.'

He stops and stares at her.

'Does your mother attend this surgery?'

'No, she died seventeen years ago. She went to the medical centre outside Lakeview and ended up being admitted to Willow View Hospital.'

'Right, Mrs Stevens. Thanks for telling me. I'll send for her notes immediately.'

'They diagnosed her as schizophrenic,' says Mum, turning the door handle and walking out.

As we reach outside, I stop.

'Mum.'

She spins around. 'What? Hurry up, there's only five minutes left on the meter.'

'Why didn't you tell me my grandmother had a mental condition?'

'I didn't want to believe you had inherited it.'

'It's treatable, though, isn't it?'

'Yes,' she says as we climb into the car and drive home.

We don't say a word to each other. I'm stunned about my grandmother's psychiatric illness and that Mum didn't think to mention it to Doctor Miller before. By the time we get home, my aunt has arrived and is sitting on the settee.

'Hiya,' she says. 'Why the moody face?'

'You're early,' says Mum.

'Yes, and I brought cakes to cheer you lot up,' she says, watching me.

'Yay, great, I need my sugar rush,' says Bella, grabbing a chocolate-covered flapjack from the box and moving into the conservatory. Next minute, the pounding of her treadmill starts up, and I escape upstairs.

Mum sits with my aunt in the kitchen. While I was with the doctor, all I could think about was getting back quickly to read Rose's book. I want to find out more. Before I open it, I reflect on Mum's comments to the doctor about her mother's disorder. I pick up my phone and Google the word 'schizophrenia' and learn my symptoms are the same. Hearing voices and seeing unreal things. Yet Martha is real to me, especially when her soft voice whispers in my ear. Does that mean I've inherited my grandmother's condition?

'Mum,' I shout, rushing down the stairs.

'Sienna, it'll have to be vanilla slice or toffee meringue coz we've demolished the others,' says Debbie, holding out a plate.

'Mum, why didn't you mention my grandmother's mental illness or say anything at the counsellors? They suspect petit mal but could it be schizophrenia?'

Mum doesn't answer but stands up, slots her plate in the dishwasher and turns around.

'Your grandmother was becoming a threat to herself and was admitted to Willow View Psychiatric Unit. It was traumatic when she died and Dad passed away soon after. Poor thing couldn't live without her.'

'You should have told me. I'm not a child and would have understood. People nowadays are open about mental conditions,' I say, licking my finger and sticking meringue crumbs in my mouth.

Mum wipes her lips.

'Oh love, I had so much happening in my life. Pregnant with you, travelling daily to the hospital to visit my dying mother and Ria didn't help me. She told me mental illness was a sign of weakness.'

'Yes, at your wedding she sat next me and remarked how it was a blessing our mum died,' says Debbie, reaching over for a cup of tea.

'Why did she say that?' I ask.

'She believed your gran dying was the kindest thing to happen to our family,' says Debbie.

'That's why I didn't tell you,' says Mum.

'What? Totally unbelievable that Nan would be so cruel.'

'I can see now that she was right.'

'Hold on, Mum,' I say.

'No, my mother wasn't the easiest person to live with. The family suffered. They didn't pick up her mental condition until we were in our teens.'

'So why do I irritate Nan?'

'Because you're the spitting image of our mother,' says Debbie, looking at Mum.

'I've wondered that, but why haven't you spoken about her before?'

I point to a framed black-and-white photograph on the wall. 'Where's that?'

'A rare day trip to the seaside. My mother's behaviour was erratic. She was in and out of the hospital and couldn't be left alone. We did our best.' Debbie sighs and places her hand on my arm. 'Try to appease your nan. She's a snob who believes your dad is too smart for my sister.'

My aunt's voice fades away as the image of Nan Ria invades my thoughts, and a heaviness tightens around my head like a band of spikes. My body tenses and I see Martha hiding behind a stone column in a dark cellar. The air is damp. A group of girls are sitting cross-legged in a circle, and their leader summons creatures to her: the scaly toads, the slow-moving worms, the slimy slugs creeping along the damp bricks. The whiff of stagnant water invades my nose, and I can't watch anymore.

My aunt shakes me. 'Sienna, what's going on? Have you a cold? You were sniffing and pulling your face. We were watching you, weren't we Tracey?'

'It's nothing. I'm tired and was resting my eyes,' I say.

'That's what she does,' cries Mum. 'I'm at my wits' end.'

Debbie hugs my mother and I hear her whisper, 'Don't worry about her. Things will sort themselves out.' She turns to me. 'I was only thinking about the wedding the other day. I remember I drank too much and argued with Ria.'

'No wonder you don't talk about it.' Mum stares at her nails.

'One minute, we were tucking into the steak dinner, and your aunt leans over to Nan saying she's suffocating your dad.'

'Why did you say that?'

'She didn't approve of the marriage and made it obvious with her sour face and tutting at everything. Yes, I admit I'd had a few drinks, but you would think she'd show empathy towards your mum being parentless, young and pregnant.'

'What happened next?'

'Nan stormed out.'

'Oh, what a shame she ruined your special day,' I say.

'We had no money and Ria paid for the whole shebang: the meal, cars and my wedding dress, so I've been obligated to her ever since. 'However…' She stops talking and smiles at me. 'I've been considering the possibility of renewing our vows. Now our finances are healthier, it would be fantastic to arrange a dream wedding. The one I never had. We'll have a special holiday. Barbados or the Amalfi coast, what do you think?' She's miles away, daydreaming and staring at a packet of chocolate digestives.

'Mum, that's wonderful, but what about Dad? Can he take the time off? He keeps stressing how busy his job is.'

'Maybe. He is owed some holiday,' she says.

I point to the packet of digestives.

'They'll not eat themselves. Open them.'

She picks up a knife to pierce the plastic wrapper. Mum and my aunt chomp on cake and biscuits while I go upstairs. Today has been a revelation. Mum has finally told me more about her mother. If I possess my grandmother's mental condition, it will explain Mum's reluctance to accept it, but what if it's not that? What could it be? I have the choice of schizophrenia, migraine, epilepsy or – I'm being visited by dead people.

Rose's book demands my attention so I settle down on my bed and open the next page.

Love spell.

Friday is the best time to create a love spell and the love goddess Freya will answer your call.

You will need:

A sprig of rosemary, a pink candle, three drops of concentrated rose oil, an untarnished black cast iron cauldron and a lock of hair from your intended.

Instructions:

Light the candle, drip the candle wax into the cauldron. Mix the rosemary with the drops of rose oil. Throw in the hair and stir.

When cool, mix to form a ball.

Hold in your hands, keep moulding the wax mixture till the face of your beloved appears.

Repeat these words:

'Love of mine, gaze upon my eyes,

Moonlight floods over your face.

I will kill her when she sleeps.

Together, for eternity, we will find peace.'

The writing is hard to decipher. Oily drops stain the page, and the sweet-smelling perfume of roses coats my fingers. The fragrance hypnotises me and my eyes close.

The kitchen door slamming jolts me. I look at my watch – I've been asleep for three hours, so I rush downstairs. My parents and aunt have dressed for their evening out and are removing a bottle of wine from the fridge.

'Sienna, you've had a long sleep. I popped in a few times, but you were miles away. Don't forget, we're staying over in the city tonight. If you don't feel well, give me a ring and we'll come back.'

'No, I'll be fine, and if you cancel the hotel, you'll lose your money. You've been planning the trip to watch *Phantom of the Opera* for ages. The tickets have sold out and it's good to have a break.' I say, meaning 'from me'.

'OK, are you sure? Isabella's sports finals are tomorrow afternoon and we'll be back in the morning. Make sure you have an early night. My phone will be on silent but in an emergency, here are numbers for the theatre and hotel. Put these in your contacts,' she says, as I tap the numbers in.

'Don't worry. Enjoy yourselves,' says Bella, going upstairs.

My mum and aunt slurp a glass of Chardonnay while Dad brings the car out of the garage.

'Bye, Sienna. Don't forget – bed early,' says Mum as they walk outside.

I wander into my sister's bedroom. The room is in darkness.

'Bella,' I whisper.

'What's wrong?' she asks, switching on her lamp.

'I know you don't like this creepy stuff but...'

She sits upright in bed and focuses on me.

'... the spirit of Martha, a young girl, is following me.'

'Stop it, Sienna, this is worrying. I'll text Mum and Dad.'

'No. They don't believe me and I don't want to spoil their night out. I've had appointments with two doctors and a counsellor, and now Mum mentioned our gran, who was mentally ill.'

'I didn't know that. Why is it a secret? Surely we should have been told in case we've inherited it,' she says and smacks her hand up to her mouth. 'Sorry, me and my big mouth.'

'No worries, I've thought about that too.'

'I've never asked you this before, but what happens when you have a vision?'

"It's peculiar. A tingle starts at the base of my spine. I blank out and see everything through sheer material. Sometimes the noises are loud and other times fuzzy images emerge when Martha reveals parts of her life. The pictures are unclear, but if we carry out the banishing spell, life will return to normal. My energy is weakening, but I'm on a mission.' Bella stares at me.

'What did you say?'

'I'm on a mission.'

'That's what I thought you said, but what do you mean?' she asks, picking up her mobile.

'I'm not positive, but an event took place in the past and I intend to discover what it was. Wicked thoughts engulf me, and Martha shows me images, which means I'm getting closer. I think Rose's book and my visions connect.'

'Her book? What's in it?'

'I haven't shown anyone because I'm still trying to work out what it means.'

'You're scaring me. Are you certain about this? We should tell Mum and Dad,' she says, her fingers over her phone.

'No. They'll say I'm making everything up. It's about time these visions and Martha left. Are you ready to chant with me?'

'If you're sure it will work. Here's the list you gave me the other day.' She reaches under her bed for a plastic bag. 'But we don't have the same equipment as when you performed it with Charlie. All I could find was a vanilla cream candle and a pencil.' She hands them to me. 'But I'm not the person who should carry this out with you. Why not do it with Charlie? She enjoys scary things.'

'I'm desperate for these visions to go and Charlie isn't around.'

My sister pulls the duvet up to her chin with only her eyes showing, reminding me of a startled deer.

'You know, I always thought you were faking it, to be the centre of attention, but now I believe you and I'm scared stiff.'

I gaze at my sister's pale, exhausted face. With the smudges of purplish shadows under her eyes and a blue tinge to her lips, I regret dragging her into this.

'Today's training session was a killer and I'm tired, so will you hurry up with this spell?' she asks, slipping out of bed and putting on her dressing gown.

'It won't be long now. Thanks for helping me. I didn't think you would, the way I've been with you,' I say, taking out the salt cellar from the plastic bag.

She shrugs and smiles.

'What's that for?'

'The salt circle will protect us. Sit down.'

She sits cross-legged on the floor, staring at me, and as I pour the salt into a circle surrounding us, the white specks vanish into the thick pile of her beige carpet. It's past midnight, and I write, 'Spirit, leave me alone,' on the piece of paper. Bella grips my hand, making me wince. We read together.

Biddy, join me and lend me your shield,
Spirit of the dead, you will not contact me again.
I ask the gods to protect me,
Remove Martha from my life.'

As I wave the paper over the candle, it bursts into flames.

'Sienna! What will happen now?'

'We need to wait,' I say.

Then…

The temperature drops and drips of water run down the wall, forming icicles. An odour of rotting vegetation, sour and sharp, seeps inside. Martha is standing motionless. Her face is distorted, as if in sorrow, and she points her finger at me and says:

What have you done? Your mission is taking too long and you have introduced the witch into your life.'

'Martha,' I cry. 'What do you mean? Tell me what to do.'

The clouds break. Thunder roars and crackles. Lightning flashes over Bella and, reflected in her dilated pupils, is a woman with a rope tied around her neck. I twist around and she changes direction, looming behind my sister. I raise my eyes. Her presence fills the room as she encircles Bella in a cloak of dark mist.

'Leave her, she's innocent. Take me,' I yell.

The colour drains from my sister's face as she wheezes. My strength wanes and I try to reach out. The putrid stench fills my nose and mouth, and I'm choking from the toxic air. The scream of a hundred spirits howls out in torment as she squeezes Bella tighter. An evil force knocks me off my feet.

'Mary, Mother of God, Flower of the Fairest, Queen of the Angels. Save her,' shouts Martha.

The oppressive air disseminates as plumes of smoke float up to the ceiling, and Bella slides to the floor. She's gasping. I kneel beside her and rub her back till her breathing slows, but there is a rattling emanating out of her chest.

'My legs are pinned to the ground, Sienna,' she squeals. 'Help me.'

A shimmering haze of watery drops envelopes my sister.

She closes her eyes and slumps her chin on her chest.

'Bella, it's me, Sienna, wake up,' I plead, shaking her.

Her bedroom door slams shut and the stench disappears.

'Bella, Bella, wake up. It's my fault for doing this,' I say, rubbing her icy hands.

She rolls onto her side and whimpers, 'My chest hurts.'

'Oh, Bella! It's my fault. When I chanted the spell with Charlie, she passed out too,' I say, noticing the pallor of her skin.

'Why didn't you tell me this?'

'Would you have still done it?'

'To be honest, at first, your attraction to witchcraft, spells, and your obsession with scary things was funny and I've been humouring you, but why did that thing want me?' she asks.

I cover my mouth with my palm, trying to remove the image out of my mind.

'The circle of salt didn't protect us, did it? Load of rubbish if you ask me. Can we chat about this tomorrow, Sienna? I'm tired. What's going on here?' she says, placing my hand over her chest. The thump of her heart is beating fast, sweat is pouring from her face, and her legs are trembling. 'Pins and needles are burning my arms and I can't stop shaking,' she cries.

'I shouldn't have involved you in this.'

'Sienna?'

'Yes?'

'What did those words, "Mother of God and Flower of the Fairest," mean?' she asks.

'Don't you remember we had a lesson about it at school? Catholics celebrate May Crowning when the statue of Mary is crowned with a wreath of flowers and honoured as the Queen of Heaven and the Mother of God.'

'Well...' she says, looking at me and biting her nails. 'Er, when I heard those words, masses and masses of colourful flowers poured from the sky and formed a barrier around me. I love you, my strange sister, and whatever happens, don't change.' She snuggles down and pulls her duvet over her head. Next minute, she's asleep.

I'm too drained to reply, so return to my room and climb into bed. I stare at the ceiling and try to get my thoughts straight. Another force is following Martha. A powerful energy risen from the underworld.

CHAPTER 22

It's early and my phone has been vibrating. I pick it up and listen to the voicemail.

'Sienna, this is the senior nurse at Monkton House. It's best if you stay at home today.'

That's it – no other message. She makes no sense, so I sink back into the pillow and notice my bedside clock has stopped at 3 a.m. Where is Bella? She usually bounces into my room, waking me up. I rest my eyes for a minute, but the crunch of wheels on the driveway and the slam of the front door wakes me. My parents are back. They're too early. Did Bella ring them and tell them we performed a spell? I'll kill her if she did. Slipping on my dressing gown, I open the front door and peer out, apprehensive about their anger but stunned when they rush in and embrace me.

'The care home contacted me this morning,' cries Dad.

'What's wrong?' I ask.

'Your Nan had another stroke during the night.' He sinks in the chair, still wearing his jacket. 'She won't survive this one,' he cries, blowing his nose.

'Don't worry, love, the medical team are caring for her.' Mum throws her bag on the chair. 'Anyway, in our rush, we missed breakfast at the hotel. What do you fancy, James, bacon and eggs?'

'How can you eat now, Tracey? With my mum at death's door?'

'She'll be fine. She always is. I don't know why we rushed away. I was looking forward to spending time in the city.'

My parents are arguing again. I accept Nan irritates Mum with her interference and the pressure she exerts over our family. But really? Is Mum not bothered about her?

'Mum, do you want a cup of tea?' I ask. 'I'll make Bella one too.'

'Oh, yeah, please, love. I've a splitting headache; too much wine last night.'

'Bella,' I shout from the bottom of the stairs.

'Sienna, please don't shout,' says Mum, rubbing her temples.

'Where is she?' asks Dad. 'Why isn't she up?'

'It's still early, James, she needs her rest,' says Mum, opening the living room curtains and moving into the kitchen.

'What time did you go to bed, Sienna?' asks Dad.

'It wasn't late,' I say, running upstairs.

'Bella, wake up. Nan is–' I shout, opening my sister's door, and notice her clock has stopped at 3 a.m., the same time as mine. She's lying under the clump of bedclothes and I wrench away the sheet. Bella is a picture of serenity lying on her back with her palms outstretched. She reminds me of the painting *Ophelia* by John Millais. There's a blue tinge to her skin and lips while a single tear lies on her cheek. Her black hair has fanned out, contrasting with the white of the pillow. I drop my head on her chest, but can't detect any movement. The similarity to Dad and Nan with their tall, slender, figures, the elegant neck, pale skin, thick eyebrows, and glossy black hair is striking.

'Bella, stop messing for once and open your eyes. You've got a busy day today.'

I try to wake her up by pinching her ear when Dad walks in.

'Isabella, wake up. Nan is ill.' He turns to me. 'Sienna? Why isn't she moving?'

A sense of foreboding flows over me. Dad throws the duvet on the floor and when there's no response, lays his head on her chest. He does it again, then takes her wrist and presses his fingers over her icy skin. His mouth opens while his eyes stare at me and back to my sister.

'Isabella, Isabella, darling, wake up.'

He pounds on her chest and counts, then breathes air into her, counts again, pounds her chest. Mum dashes upstairs and Dad yells at her. They're making too much noise; it grates in my ears and I screech a penetrating cry. A scream to wake the dead. *Yes, I will wake her up.* Dad is holding her, rocking her back and forwards. He mumbles in her ear and sobs, clutching her to his chest.

'Phone, phone,' he shouts, tossing his mobile at Mum.

'What happened, Sienna?' Dad asks. Mum is staring at the bed so he grabs the mobile off her and barks instructions. She grabs hold of Bella's hand and slumps to the floor.

'Ha ha, Bella, the joke is over.' I bend down and whisper that she has to keep last night's activities a secret. Her eyes are closed and I'm sure she'll wake up soon. If she wants to win her race, she needs to hurry and get changed. I move over to the wardrobe and take out a sports bag with trainers and tracksuit. She'll want her lucky pink hairband to tie her hair back or else it will be distracting.

The doorbell rings. I rush downstairs and open the door. Two people in green uniforms charge upstairs and the house reverberates with the thumping of her chest, reminding me of the pounding of her treadmill. It seems to carry on for ages. The paramedics stand up and walk over to my parents. I watch them shake their heads. Then Mum screams while Dad holds her. She sinks to the floor and clutches Scottie, Bella's old stuffed toy dog. Rocking backward and forwards. Dad walks out of the room. She stands up and places her hand on my cheek; her smudged mascara making shadows under her eyes.

'Sienna, do you want to say goodbye to your sister?'

'But Bella is sleeping, isn't she?'

Mum gathers me in her arms.

'Oh, darling. Your sister has gone, sweetheart,' she sobs. Her face is blotchy and swollen.

'What? Gone where? She was fine last night.'

Dad returns with a glass of water and gives it to Mum.

'Sienna,' he cries, bubbles of mucus dripping out of his nose. He sniffs and blows into a crumpled tissue.

I caress my sister's face and stroke her hair.

'What's wrong with her?' I ask the paramedics. The older man pats my arm.

'We're taking your sister to the hospital now, love,' he replies, nodding to his colleague.

Dad joins them, but Bella is asleep, and they're wrong. She's going to jump up and shout, 'Fooled you.'

I kiss her lips. This isn't her; it's an empty shell. A plastic mannequin lying on a bed. Happier times flood my memory. Walking to school, as she skips on ahead. She couldn't keep still. Watching her run at the athletic club. Her ballet performance at the local theatre. Holidays, weekends away, London sight-seeing. Relaxing in the garden and developing a relationship. But why did I spoil it by chanting the spell? My guilt overwhelms me. Sinking to my knees, I howl in a state of disbelief and misery.

'Isabella, I wish it was me,' I cry, holding her unresponsive body.

I'm annoyed with Charlie for introducing her stupid spell. How foolish we were, dabbling in things we don't understand. My parents are shouting at each other. The noise is hurting my ears. The paramedics place my sister on to a stretcher. My mother rocks backwards and forward on the floor while Dad slumps on the chair.

'No wait,' I say, wrapping a blanket around her. My poor sister, she's frozen. My heart shatters into a thousand pieces as an icy shard pierces my soul. I want to suffer for the hurt I caused her. Tears stream down my cheeks. The pain is raw. She tolerated my temper and tantrums. What was it she said?

'I love you, my strange sister, don't change.'

They try to drag me away, but I refuse to let go. They release my grip, finger by finger. I howl, scream, and claw at them. They press a sharp needle into my thigh and icy liquid flows into me as I sink to the floor.

***

The next morning, I'm lying on my bed, still dressed. My head is throbbing. I'm gasping for a sip of water, and that's when I remember.

I killed Bella.

Whatever the medics gave me has left a metallic taste in my mouth, making me thirsty. I stumble out of bed and into Bella's room. Mum is clutching my sister's pillow and humming to herself.

'Are you OK?' I ask.

She twists her head to stare at me.

'Am I OK? Am I OK? What a question. You can't imagine my sorrow,' she cries, placing her hand over her chest. 'My baby's voice surrounds me. She glides towards me with her hair wafting in the breeze and her adorable smile reaching out. Isabella was the kindest person, her soul as fragile as butterfly wings.'

'Mum.' I stretch out my hand towards her.

'Don't, not now, I'm not ready,' she says, and continues. 'Isabella was adorable and people told me to enter her for baby competitions, but we didn't want you to be jealous. We gave you both similar toys and clothes. But you were envious, weren't you, Sienna? You resented your sister.'

'No, that's not true. I loved Bella,' I say, trying to reassure Mum.

What a lie. I'd been nasty by teasing and bullying her. My mind drifts to a memory of creeping into Bella's room and scaring her with my stories of witches. I concocted a nasty potion of vinegar, lemon juice and milk, and made her swallow it. She thought it was a special magical recipe to help sprint faster than the other girls. When she coughed and spluttered, I pinched her and ordered her to keep quiet.

She's dead, and it's my fault.

Dad plods up the stairs.

'Tracey. Are you coming with me to the care home?'

'I'll go with you,' I say.

'No, you need to rest.' He puts his arm around me and rubs his watery eyes.

'Why not? I want to see Nan.' I don't want to stay in this house on my own.

'James, Sienna should be with us when we break the news.'

'No,' says Dad. 'She'll probably blame her.'

Mum stands with her hands on her hips and glares at him. 'So you're finally admitting her attitude towards our eldest daughter isn't a good one? I'm staying here.'

The hall phone rings and I rush to answer it. It's Aunt Debbie.

'Oh, my poor dear. This is dreadful. How awful. A tragedy. Unbelievable,' she says, her voice breaking up. 'I'm so sorry. I'll be with you soon.'

Dad drives to Monkton House on his own while Mum stays in Bella's room, but I can't settle. I wander around, picking up her trainers, straightening her running magazine on the coffee table, and spot a solitary sports sock on the floor. I hold it in my hand and collapse, resting my head against the cushion. It's late when Dad returns and shouts for Mum. He picks me up from the floor, places me on the armchair, and passes me a tissue.

'Nan is at the hospital, having tests,' he says.

My parents sit at opposite ends of the settee, unaware they've left the middle seat empty for Bella.

'Aunt Debbie is coming soon,' I say.

My heartbeat increases and I panic, thinking that the police will arrive and take me to prison. My poor sister.

'I didn't mean it.' I stand up and pace around.

'What did you say?'

'Nothing. Dad, I meant to tell you Nan was weakening, and it slipped out of my mind. And the way I treated Bella was terrible. I was a mean sister to her,' I say, rubbing my eyes.

The doorbell rings. Mum rushes to answer it and Aunt Debbie dashes in. They burst into another bout of sobbing and cling to each other.

'Hush, Sienna, come here.' I collapse into Dad as he enfolds me in his arms and talks softly to me.

My tall, powerful father is broken into bits, but his words of comfort make no change to my mood. It's my fault Bella is dead. I move away from him. I don't deserve his compassion. The room is quiet. Dad stands up and switches on the kettle. Mum reaches to the top shelf in the cupboard and picks out a packet of biscuits while my aunt scrolls through her phone. What are you doing? I want to scream at them. They act normally while I sit on the chair and reflect on the spells and information in Rose's book. Are they connected to Bella's death? The weight of blame pushes down on my head. Black thoughts flow over me. A gentle breeze whispers in my hair. *'Your power is strengthening. Use it.'* My body itches as if ants are crawling over me. I scratch, scraping away the skin on my neck, blood covering my fingers. A pungent tang of herbs; an earthy, bloody stench; earthworms wriggling amongst the grass. My parents stop what they're doing and gape at each other. I watch Mum stick her hand up to her mouth. I sink to the floor and cry for my sister. All the times I was jealous of her and wanted her gone. Now she has. Was it Charlie's spell that killed her?

Dad strides over to me and holds me tight. The familiar scent of lemon aftershave wafts over me. My hands pummel his chest. I brought death into our lives and it was my fault Bella died.

'Don't worry, don't worry, we'll help you,' he says.

I'm unsure what he will suggest next. Dad is holding me tight but my outburst worries me. Am I having a breakdown? Are they right and I have a mental problem?

'Sienna. We understand how hard this is, and you're suffering, but we need to consider the next steps,' he says.

'What next steps?'

I pull away from Dad's grip.

'To plan Isabella's funeral. We need your input, choosing her favourite flowers and names of her friends.' He strides over to the sideboard and picks up a leaflet.

'What the hell is this?' I rush over and snatch it from his hands. 'Funeral planning checklist?' I read. 'No. It's too early. This is for old people and not my baby sister.'

Mum lets out a shriek and rushes into the kitchen while my dad follows her. My phone has been charging. I play the voicemail: Charlie is begging me to pick up, concern in her voice.

'Sienna, where the hell are you? I've not been able to get in contact. After the exams finished, guess what? Dad sprung a surprise holiday on us. A cruise to the Far East. I had no time to tell you, but I'm home now. The connections were terrible, and I didn't want to worry you, but we stopped over in India. Guess what happened? We passed this old man, a fortune teller, who was holding out his hand for money. He grabbed mine and said he saw a girl falling. I thought of Octavia and was terrified so I ran away. His message has been tormenting me for ages. So, I phoned Gran. She wanted the name of the person we chanted to. I couldn't remember it and said Biddy Blog. That's when she lost her temper and said if it was Biddy Bishop, we're in trouble. Gran told me not to repeat her name. But who did we summon with the spell against Octavia? I'm frightened and I need to go. Dad is here. Phone me.'

Another voicemail message.

'Sienna, I'm serious. Are you listening? Where are you? I've tried phoning your sister, but she's not answering either. Yes, fine, Dad.' Her message cuts off.

Five minutes later.

'Sienna,' she whispers in a frightened voice. 'Whatever you planned to do with your sister, DO NOT, and I repeat, DO NOT use that spell. I can't say her name, but it begins with B. Google it, Sienna. Please text me and tell me you're safe.'

I open my laptop, type the name in the search engine, and immediately regret it. Biddy Bishop was a Salem witch who murdered her two husbands by using a variety of herbs and poisonous sap from the lily. If anyone disagreed with her, she created a spell to kill them. It was alleged that if people argued with her, disaster would follow them. People were found dead with nails stuck in their eyes. She worked with the devil, causing chaos wherever she travelled, and was convicted of her crimes and hanged.

I can't read anymore. My eyes are smarting. I'm puzzled by this information. Why did we chant her name? I remember the spell came from the magazine Rose found in Drumbeg Manor. I'm too exhausted to consider Charlie's message. It wasn't our fault Octavia died; she tripped and fell down the stairs. Tomorrow, I will throw anything connected with the supernatural in the bin. This subject is too immense for me. I'm frightened by the malevolence I've unleashed with my interest in the occult.

The phone rings.

'Oh, Charlie, you're home,' I cry and tell her about my sister.

She doesn't interrupt, but sobs uncontrollably.

'It's my fault – I found the spell in the magazine and I'm sorry about Bella,' she whispers. 'You're stronger than me. I would have crumbled by now. I've got to get my head around this. Talk to you later.' She ends the call and I'm left with an empty feeling.

Walking away, I spot a school photograph on the wall. It's one where I'm standing behind Bella, my hand perched on her shoulder. The difference between us is obvious: she's stunning with her dark eyes and shiny hair. I'm a mess. Why didn't the photographer mention my creased shirt and frizzy hair? Bella is beaming compared to my rigid smile. Why did my parents waste their money on this? Placing the photo back on the shelf, I notice she has one hand in front of the other on her lap, but it's her middle finger that stands out.

She's flipping the bird at me. She got me that time. I laugh until my sides ache. Oh, my beautiful sister. How can I make it up to you? Send me a sign. Anything.

CHAPTER 23

Three days later.

Dad is in his study, and Mum is still in bed. The last few days have been a whirl. Thoughts of the spell cloud my mind with a painful anxiety that I killed Bella. The doorbell rings while I'm downstairs nibbling on a piece of dry bread and skimming through photos of my sister. Matt is standing on the doorstep.

'Sienna, how are you? No, sorry, what a stupid question,' he says, clutching a bunch of red tulips.

'Sorry I've not been in touch. How did you find out?' I ask, watching the petals drift to the floor.

We enter the living room, Matt leaving a trail of petals behind him.

'Somebody has posted news about your sister on Facebook; they're saying you killed her and the police will convict you.'

'What does that mean? Who would write such horrible things?' I ask, grabbing his arm.

'Gossip spreads fast here. It could be a girl from school or a neighbour who noticed the ambulance.'

Matthew peeks behind him at the twitching of the curtains from the window opposite.

'The trouble with this village is there are too many nosy parkers. I'm sorry again about Bella. Was she ill? She was always so sporty.'

'No, she never had a day off sick till the night of the Ouija board,' I say. 'Follow me and I'll get a vase.'

My mother is at the kitchen table, poring over Isabella's baby photos.

'Mum, Matt is here. People are trolling me and saying I hurt Bella.'

'I have no idea what trolling is,' she says. Her face is flushed and she keeps licking her dry lips.

Dad enters the kitchen and pours a glass of water. He turns towards me, his shoulders hunched, and flashes a quick smile.

'Don't listen to idle chatter. When we receive the results from the post mortem report, we'll understand why she died,' he says.

I edge away, hoping the guilt doesn't show in my face, and shudder at the thought of what they will do to Bella.

'She'll be freezing; my baby needs me,' wails Mum, twisting her tissue into sodden clumps.

'James, when will we get the report?' asks Debbie as she walks over to Mum.

'The doctor told me that because of her age, they regard it as urgent, so it shouldn't be long now.'

'The idea of arranging my sister's burial is unbelievable. Where do we begin? I keep imagining her strolling in, dropping her trainers and rucksack on the floor, and pouring herself a glass of milk,' I say.

'Sienna, I'm going now, but if you need my help, please phone me,' says Matt. When we get to the door, he bends down and kisses my cheek. This time I don't blush.

After Matt has left, we gather on the settee, each with our memories of Isabella. I start first.

'Bella on the sports track. Afterwards, she gave me her medal and said, 'You take it, sis. I've won loads. Why don't you jog with me?' She tried to persuade me to train with her. I should have been kinder to her. Why didn't I snap out of my grumpiness?' I ask them, but they don't answer.

I recall once she wanted me to help her with homework and searched for me in the school library, but as soon as I spotted her, I crept out. She was late coming home that night, and was told off, but didn't snitch on me.

'She was cute when she started primary school and lined up her teddies. She made up a class register and shouted out their names, mimicking the teacher,' says Mum, standing up to show Isabella's actions. We smile and carry on reminiscing.

'She tried on her new school uniform and danced around the room, happy to be following in your footsteps. Sienna, you promised to watch over her,' says Dad.

'Did I?'

'Yes, you showed her the different classrooms, didn't you?' he asks, studying me.

'Mmm. Yeah. Mind you, Bella made friends easily and didn't need me,' I say, hoping they missed the uncertainty behind my words. The sound of a ringtone distracts him.

'Who's that?' He picks up his mobile and moves next to Mum. 'That was quick.' We watch his skin turn ashen and a tiny muscle in his cheek twitch.

'Thank you for letting me know,' he says, turning towards us. That was Dr Miller on the phone. He said young people dying suddenly require immediate action, and the coroner treated it as an emergency.' His voice sounds far away.

My mother utters a cry. I lower myself in the chair and pick at the rough skin around my nails. What did he mean? I groan. My aunt is examining me. How many years will I get for killing my sister? Will my parents visit me in prison? Should I tell them she died from chanting a spell? They'll say I've lost it. This is it. I breathe in and bow my head. My aunt is staring at me. Dad's voice is muffled as if underwater.

'Natural cause of death… sudden death syndrome.'

'What's that?' I ask, lifting my head.

My parents are weeping and holding each other.

Aunt Debbie stands up and rushes over to me.

'Sienna, listen.'

'Isabella died from long QT syndrome,' he says. 'Which means she had an undiagnosed heart condition.'

'James, what does that mean? Why wasn't this spotted?' asks Mum.

'I should have noticed her breathlessness when we went jogging. She trained too often, didn't she?' Dad is staring at Mum. 'It's my fault – I pushed her too hard.'

'What is long QT syndrome and will I catch it?' I ask.

'The doctor explained it's an increased, irregular heartbeat and can be inherited.'

Debbie turns to Dad. 'So, Isabella died from natural causes?'.

'But how?' I ask.

'The doctor told me it could have happened any time.'

'If we'd paid more attention to those dizzy spells of Isabella's instead of dismissing them, she could have been treated,' says Mum.

'We'll never know now, Tracey, but we need to collect the death certificate,' says Dad, rubbing Mum's back.

'Don't you remember we phoned for advice about Isabella's breathlessness, and couldn't get past the blasted receptionist,' she cries. The next minute, Mum is screaming and collapses on the floor. 'Isabella, Isabella, come back to me.'

My aunt rushes over and wraps her arm around her. The idea of being in this room without Bella is torture. I need to talk to my friends, so phone Matt and ask him to meet me in the park and then I text Charlie.

'Mum, Dad, I'll be back later,' I say, moving towards the door and picking up my key.

Debbie follows me. 'Don't be too long. Your parents need you.'

I stroll towards the park near the school. My sister lived for fourteen years. How can that be fair? She will never have her first boyfriend, win races, and achieve sporting success. However, she will always be a winner to me and my parents. Mr Singh the newsagent is polishing the glass in his shop door and stops when I get closer.

'Many apologies about your sister. Stay here.' He enters his shop while I wait. A few minutes later, he opens the door and stands in front of me.

'I often saw you on your own, and told Isabella to help you.'

'What do you mean?'

With his hands clasped, he bows his head.

'You are a lonely soul, always observing. A wanderer, who needs protection.' He sticks his hand in his pocket. 'Wear this. It will keep you safe.' Mr Singh passes me a bracelet. 'It's a Hindu amulet strung from tourmaline beads and made of Indian silver from Rajasthan,' he says, fastening it over my wrist.

'What is tourmaline?' I ask.

'This gemstone has many properties, such as relieving stress and increasing mental alertness. It will strengthen your immune system,' he says. 'Your sorrow resembles Garuda, the king of birds working with Vishnu, to fight injustice and destroy evil. Your melancholy resembles the bird and will fly away. All I ask is, when your hurt has eased, pass this bracelet on to another tortured soul.'

'How will I tell?' I ask.

'You will feel it here.' He places his palm over his heart.

'Thank you,' I say. 'I'll treasure this always.'

'Take care.' He bows and strolls into the shop.

Further along the path leading towards school, I notice Matt sitting on a bench. He hasn't spotted me yet, so I spend a minute or two observing him. As I step towards him, he twists around.

'Sienna,' he says. 'Apologies for barging in on your family with that pathetic excuse of a bouquet, but I was desperate to be with you.'

'Matt, I'm glad you came.'

'I've been worried about you,' he says, gripping my hand and fiddling with the bracelet. 'Is this new?'

'It's from Mr Singh. Here's me criticising him for being a miserable old sod and he does something nice.'

Matt grabs both hands and stares deep into my eyes. 'You don't realise that people like you.'

I shrug. 'I've always felt different, as if I don't belong.' Before we can carry on with our conversation, I spot my friend.

'Oh, here she is. Charlie!' I wave at her.

We stand up as she rushes over.

'I'm so sorry, you poor thing. Terrible news,' she says, rubbing my arm.

'Here, drink this.' She opens the tab on the can of Coke and passes it to me.

'Thanks,' I say.

I'm in the middle of my two best friends. Matt is holding my hand as I talk about my sister. He squeezes mine.

'I need to tell you a secret,' I say. 'You know already, Charlie.'

'What?' asks Matt.

'Bella died because I chanted a spell and we summoned...'

'Stop!' shouts Charlie.

222

'Sienna, what were you going to say?' asks Matt.

I shake my head.

'The doctor told you the reason Bella died, and I know it's hard to accept, but you need to get the idea that you were responsible out of your head.'

'Matt's right,' says Charlie. 'Let's sit down.' She points to the school's playing field where the blossom trees are flowering.

'I'll never see my sister again. Oh God, this is unbearable. Why did she die?' Matthew places his arm around my shoulders, and I lean into him and study Charlie strolling through the grass.

'Stop!' I shout.

'What's wrong?'

I gesture to a ring of flowers. 'It's a witch's circle.'

Matt frowns at me. 'I thought your obsession with the paranormal was over?'

'Wait a minute.' Charlie picks up a flower. 'This is familiar. Have you got my gran's book with you?' she asks.

'No, it's back in my room.'

'This is identical to the petal on the first page.'

'Let's have a look.' I hold up the flower and study its fragile petals.

As we advance deeper into the woods, masses of white fluffy clusters catch our eye.

'They look like cow's parsley,' says Charlie, wrinkling her nose.

'I'll have a search,' says Matt, scrolling through his phone.

'Anything?' I ask.

'Nope, can't see it,' he replies.

'I'll take a photo and post it on Facebook. Someone may identify them,' I say, taking out my mobile. 'Help me pick them and I'll gather a bunch. Mum might recognise them.'

'Yes, and I'll tell Rose we may have found them,' says Charlie.

'Found what?' asks Matt, studying us.

'Well,' I say. 'It began…'

'… with the flowers in her spell book,' continues Charlie.

We gather handfuls of the sweet-smelling blooms. They're fragile, with frilly white petals around a centre of navy blue.

'How strange. They're stuck together like candy floss, but if you look closely, they're miniscule lilies grouped as one flower. Hey, Charlie, can you remember from science lessons the name of the insides of flowers?' I ask.

'Stigma?' she says.

'Yes, stamen, pistil, stigma, ovule and the insides of the petals are blue but this pollen is blood red. That's unusual,' says Matt, peering at the flower. 'What?' he asks, staring at us.

'How romantic, Matt. Sienna will always rely on you to blind her with science,' says Charlie with a grin.

As we are nearing home, I grab their hands.

'Thank you for being with me today.'

Charlie waves. 'I'm going to investigate these flowers.'

Matt accompanies me to the door. 'How are you now?' he asks.

'I'm OK, no, I'm better than that. The night before my sister died, she made a strange comment. She told me to live my life.'

He holds my hand. 'You need to follow her advice, don't you?' He bends his head and our lips connect with a kiss tasting of sugary Coke and chewing gum. His lips are soft and his body presses against mine. The flowers stain my pale T-shirt, but I don't care. 'Sienna, I can't stop thinking about you,' he whispers as Dad opens the front door, spoiling the mood.

'Sienna, it's visiting time for your Nan. Let's go,' he says, closing the door behind him.

We get into the car and Matt strolls along the pavement. He waves at me as we pass him, and my fingers reach up to stroke my lips, remembering his kiss.

At the hospital, Dad rushes in through the double doors, his shoes slipping along the shiny floor. When we enter the ward, a nurse points to a screen around a bed.

'Mrs Stevens has finished,' says the nurse.

She pulls open the curtains to reveal Nan sitting up.

'James, you came. And where is my little Bella?' she asks, peering behind me.

Walking towards her, I present the bunches of flowers we picked from the wood.

'No. No, take them away, Martha! Danger – danger! Lilies are coming for you.'

'For goodness' sake, not again. Wait outside and get rid of those blasted flowers,' says Dad.

What on earth is wrong with her? Now she's calling me Martha. When will this nightmare end?

CHAPTER 24

The sun streaming into my room awakens me. I stretch and enjoy the silence but then remember. Seeing my new dress hanging outside the wardrobe reminds me that today we bury my sister. My stomach is churning. Saliva fills my mouth and I want to be sick. I sit up as Dad enters wearing his sombre black suit.

'Where's your multi-coloured tie? We agreed she wouldn't want it to be a depressing day,' I say, as he passes me a cup of tea.

'I changed my mind. Black is a mark of respect.'

'Do you want me to look for darker clothes?'

'No. Isabella will appreciate you wearing a dress instead of your jeans.' The corners of his mouth turn down as he struggles with his cufflinks. Mum enters and perches on the edge of the bed.

'I'm wearing my summer dress too, the one with the palm trees. Do you remember when Isabella was younger, she picked it out for me at Santa Eulalia market?' says Mum. She's still in her dressing gown, holding on to her coffee mug. 'Do you want help, love?' she asks, pointing to his shirt cuffs.

Today is the worst day of my life. Nothing compares to this. It took us ages to choose the cars, coffin, clothes, colour of flowers and music. Families don't discuss funeral arrangements, do they? It's tempting fate. Which makes me wonder what would happen if my parents died and I'm left alone in the world, an orphan. Who would I live with? Aunt Debbie? I brush away a tear at that thought.

'Sienna, try to stop your daydreaming, at least for today,' says Dad.

I stare at the wardrobe mirror. I look a sight with my short, stubby legs poking out of a flowery pink dress as sweat pools under my armpits. My red shiny face, freckles, and blasted ginger hair are the bane of my life. I slap concealer over my birthmark and hope nobody will notice. How selfish to be thinking about this now. I lie on the bed, unable to say goodbye to Bella, but the doorbell rings, and they're here.

A convoy of funeral cars arrives to transport us to the crematorium, and we climb into them. My fingers are shaking, and the door handle slips out of my grasp. This is unreal. My parents hold hands as we drive through the village, and people lower their heads when we pass. The older neighbours are making the sign of the cross. Bella told me her ambition was to be a top athlete, enter the Olympics and win medals. She trained regularly to achieve her dream and boasted that one day she would ride through our village in an open-topped bus, with the crowds cheering her on. This will never happen.

The amount of people lining the streets is amazing. She would have enjoyed the fuss. I'm alone in the back seat, as an energy flows over me and the imperceptible pressure of fingertips trail across my hand.

'I hope you're watching, Bella; this is for you,' I whisper into the air. My lip quivers at the enormity of the event. Why did my sister die and not me?

The cars pull up outside the chapel. Her favourite song – *Angels* by Robbie Williams – is reverberating throughout the building. She lies in an oak coffin with mounds of flowers perched on the top. I designed the wreath made from white lilies, pink roses, mimosas and baby's breath, fashioned in the shape of a heart. The pallbearers lift it out, checking the flowers are secure and not slipping off the shiny wood.

Dad blows his nose on a white handkerchief. My mother is weeping, and people stare at me, as I hear Bella singing along with the song.

We walk behind her coffin, but my mind is blank. The chapel is crowded with people sobbing. I'm sweltering in the heat and tug at my collar to waft in cool air as the polyester material sticks to the back of my legs. This dress being pink and girly would suit Bella. A full-length window lies behind the altar and the sun blazes through the glass with an intense heat. The blossom trees shedding their petals and floating to the floor catch my eye. A slight wind echoes in my ears. In the distance, shining with silvery sparks, glows the figure of my sister covered in a diaphanous veil, floating towards me. Tendrils of gossamer drift across my face with the hint of her flowery perfume seeping into my nose.

I bend my head as she places her lips by my ears and whispers, 'My sweet, strange sister, live your life. Be strong for me.'

The image floats away, and the iridescent shimmer of a will of the wisp evaporates. During the service, people recite poems and praise her. Teachers and support staff have cut their summer holidays short to attend. The principal compliments Isabella's strengths, and her kindness towards others by giving up her break time and mentoring younger pupils. My perfect sister. Even in death, they worship her. A voice in my head is telling me I'm being unkind to have these thoughts. I want to answer back that I can't help it, but this voice won't stop. Mum holds my hand and Dad grabs the other. Large photographs of Bella are next to the coffin, with her sports medals and trophies on the steps. The athletic coach's voice quivers when she praises my sister's commitment, her confidence, and her successes. I sense movement beside me as Dad stands up.

'Sit down,' I mutter, trying to haul him back.

'Hush, love, he wants to say a few words.' Mum squeezes my arm.

Dad ambles up to the lectern. Isabella is next to him with her head on his shoulder, and their dark hair merging. Her radiance shines through a silver cloak of crystal beads.

He clears his throat.

'Isabella was our second daughter and a treasure. You speak about her kindness. However, to us she was a teenager and not perfect, and would have a strop if she lost a race or when her sister ate the last piece of chocolate.'

The crowd murmurs. I scan the congregation and notice a few people smiling, and I'm glad Dad's eulogy is easing the sorrowful mood.

'A light of our life has been extinguished, but her spirit will live on in her sister, Sienna.'

I choke from the poignancy of his words, and consider what he means. Does he know she's with me? Her presence will help me change and become a better person. Dad holds out his hand and we join him as one family. Isabella's other favourite song, *A Thousand Years* by Christina Perri, is playing in the background as the coffin slides along the runners. The thick velvet curtains draw together and I want to wrench Bella out.

'She can't leave me, she can't,' I sob on Dad's chest. I stare at the window where a butterfly is flapping its wings.

'Say farewell to your sister. She's ready to depart this earth now and I will watch over her for you,' murmurs a familiar voice behind me.

I spin around, but there's no-one there. The butterfly flies away from the window. Martha leaves behind trickles of muddy water before she vanishes. The service is over and as we mill outside the chapel, Bella's friends surround me.

Abigail, the ringleader, puts her hand on my arm and says, 'Hi Sienna. We're sorry about Bella and thanks for inviting us coz we wanted to show our respects. She's my best friend. Oh no. I mean, was. Oh, I don't know what to say. Oh my God, how can you stand it?' She sniffs into a tissue as the girl next to her joins in. 'Bella talked about you all the time. She was proud to be your sister because you're loads cleverer than her.'

'You're having a laugh, aren't you?' I say.

The heat is making me woozy, and my eyelids twitch. People are chatting. I want to escape and follow Martha, but she has left me.

'No, it's true. She worshipped you and would have done anything for her big sister,' Abigail replies.

The misery of being unaware of her thoughts cuts me into pieces. The silly arguments and jealousies. Time squandered. Mum squeezes my arm and I climb into the funeral car with her and Dad. The mourners follow us home for refreshments, but I don't want to meet anyone. I want to hide away in my room, and scream out it's my fault, I killed her. I pick up a plate of egg mayonnaise sandwiches and hand them out. People keep saying how proud Bella was of me. Why didn't she tell me? Why didn't I celebrate our differences instead of being nasty and bitter? What a waste. From now on, I'm determined to follow in Bella's footsteps, be kind, cheerful, and help people in need. Perhaps I'll gather food for food banks or stand on the street corners and collect money for heart charities.

Matt strides over to me. His black tie is tight against his collar and he rubs the pinched skin on his neck. I long to reach up and undo the top button for him.

'Thanks for coming today. We appreciated it,' I say, sniffling and searching for a tissue.

He hands me a glass of water and I study the people gathering on the lawn and chatting as if they're at a garden party. Smiling and drinking glasses of wine. Dad is with a teacher and he laughs. A gut-wrenching belly laugh. Leaning backwards and forwards, his mouth open wide, wiping the tears from his eyes. What's funny? How dare he laugh? Today of all days. I'm livid and want them to go. I reach the handle to open the back door for air when Matt places his hand over mine.

'I'm sorry about your sister.'

'It's my fault she died.'

'Not true. She died of natural causes.'

'Matt, how can the death of a fit and healthy fourteen-year-old be natural? She'd still be alive if I hadn't involved her in that spell,' I say.

'Sienna. This may not be the best time, but here's something for you,' he says, thrusting a small box into my hand.

'Thanks.' I stick it in my pocket, distracted by the crowd milling around.

Isabella's friends keep clutching me and giving me their mobile numbers, asking me to keep in contact. I'm exhausted and glad to escape to the comfort of my room. I open the box Matt gave me and nestled amongst crumpled tissue paper is a pair of shiny green peridot earrings. Inside the box is a piece of paper, which reads:

'Sienna, this gem signifies strength, and will protect you from nightmares. Matthew xxx.'

I study his message and try on the earrings. They sparkle against my skin. The thought of Matt buying them for me makes me happy. I clasp my pillow, picturing my sister and revisiting memories of her. *I promise you, Isabella, I will change my life, and your death will not be in vain.* The ache for her is tearing me apart and I can't stand being on my own any longer, so I go downstairs. Charlie and Rose are chatting with the form teacher.

'Do you want a drink or a sandwich? There's plenty over there,' I say, gesturing to the buffet table, overloaded with enough food to feed the village.

'No, we're fine, thanks,' says Charlie as my parents come over.

'Mum and Dad, this is Rose, Charlie's grandmother.' They shake hands with her, and thank her for coming, then Isabella's friends interrupt them and they drift away.

'Rose, Charlie. It's a lovely evening – let's move into the conservatory,' I say.

'Not me, Sienna, I'm tired. Are you coming home, Charlie?'

'Gran, if it's alright with you, I'll stay here and organise a taxi back.'

'Sienna, will you say goodbye to your parents for me? I'm sure we'll meet in the next few days before I head back to Ireland.'

As I embrace her, I notice her deepened wrinkles and pain etched over her face.

'What's wrong with your gran?' I ask Charlie after Rose staggers out of the room.

'Her migraines are increasing and I'm worried because she's been saying…' Charlie stops and grabs a glass of squash. I refill my drink and wait for her to continue.

'What?' I ask.

'OK, this is odd, but she's been repeating the same words as your nan.'

'Which ones?'

'The thing about lilies.'

'We've been on the search for the flowers from her book but maybe she's become obsessed with them.'

'No, it's more. Dad was worried about her and he employed a night carer.'

'She's not that old,' I say.

'Yes, but the thing is, the carer phoned Dad the next day and, well…'

'Charlie! What?'

'Gran has been waking up at night, opening the curtains and shouting.'

'Shouting? Shouting what?'

'She's been screaming, "Watch out for the lilies," and scaring the carer.'

'Perhaps she heard me mention my nan using those words, and she repeated it.'

'No, it's more than that.'

'What could it be?' I ask.

'The carer said that a stench of burnt matches surrounded Gran. The plugs were off and there were no appliances smouldering. Dad called the fire service in to make sure the cottage was safe.'

'What does the smell of burning mean?'.

'It's a mystery. Rose told me about her psychic insights or 'funny turns', but doesn't remember walking into the lounge. The problem we have now is that the carer resigned, stating the cottage is haunted.'

I stare at her, worried about Rose being alone.

'Is she living with you here in Lakeview now?'

'Yes, it's best to stay with us for a while till Dad decides what to do.'

'What does the doctor suggest?'

'He wasn't very sympathetic and said her erratic sleeping was because of her age. I haven't told Dad about the spell book because she was fine before giving it to us. Well, *you,* actually. We're thinking of having her live permanently with us.'

'Your gran worries me.'

'So if you were that concerned, why didn't you get in touch?'

I look away. Charlie has been the one difficult to contact.

'I haven't been honest with you.' She stands up and gulps her drink. 'You know, when I mentioned visions with murky shapes, swirling around and hands trying to reach out, I…'

'What?'

'I was lying.'

'Even about coming from a long line of Irish mystics?' I ask.

'Yes, I said that so you would be my friend, but I don't have a psychic bone in my body. My gran is the one with the gift of sight, not me.'

'Right then.' I stand up. 'You've been pretending you're my friend? Why? To make me out a fool. Do you tell the kids at school things about me? Is that why you sit next to me in class? Did you tell Paddy to make up the message? I've been a mug,' I cry.

'I didn't know he would say those things,' whispers Charlie.

'Let yourself out.' I march away from her.

'Wait, Sienna.' She grabs hold of my arm. 'You've no idea how much I wanted to copy you. You're an individual and don't follow the crowd. I wanted you to think I was different and lied about my paranormal ability. At Gran's, you connected with her, but she's disappointed with me because of my lack of mystic tendencies. There, I've told you. If you want me to leave, I will,' she says.

'Oh Charlie, you daft thing. It doesn't matter if you're not psychic. I'm fed up with these visions and not being able to do anything about them. The doctor suggests it's petit mal epilepsy, so I may not be psychic after all. Also, Mum has told me that my grandmother had schizophrenia. Something else to consider.' I look down and swirl the melted ice cubes in my glass.

'That's nothing to worry about because both conditions are treatable.' She places her hand over mine as Dad walks in.

'Hello, you two. Some good news at last: your nan has made a recovery and is being transferred back to Monkton House. Will you go to see her when you can, please?'

'Er, yes, soon,' I say.

'Can I join you?' asks Charlie.

'How lovely. She will appreciate the company, but take your nose rings out before you go, won't you?' he laughs.

When her taxi arrives, I walk with her to the door.

'Thanks for being honest with me. That's what best friends are for,' I say, smacking her arm playfully.

My parents are still circulating, and I escape to bed and dwell on my sister and Charlie. Considering I'm psychic, reading people's emotions is a skill that needs developing. I make a vow to be kinder, less selfish and more sensitive to others' needs.

CHAPTER 25

My sister's death has affected us in different ways. I loll about in my pyjamas while Debbie and Mum go on long walks. When they return, the first thing they do is open a bottle of wine. Dad stays upstairs in his study and surfaces only to eat. I'm having a coffee in the lounge when the doorbell rings. Charlie and Rose are standing outside.

'Come in,' I say.

'Is this a good time?' Rose asks.

'It's fine, I'm glad you're here coz these last few days have been difficult. Come into the lounge.'

'Sienna,' says Rose. 'Charlie told me the flowers you found in the school playing field are identical to the ones stuck amongst the pages in the book. Can I check it out, please?'

'Of course. Wait here, the book's in my room.'

I rush upstairs. When I come down and hand it over, I breathe a sigh of relief, glad to get rid of it.

'Rose, the pages I've read are sickening, and whoever gave it to your parents has a weird mind,' I say, handing it to her. 'By the way, my nan had a peculiar turn when I gave her the flowers, so I brought them back home with me. They're in the vase over there.' I point to the sideboard. 'Let's compare them.'

We examine the flowers.

'They're identical,' gasps Rose.

'Yes, you're right. I sent a photo of the flower to our local Facebook page. Several horticulturists contacted me and told me they are unique – they grow in the Lakeview area of the Cotswolds. They're named Lilliarosa or *Lilliarosa origianaus*.'

'That's an unusual name, isn't it?' asks Charlie.

Rose shakes her head. 'I've never heard of them, so why are they stuck in my book? They came from this area and I want to find out who picked them.'

'Gran told me about a dream she had last night. She saw the flowers surrounding a large building that looked like a stately home. When she described it, I immediately thought of Monkton House. She asked if she could join us when we visit your nan there.'

'Will your parents be OK with that?' asks Rose.

'Of course. I'll get dressed while my aunt makes you a coffee. Won't you?' I shout through to the kitchen where Aunt Debbie is washing up.

Ten minutes later, I return.

'Ah, here she is. I'll take you to Monkton before carrying on into town; your parents can have time on their own,' she says and shoves the toaster back in the cupboard.

'That's cool, thanks.'

We climb into my aunt's car. Debbie has never been to the care home before, and I direct her through narrow lanes. A laundry van tries to squeeze past us.

'What the hell? Bloody white van driver. What a nuisance. Is this the only way in?'

'Yes, 'fraid so.'

'I wouldn't want to visit here at night. Can't they afford a decent road? This desolate countryside is creepy,' she says, driving up to the entrance and switching off the ignition. 'Here we are. Wow, I never knew this old Gothic structure was lurking here. Looks like it belongs in a horror film. Give me the city any day.'

'It's always been here,' I say as the cawing of birds drowns out my voice.

'What the hell is that squawking?' she asks.

'Ravens,' I say. 'It's strange but since I've been visiting here, their numbers have doubled.'

'What? Are you sure? Yeah, spooky the way they're circling around – and look.' She points to the roof. 'They're sitting and waiting. God, are you sure they're not watching us? It reminds me of that film *The Birds* by Hitchcock.'

Debbie is fumbling with her car window; the electrics have stuck and she can't open it.

'What the hell? This has never happened before. It's a new car. Never mind. Sienna, get out and punch the pass code in.'

I jump out of the car and press in the numbers on the control pad. The gates open automatically, creaking and shuddering.

I get back in the car. Debbie nudges me, and I turn round to see what she's on about. Rose's face is an ashen grey, and she's sitting upright, her large handbag clutched firmly against her chest. She's staring at the house and pointing up at the roof. I follow her gaze towards the stone figures perched on the edges of the turrets. Figures made of granite, dressed in long gowns, their heads covered by hoods, holding their hands in prayer.

Debbie prods me again.

'What are they?'

'Anne Duncan told me they're monks. The religious figures who owned this property years ago. She showed me a photograph from her book.'

'Who's Anne Duncan?' asks Rose.

'She's researching the history of this area,' I say, turning around in my seat to face her. 'We'll pop in to see her before Nan.'

Debbie stops the car. Rose flings open the door and points her finger in the distance.

'Look,' she says, as she gets out. I follow her gaze. Amongst the base of trees are masses of white flowers clumped together. Their fluffy display reminds me of clouds.

'They're weeds, Rose – cow parsley,' I say.

'No, over there.' She points, and heads towards the nearest tree.

'OK, I'm off, Sienna. Are you sure you'll be alright with…' She nods her head towards Rose, who is on her hands and knees picking the flowers.

'Yes; we'll chat with Anne Duncan and maybe she'll tell us more about the flowers that grow around here.'

'Right, see you later.' She waves and drives away.

Nan's carer opens the front door and heads towards us.

'I've brought my friend's gran with me,' I say to her.

'Good to see more visitors during the day. Right, I'm off home now. I've finished my shift. The speed of your nan's stroke alarmed us. We believed something spooked her,' she says, moving away.

'What does she mean?' asks Charlie as Rose walks towards us with her hands full of white flowers.

'You look like a beautiful bride, Gran.' Charlie wraps her arms around her and rests her chin on her shoulder.

'Get away with you. These are for my research. I'm determined to resolve this mystery, and you're my helpers.' She looks at us and buries her nose in the bunch of flowers.

We enter Monkton House and it hits me again: bitterness and

regret, tasting of almonds and tears. Rose is standing still, her arms full of white blooms, staring up at Jesus on the cross. His eyes are closed.

'At first it's a shock when you see how realistic the figure is, but you become used to it dangling from the ceiling,' I say.

'Who's on duty?' asks Charlie. 'It's too quiet. Anyone could sneak in here.'

The reception area is empty. The desk is unmanned, and behind it is the matron's office. I peer through her side window, but she's not there.

'Anne Duncan first,' I say.

As we open the double doors, Matt walks towards us.

'Hi. I saw you from Anne's patio.'

'Where are the carers?' I ask.

'They're short staffed this week, with people on their holidays, and a resident in the home is…' he whispers, '… dying.'

'You're sweet, dear, but you don't need to protect me from death. I'm Rose, Charlie's gran, and you must be the hunk the girls talk about. Or should I say, one particular girl,' she grins.

'Gran!' shrieks Charlie.

'Rose,' I whisper, covering my face with my hands as the heat creeps up my neck.

'Right ladies, allow me to escort you,' he says, holding Rose's elbow and ushering her along the corridor.

'Ooh, aren't you the gentleman?' She laughs. 'It's no wonder Sienna blushes when your name crops up.'

I try to glare at Rose but we end up laughing as Matt grins and pretends to doff his cap. A few residents are shuffling along the hallways and acknowledge me as I pass them.

'Are you going to read to me again, Sienna, love,' asks one old lady. 'I liked that Patricia Highsmith. What was it now? *Ripples Game*?

No, let me think.' She peers at me while her carer waits patiently. 'I'll get it in a mo. That's it, *The Talented Mr Ripley*. Yes, you'll read the next one. *Ripley's Game*? Yes, that one.'

I smile at her, but it saddens me she won't remember our chat next time we meet. We knock on Anne Duncan's room.

'Come in.' She opens the door. 'Well, well, finally,' she says, stretching out her hand.

'I'm Rose.'

'You're identical to Martha, dear,' says Anne. 'I've been waiting to meet you, and here you are.'

'Should we fetch a nurse?' Matt whispers to me.

'No, I want to listen to her.'

'Well, I need to go. The matron has asked me to sit with a resident, but she'll probably be dozing. I'll catch you later.' He waves his hand and walks out.

'Sit over here,' says Anne, gesturing to her bed. Rose is still gripping the bunches of white flowers. Charlie and I plonk ourselves down, taking care not to mess up her immaculate white crochet bedcovers. Rose drags a chair out from under the desk and joins us, but then closes her eyes and hums a familiar nursery rhyme.

'What's wrong, Gran? What's that tune?' asks Charlie.

'I don't know. I can't get it out of my head,' she says.

'Are you sure you're OK, dear? Your face has turned greyish. I remember that song. *Lavender blue*. Gosh, you're going back years, aren't you? *Lavender blue, dilly dilly. Lavender green*. Loved the words but not heard that since I was a youngster. Anyway, I'm Anne Duncan, the author of this book,' she says, gesturing to the hardback on her desk. 'I decided to write it because of my background. When my parents died, the authorities sent me here.'

'Oh, how awful for you,' says Rose.

'You're right. Mrs Goldman ran the orphanage, but she was a terrible woman.' Anne Duncan peers at us over her glasses. 'She had a daughter a few years older than me. It was upsetting, losing my parents. I was younger than the other girls and cried at night while two friends comforted me. One was Martha and I can't recall the name of the other one. After the dreadful event, when parts of the house burnt down, they sent me to another orphanage and lost contact. Years passed, and I became a historian at Oxford University. My health failed and with no family to live with, I accepted a place here. Although Monkton House is now a care home, it hasn't changed and still holds memories.'

'Hold on, Anne – you said Martha lived here?' I say.

'Yes, I've told you that before, haven't I?'

I shake my head.

There's a knock and a carer pushes open the door with her hip.

'Time for your tea, dear.' She hands Anne a cup. 'Would you like one?' she asks us.

'No thanks,' I say.

The old lady stirs her drink, and I remember the ledger we found in the library.

'Anne, what was in the journal?'

She places her teaspoon on the saucer and says, 'Ah yes, it's Latin, so I sent it away to a friend of mine, a professor of languages at Oxford University, who translated it. He explained it was normal practice to transcribe into another language to conceal evidence from the public. His research shows the staff employed at the orphanage originated from an old sect who still spoke and wrote an ancient form of Latin. One of them must have recorded what she saw.'

'What could be so awful that it needs hidden?' I ask.

Anne picks up her jotter and opens it.

'I've found out this orphanage operated as a money-making business. They gave babies up for adoption and commanded the highest prices. Here is a list of the girls who gave birth and the adopters of their babies.' She reads out a couple of girls, but the babies are unnamed:

'Maisie Walker. Baby girl. Adopted by Mr and Mrs Sullivan, London, England; Sarah Kelly. Baby boy. Adopted by Mr and Mrs Doyle, County Clare, Ireland. There are others but they will need checking against documents.'

'What does it mean?' I ask, staring at the journal in front of me.

'An illegal practice of buying babies from desperate girls took place here.'

Rose yawns.

'It's interesting history, Anne, but I'm sorry to say that I'm very weary – I suffer from migraines, which wipe me out. Sienna, I'll just say hello to your nan and then I'll go home. I'll give her these flowers,' she says, picking at the blossoms which are shrivelling in the room's heat.

'There's more to explore,' says Anne. 'I'll carry on with it. My friend is sending me further details. I'm sure we'll meet again, Rose.'

As Charlie's gran makes her way out the door, Anne narrows her eyes.

'What's wrong?' I ask.

'She's the spitting image of Martha.'

'That's impossible,' I say. 'Rose is from Ireland.'

'Martha went missing. Her disappearance was hushed up, and I was sad because she was kind to us younger girls. Oh well. Perhaps my eyesight is failing me. I know Martha wasn't from Ireland. Tell you what, I'll phone the professor and ask him if he has completed his research. See you later, dear.' She closes her notebook and I stand up.

Charlie and Rose are waiting outside the room for me.

'I'm going to Nan's now. Are you coming?' I ask. Rose is holding on to Charlie's arm. They follow me as I knock on Nan's door then enter.

'Hello, Nan. I've brought visitors with me,' I say.

She's leaning against a mound of pillows with her hair combed, and a large, floppy, striped bow gripping her wiry grey hair off her face. She resembles a little girl, and this childish appearance would have annoyed her at one time. She widens her eyes while her mouth twists into a crooked smile. Rose is behind me and walks forward with the bunch of white flowers clasped in her hands. When Nan spots Rose, she opens her mouth wide and yells, 'Martha! Run or she'll catch you!'

'Who, dear?' Rose asks, holding her hand. 'Not again,' she says, raising her eyebrows to me and Charlie.

'Hello, Sienna. Are these your friends? Oh, what pretty white flowers you've brought me and they smell like… mmm what was it, now? Er, let me think. Stick them in the vase, please. Who are you?' she asks, peering at Rose.

'I'm Rose,' she says, holding her hand.

The carer knocks on the door and enters.

'I'm not following you,' she laughs. 'But your nan needs her medication.'

'Rose is a pretty name,' Nan says and coughs as she swallows her tablets.

'Dad will drop by soon,' I whisper, and kiss her cheek. 'She'll be OK,' I say to the others.

'That's it, marzipan from a wedding cake. They smell of almonds,' Nan says and slumps back down in the bed. We open the door to leave.

'Can you sense it?' I ask Rose and Charlie.

Rose runs her fingers along the exposed granite bricks.

'Yes. Unhappiness.' Her face pales, and she stumbles. 'The cries of young girls are enclosed in the nooks and crannies of these stone walls, and the power is strengthening. We must eradicate the malevolence,' she cries, gripping my arm and staring at me.

'Gran, what's wrong?' asks Charlie.

'It's consuming my energy and I need to escape.' She holds her head in her hands.

'I'll phone for a taxi,' says Charlie, getting out her phone.

I grab Rose's sleeve. 'Don't worry, I'll figure this out.'

She sniffs and pulls a lace handkerchief out of her pocket. While Charlie is talking, Rose pulls me down and whispers, 'We associate a bitter almond smell with the poison cyanide, found in flowers and plants. How does your nan know this? Be careful, Sienna. Your sensitivity is off balance. If anything happens, you need to escape before the wickedness attaches itself to you.'

We return to the reception area and wait outside as the taxi drives through the gates.

'I'll see you later, Gran,' says Charlie, ushering her into the car.

We go back inside. Silence throughout the house. Waiting for me. We head off to find Matt. Charlie is following me, but the passageways are similar and I'm afraid of losing my way. The pulse of the house is telling me I'm close. I follow a repetitive humming and end up in front of a plain oak door. I press my hand on the wood. Heat, destruction, and death wait behind it. It creaks open and my eyes adjust to the gloom. The stench of old age drifts towards me. An elderly woman huddles in a hospital cot, which is connected to a mass of snarled wires. Matt is on the edge of a plastic chair by the side of her bed, reading to her from a black leather book. The front cover has a gold cross with the words *Des Bibliis* embossed across it.

The old woman raises herself on her frail elbow. She's emaciated with dehydrated skin. Her long hair is a mass of tangled grey knots. Her face is cadaverous, her cheekbones stick out and her deep-set eyes seem buried into her skull. Those beady eyes scrutinise me and the image arrives in a flash.

This is the girl who killed Martha.

Her name is Lilith.

My body is on fire. Spikes of fear pierce me as I watch Martha's last day. She whispers:

'*Sienna. Help. I'm underwater. I can't see. My heart is beating in panic and my limbs are too heavy. The strands of moving weed tangle against my legs, dragging me deeper. The reek of the muddy pond is overwhelming. It would be easy to sink; close my eyes, and free me from this world, but he is waiting. My lungs are burning as I inhale the cloudy liquid. I'm exhausted now and want freedom from this torment. I see him. He's coming for me. The blanket of water is closing in, and I catch my last breath till peace flows over me. Finally, you have found her.*'

Matt stands up and places the bible on the chair.

'What are you doing here, love?' he asks, rushing over to hold me. His concerned voice weakens me.

My legs buckle as I say, 'This… this… is the person from my visions.'

The old woman scrutinises us and, stretching out her withered hand towards Charlie, she says, 'Martha, Martha, forgive me. It was the witch who told me to torment you. We were friends once; can we try again?' Her scratchy voice hisses.

'I'm not Martha. Leave me alone!' Charlie shouts back at her.

I twist away; the fetid stench makes me sick, and I cover my nose and mouth with my hand.

'Sienna, grab this,' says Matt, passing me a bottle of water. I swig it down and stand in front of the old woman. She reaches out for my hand, but I keep my distance.

'What did you do to Martha?' I ask.

She raises her head as the door opens.

'Sienna and Charlie, you need to see this,' says Anne Duncan, peeping her head around the door. In her hands is a black and white grainy photograph.

'Ah, you've finally found me. Are you here to listen to my confession?'

'Who are you?' asks Anne, standing next to the bed.

'Don't you recognise me? I remember you sneaking around, too young to play with us older girls,' she says, and tries to pull herself up. 'My name is Lilith Goldman, but everyone calls me Lili, after the flower.' She attempts to laugh but blood-stained saliva sprays from her mouth.

'Here.' She waves towards a large old-fashioned brass key lying on the bedside table. 'Open the chest over there and take out my journal. I wrote my version of events before my mind blurred. You need to read it,' she says, pointing at Charlie.

'OK, here goes.' She picks up the key and unlocks the padlock. Lifting the lid and lying on top of an old grey dress is a tattered book.

Opening it, Charlie reads.

Today is a terrible day and my thoughts need writing before the madness controls me. Whoever is reading this will discover what happened here at this house of hell. My mother purchased this place cheaply. It was once a monastery. Nobody would buy it after the monks absconded, leaving it in a state of disrepair. The staff did my bidding. Anything I wanted they gave me or else my mother fired them, but I bored easily. Those simple girls idolised me. I could fool them, but not Martha. She refused to conform to my leadership and join me.'

The old woman coughs as her eyes glare into mine.

'I remember it like it was yesterday,' she says.

'Stop,' says Matt. 'This isn't right.' He plumps her pillow and raises her up.

'No, carry on,' she says. 'I want my story told.'

Charlie turns to the next page.

'Martha differed from the other girls. She was my friend, but then caught the eye of Joe, the gardener, and it angered me because I saw him first. Joe had taught me how to cultivate flowers from seeds and cuttings. Before she arrived, I had spent a lot of my time with him in the greenhouse, learning the names of flowers and herbs. He showed me the poisonous ones and warned me to keep away from them. I didn't listen to him. It was Martha, always Martha, he wanted. I tried to persuade my mother to expel her, declaring she wasn't carrying out her chores and obeying instructions. That wasn't true, so I needed another way to eliminate her.'

'Stop reading, Charlotte. What do you mean?' asks Anne, turning to Lilith.

'Those simple girls trailed after me and competed for my attention. They were my puppets, and I played with their emotions. They were worried my mother would banish them to a life on the streets and I manipulated their fear to my advantage. They spied on Martha and reported the times she met Joe. To them, I was their saviour.' She coughs again into a soiled handkerchief.

'So, you knew Martha?' I ask.

The old lady ignores me and closes her eyes.

'Carry on, Charlie,' I say.

'On Sundays, the local priest arrived to say mass, and we trooped to the chapel. Meanwhile, I persuaded my mother that my group needed to spend the time studying instead of praying. She allowed the cellar of the orphanage as our headquarters, and I convinced her it was a reading club. Mother had no idea what we were up to.' Charlie stops reading.

'The tunnel to the crypt is underneath this room,' Lili says, pointing a finger to the floor.

'Underneath this room?' I repeat.

'Yes, it led to the monks' chapel. Carry on, dear,' says Lili.

'First, we destroyed the religious evidence and painted the room jet black, but the ceiling was damp and water dripped down the walls. It was our special place. I found heavy velvet curtains to drape over the door, and lit candles and held meetings with my followers. We studied the art of witchcraft and invoked spells.'

At the mention of spells, Charlie stares at me, while the old lady's lips turn upwards into a sly grin.

'All I wanted was a love spell to lure Joe.' Lili then clams up, and I stare at the spittle drooling from her mouth.

A sense of danger flows over me. Anne Duncan is wiping her eyes and reaches for the plastic chair near the wardrobe.

'Witchcraft?' Matt stares at me, narrowing his eyes. 'This isn't right, Sienna.'

Anne perches on the end of a chair, her eyes shut. I look at Lili.

'The painting in the hallway – is it your mother?' I ask.

She nods her head and points at the book in Charlie's hand.

'Continue reading.'

Charlie starts again. *'My mother thought Martha came from a wealthy family, but it was the opposite. Poor as a church mouse. After Martha's mother died, the father gambled away his meagre wages. He died soon after they sent her here. She was intelligent and understood what was happening. She saw girls arriving and kept in separate rooms, away from others. Martha planned to inform the authorities.'*

Charlie pauses and looks up as the old woman points at her and says, 'Mother wanted you.'

'I'm not Martha. You're confused,' whispers Charlie, closing the book.

'The meetings became intense. We designed our own special ritual and launched the ceremony by ringing a bell. We recited the Lord's prayer but....'

'What?' I ask. The room is too hot. It's impossible to breathe, and the stench of putrid water makes me gag.

'... we chanted it backwards.'

'This is sacrilegious. Don't listen anymore,' Anne cries, sticking her hands over her ears.

Lilith laughs, pointing a bony finger at Anne.

'Oh yes, always a weakling, scampering away, and hiding under the bed. You told Martha's friend what was happening. What was her name? Oh, I can't remember. My followers became a powerful group.'

'You should have ended it!' I shout.

'You may be right, but I enjoyed the control and the attention. We concocted spells using herbs and poisons, and I created one so Joe would fall in love with me, but it was useless.' She coughs out drops of blood which stain her handkerchief. The room is stifling, and the stench of dead lilies surrounds us. I stare at her as the realisation dawns on me.

'Did you create a spell book?'

She ignores me and waves her hand at Charlie.

'Mother welcomed girls who found themselves in trouble with the local lads, and she tricked them by offering shelter and warmth. She travelled around the country, locating girls for the orphanage, intent on making money from adoptions. She ignored me as the school increased in numbers and became greedy for wealth and prestige. The babies were born, adopted, and sent abroad.'

'Sienna, I don't like the sound of this. Let's go,' says Matt.

'Wait, listen to this,' says Charlie, turning to the next page.

'I increased my group of followers and told them to obey me. They had no relatives and lived in fear of dismissal. Mother didn't want to keep anyone who

would inform on her illicit deeds. She believed my opinion of each girl. The group grew and became our secret coven. I desired higher supremacy and told them to…'

'To what?' I whisper to Charlie.

'… surrender to me and carry out my commands.'

The old woman stares at me, her beady eyes dulling as she murmurs.

'We summoned Biddy Bishop through the Ouija board.'

'Who the hell is she?' asks Matt.

Charlie bites her nails as I tell him.

'She was an Irish witch accused of witchcraft and hung.'

'Carry on, Charlie, what else does it say?'

'During the Ouija session, I asked Biddy Bishop to give me the secrets of the herbs and to eliminate Martha, but two girls followed us into the crypt. They spied on our ceremony and vowed to report us.'

The room is hushed apart from the crackle of the page turning. Matt is by my side. His face has a chalky tinge, and he grips my hand.

'Joe adored her, and I was jealous. He was mine first,' the old woman whispers. Her voice is cracking with tiredness, but she slams her hand down on the bedcover.

'Carry on, Charlotte,' says Anne, moving towards her with a prayer book clasped in her hand.

Charlie reads the next page.

'I scribbled Martha a note, telling her that Joe would wait by the lake later that afternoon. She followed me to the cellar instead and witnessed the Ouija session. I was furious. She had disobeyed me and had watched our rituals. When Biddy Bishop showed herself to us, the other girls became hysterical, screaming, shouting, pulling, scratching each other and scrambling over themselves to flee. They hid in the darkest parts of the cellar. I yelled to Martha that Joe was in the summerhouse by the jetty. She trusted my word and hurried towards the lake. Biddy Bishop was with me when I followed Martha. It was an accident. I tried to

grab her, but pushed her instead. She slipped on the ice and fell through the decayed wooden slats. There was a girl hiding in the bushes and she ran away. I rushed back for help, but in my haste to escape I ignored a critical rule.'

'Which was?' Anne asks.

'To extinguish the candles.'

Anne drops her head in her hands and says, 'So, that's how parts of the orphanage burned down?'

'What happened to the girls?' Matt turns to Anne.

'They sent them to relatives or other orphanages.'

'I had no-one to go to,' says Lilith, her voice weakening.

'Why are you still living here?' I ask.

'The fire service rescued me. My mother died, and this property became mine. The surviving staff enabled me to live here,' she cackles. 'People soon forgot about the mad girl tending to the garden. Different organisations wanted to buy this building. I rejected them until the local diocese made me an offer I couldn't refuse and turned it into a care home. Don't you find that ironic? They were unaware of the depravity that had taken place here and left me alone. Time drifted away from me, but my behaviour towards my friend has tormented me. All for the love of a man. Tsk-tsk,' she splutters. 'I'm telling you, girls, they're not worth it.'

Matt studies the old woman. 'Please, pass me a sip of water. I have wasted my time drowning my sorrows in the bottom of a gin bottle. It's killing me.' She coughs, spitting droplets of watery blood and phlegm on her bedclothes. Matt holds her head up and dribbles the bottle of water into her mouth. Even after listening to her ramblings about witches and evil, his compassionate nature shines through.

'Carry on, Lili,' he says, dabbing at her lips.

'I'm forever reminded of my wickedness. Of my human weakness. I was cruel to Martha and didn't appreciate her strength, but now she's coming for me. Leave me be. I'm exhausted.' She waves her hand at us.

'It's hard to accept supernatural events involving witches took place here,' says Matt, glancing at the door as the clomping of footsteps approaches.

CHAPTER 26

The door opens – Matron is standing there with an agency nurse by her side.

'What are you doing here and bothering one of our residents?' she asks. 'Right, Anne, you need to return to your room immediately. Sienna and your friend, leave now before you upset Lilith even more. Matthew, thank you for keeping her company, but now it's time for you to go.'

I storm out of the room, with the others following behind me.

'Slow down, slow down. I'm not as young as you,' says Anne, holding on to the door frame and panting. We troop into her room. I stand with my arms crossed as Charlie flops on the bed and bites her nails.

'I've been at Monkton for the last few months and was unaware Lilith Goldman was living here.'

We don't answer her. Charlie sniffs away her tears.

'I wish she hadn't forced me to read her journal now. Why me?'

'She became involved in witchcraft, and through the Ouija board she summoned Biddy Bishop, the witch from Salem,' says Anne. She shudders. 'I had no idea this was taking place.'

'Who was hiding in the bushes?' I ask her.

Anne shrugs. 'But what should we do now?'

'For months, the visions and voices spoke of Martha's story, but now we have found her. I don't know what to do next.'

'I think Martha is my great grandmother,' whispers Charlie.

I stare at her. 'What! No way. Really? Where's the proof?'

'Rose's spell book. Lilith said she…'

Matt interrupts. 'Charlie, she didn't admit it. When you asked her, she didn't reply.'

'We need to go back to her room and find out more,' I say.

'It'll be tricky now the matron is on our case,' replies Charlie.

'Not if we return at night.' I study them to gauge their reaction.

'Count me out,' says Anne. 'There's no way I'm visiting that woman at night. Who knows what evil spirits are lurking in her room. I'll open my patio doors, and you can sneak in through there. Be quiet, mind you.'

'Mmm, I'm not sure about this idea of yours, Sienna. What do you hope to gain from seeing her again?' asks Charlie.

'I'm waiting for my professor friend to come back with more information.' Anne holds up the photograph. 'This is what I wanted to show you,' she says, passing it to me. It's a picture of three girls with their arms around each other, smiling into the camera.

'There's Martha, with Lilith in the middle, but I'm not sure what happened to the other girl,' says Anne.

I scream. 'Martha. Martha. She's the girl who's been following me.' I hold the photograph and study it. 'It's unbelievable. This photo proves that she was real.'

Anne's carer knocks on the door and enters, so we walk away and wait in the empty foyer.

'It's too quiet, isn't it? Where is everyone?' asks Charlie.

'I'm not sure. This reception area is usually buzzing with admin staff and visitors. Do you want to wait for the minibus?' asks Matt.

'I'll phone my aunt; she'll pick us up,' I say.

'I don't know about you two, but I'm finding it difficult to understand what happened here,' says Matt as he opens the large oak door. We walk outside.

'Is Lilith telling the truth? Did she really summon a witch?' whispers Charlie to me.

I nod my head. 'Yes, it's the same one. What if we've woken her up?'

'OMG, don't say that! Is she here, following us?' asks Charlie, turning around.

'I don't know but we need to be careful and not say her name or think about her.'

'I can't stop thinking about her now that you've told me not to. God, Sienna, why did you start all this?' she says, stomping off.

'Me? Start all this?' I yell, but she's left.

I find her and Matt sitting on an old wooden bench outside. It resembles the same one from my vision of tearful girls. Secrets held amongst the walls. Matt can't sit still and paces while I want to escape from the task ahead. A car drives along the path. Gravel scatters in a cloud of dust as Debbie pulls up and we climb in.

'What's with the pale faces? Did you see a ghost?' She grins as we climb into the car, but her smile vanishes as I narrate Lilith's life. My aunt is silent. We carry on along the road to our house and she stops the car in a lay-by and frowns at us.

'That's enough. She's either a talented storyteller or a lonely old lady suffering from dementia.'

'But I read them from her diary,' says Charlie.

'I think she was bored living in the house alone. She made it up and wrote a story. Have you got the diary with you?'

'No.'

'You didn't embellish it as you were reading, did you?' asks Debbie, staring at Charlie in the mirror.

'What? Are you saying I'm lying?'

'We were there. We heard it all,' I say. But we didn't see the pages and now I'm wondering whether Charlie made it up. Would she do that? I twist my head and watch Matt patting her hand.

Damn. I turn away and look out the window. That's all I need; those two getting close.

'Next time you go in to visit your nan, why don't you pick up Lilith's journal and I'll have a gander at it?'

Matt touches my shoulder and I turn around.

'I'm not sure the matron will let us back in there again, but your aunt is right. Can you drop me off here, please? Thanks for the lift.'

'Me too. I'll take the shortcut home with you,' says Charlie. 'WhatsApp later?'

Debbie pulls in and my friends jump out and walk along the pavement together. She peers through the window and grips the steering wheel.

'This has to end now. I've told your mum you shouldn't go back to the care home again and I'm not sure about Charlie. You're highly receptive to the atmosphere there. Remember, we're grieving for your sister and this nonsense doesn't help.'

'Mm-hmm.' I look out the window. Why did I bother telling her? She starts the car and we carry on along the road in silence.

When we get home, I go upstairs and lie on my bed. A black mood of despondency sweeps over me as I struggle to understand the story Lilith Goldman told us. I receive a message from Charlie and Rose about meeting tonight and Matt texts to say he will help us. I'm fidgety, pick at my food at dinnertime and tell Mum I'm tired. Later, I hop into bed wearing my dark tracksuit, fleece and trainers, and cover myself with the duvet, hoping Mum doesn't notice. She knocks on my door and walks in.

'Good night, love. How are you coping?' she asks, placing the back of her hand on my forehead. 'You're flushed.'

'I'm fine. You go to bed too, Mum; you need your rest. It's been a horrible week.'

'I know. This was unexpected. You're not prepared for your children dying before you.' She dabs her eyes with a tissue.

The mattress sags as she perches on the end of the bed. I pull the duvet up and hope she doesn't stay. I haven't stopped thinking about Bella, but this mystery needs solving. Placing my hand up to my mouth, I pretend to yawn.

She stands and edges towards the door. 'Call me if you need anything.'

'Yep.' I burrow my head under the cover. It's wrong deceiving Mum, but I need answers tonight.

I'm tired and rest my eyes for a moment. It's after midnight. My phone vibrates with the one-word message. 'Outside.'

Opening my bedroom door, the landing is in darkness, so I press the light on my mobile. Tiptoeing downstairs, avoiding the creaky bottom step, I undo the latch. I'm outside and my breath puffs out icy plumes of smoke. The night air is frosty for this time of year, and I'm having second thoughts. Rose is in the driver's seat of an old Metro. Charlie is next to her, and Matt is sitting in the back. Everyone is wearing dark clothes. I climb into the car, taking care not to slam it.

'I'm not sure this is a good idea. Lilith Goldman is dangerous,' whispers Matt.

'I'm desperate for these voices in my head to go and she holds the key to my problems,' I say.

'Sienna, I'm a rational person, yet what she told us made my skin crawl. The idea of summoning a witch is bizarre. Perhaps your aunt is right, and she made it up.'

'Maybe, but what about those papers we found, with the names of witches and the strange drawings? It was her signature.'

Rose drives carefully, avoiding the potholes, and we enter the forest.

'Gran is adamant about coming with us, so bear with her,' whispers Charlie, twisting around and catching Matt holding my hand.

'Where did she get this car?' I ask as we bounce along the rutted lane.

'It's Mum's, but she lets Gran drive it.'

Matt bites his lip as we get closer. 'I'm not sure now. This is wrong.'

'It needs to be done,' replies Rose. 'Help is on our side. Take it out please, Charlie.'

She opens her gran's bag and withdraws a plastic bottle in the shape of the Virgin Mary.

'What's in the bottle, Rose?' asks Matt.

'Holy water.' She crunches the gears as we drive through the woods.

Charlie raises her eyebrows at me. We arrive – Monkton House is waiting for us. It looms menacingly, shrouded in darkness apart from one solitary light in the downstairs room.

'How will we enter with those security cameras?' whispers Matt.

'Anne said they're dummies, and for show, to fool burglars. We could enter through the front gates, but I guess it connects the keypad to the office.'

'Are you sure? I don't want any trouble with the police,' says Matt.

'You won't. The carers are probably dozing in the staff room. Anne is leaving her patio doors open so we can go in through them.'

'Rose, switch the headlights off and park under that tree.' I point to the large oak tree. 'There's a broken plank in the fence we can squeeze through and nobody will see us,' I say.

She grins at me and stops the car. We tiptoe out. A menacing silence stills the air. The moon casts its glow onto the lake. I shiver and rub my arms, picturing the girl who drowned there. We force our way through the broken fence and end up on the grounds of Monkton House. The patio door opens and Anne, wearing her woollen dressing gown, waves at us. Hurrying across the damp grass, we tiptoe into her room. She's clutching the ancient ledger and gestures for us to sit.

'It was happening under my eyes and I didn't know.'

Matt grabs my hand.

'This is the professor's report. He's found that the state sent orphaned children during the war to Monkton House to be cared for. Mrs Goldman changed the building into a mother and baby home, and pregnant girls arrived. The girls thought they were safe, but the minute their babies were born, they were adopted. Parents would pay any price to own a new born baby and Mrs Goldman became a rich woman.'

'Lilith was right,' I whisper.

Anne peers at me over her half-moon glasses. 'I spent my time over in the school wing, so this is news to me.'

A thin leaf of vellum paper floats out of the tatty leather book.

A shuffle of feet outside the room.

'Hush, be quiet or we'll be in trouble,' I whisper.

'I've found more lists of girls' names,' Anne says, passing us the papers.

We flick through the pages. Anne hands over a piece of paper and says, 'Here is the evidence which reports that two girls, Martha and Henrietta, both fourteen, joined the orphanage in 1946. This will be a shock to you and your family, Sienna, but the evidence shows Henrietta is your grandmother.'

I jump up. 'No way. Sorry, but you're wrong, Anne. My nan's name is Ria.'

'That's right. Ria is short for Henrietta. The records state that she survived the fire and was fostered out to a variety of different families.'

'That's impossible. Are you positive? She's never spoken about her past or that she came from an orphanage. Wait till I tell Dad,' I say. 'Here, let me read your report.' I gesture at the documents in Anne's hands.

'There's something else,' she continues, studying Rose.

'Rose, with the information from the ledger, and the help from the professor, we discovered Martha was an orphan. Her mother died first in 1945 and her father a year later. The girl was penniless, and the state sent her here.'

'Why is this relevant to me?' she asks.

Anne clears her throat and carries on. 'The records show Martha had a relationship with a young man, age eighteen. He was the assistant gardener and his name was Joseph Malone. In 1948, aged sixteen, she became pregnant and gave birth, naming her daughter Rose after her favourite flower. We've found information proving they're your parents.'

Rose gasps and rubs the back of her neck while we stare at each other.

'Where's the proof it's me?' she asks.

'There. Is this you?' We peer over her shoulders at the page as Anne points to the names of Rose's adoptive parents and the date they took her to Ireland.

'Martha is Rose's mother, making her my great-grandmother. How unbelievable is that?' she cries, looking at me.

Anne continues reading from the ledger. 'Amongst some old documents, I've found love letters they wrote to each other, showing they planned on eloping. I'm sorry to say but your mother, Martha, died soon after you were born, and Siobhan and Niall Kelly travelled from Ireland to adopt you.' Rose is shaking her head and fidgeting with the sleeve of her cardigan. 'These belong to you.' Anne hands Rose a bunch of envelopes tied up with a faded blue ribbon.

'No. This is a lie. Why are you making this up? Show me the proof. I'm not adopted, I don't believe you,' she says and clutches the envelopes to her chest.

Charlie rushes over to her gran and hugs her.

'Didn't your parents tell you?' asks Anne.

Rose bites her lips, and her face changes as if she remembers.

'I didn't resemble them, but that didn't bother me. However, I couldn't find any photographs of me as a new born. Also, when my son, Brendan, was born, I asked my mother whether I was breastfed. She didn't reply, and went into the kitchen. Women in those days didn't discuss private matters, but they should have told me I was adopted. Now they're both dead and it's too late to tell them how much they meant to me.' Rose is weeping again. 'They gave me their love and treated me as a daughter.'

Anne leans over and pats Rose's knee. 'Dear, you *were* a daughter to them.'

I reflect on the information that's come from Anne. Matt is sitting on the chair, reading through the ledger. He's restless and keeps moving around, fussing with the cushion and tapping his fingers on the arm of the chair. What do you say to a person in their sixties who finds out she's adopted? We're quiet, waiting for someone to break the silence. I'm exhausted and rub my gritty eyes.

Anne faces me and says, 'Can you help me collate this information and type it up for me?'

'Yes, I'll do that, but the reason I came here was to see Lilith

Goldman again. Matt, will you wait for us in the car? You can be a lookout and text me if you see anyone. It won't take long. Charlie and Rose, follow me.' I gesture to them, but Matt stands up and storms over to me.

'Sienna, you must be bloody joking. The only reason I'm with you tonight is to learn more from Anne Duncan's research. I must be mad, and I don't understand why you're even contemplating prowling down those corridors again. They're spookier at night and you'll get caught. Tell her not to do it,' he says to Rose.

'No, you won't persuade her. Sienna has witnessed images of Martha's life. Now I know about my mother. I want to help Sienna.'

'What will you do? You won't harm the old woman, will you?' asks Matt.

'From the moment I entered Monkton House, it's been summoning me,' I say.

'I don't agree with you, Sienna, but if you're not out in fifteen minutes, I'm coming in,' he says, opening the patio door and walking out.

'He'll have to change his views if you want your psychic skills to develop,' says Rose, studying me.

'Here, you may need these.' Anne hands me a necklace of rosary beads. 'Be careful now.'

I grab them, drape them around my neck, and open the door. It's deathly quiet; the carers will be in their staff room. A sense of finality radiates throughout the area. This time, I use the glare from the wall lights to work out where I am. Although it's pitch black, the incessant beeping of the machine leads me to her room. We walk down the deserted passageways and use our fingers to feel the way along the smooth plaster. As I touch the unevenness of exposed bricks, the temperature drops and I rub my arms for warmth. Then the atmosphere changes and I know I'm getting closer as the building's pulse rings in my ear and a suffocating heat overwhelms me. I open the door. She's awake.

'I've been waiting for you,' she croaks. 'After all this time, I finally get to meet Martha and Joe's daughter. Come here, my dear.' She holds out her hand to Rose.

A silver haze descends from the ceiling and covers the room. I remove the rosary beads from my neck and place them on Lilith. I'm paralysed with fear as the vision of hands stretch towards me.

'This is weird. Come on, Sienna, let's get out.'

'No, not yet.'

'Look, she hasn't long left,' whispers Charlie.

I see her cavernous skull, the wisps of grey, matted hair, drool dribbling from her mouth and the rattle of death in her lungs.

'Martha, where are you? Save me from this eternal torment. Dear Lord, into your hands, take my spirit. Absolve my sins and set me free,' Lilith screams and stretches out her arms.

The acrid stench of fear surrounds me, as we advance towards the old woman. Standing behind her metal headboard is the figure of Martha, dripping with water. Her hair is matted with green weeds. Her skin is a mottled blue and her marble white face is devoid of emotion.

'Lilith. Why were you cruel to my mother?' asks Rose.

'She was my great-grandmother,' cries Charlie.

I grab their hands and we point them towards Lilith.

Martha's presence floats to our side and murmurs in my ear. I repeat her words: '*All you have to do is say you're sorry and I will release you from your suffering.*'

'My weakness and jealousy was my downfall,' croaks Lilith, spitting out blood-stained mucus onto the white sheets. With a stony glare in her dead eyes, she points her bony finger at me and says, 'You know what jealousy can do to a person, don't you, Sienna?'

I sink under her gaze as my strength drains from me, and the image of my sister appears.

'Wait,' says Rose, holding up the spell book and looking at the old woman. 'Is this yours?'

Lilith stares at Rose.

'Yes,' she whispers. 'I was wicked. Corrupted by the witch of Salem.'

The door blows open and an old lady in a long white nightdress stands there, holding an armful of white flowers.

'Nan, what are you doing? This is dangerous. Please go back,' I say, rushing towards her.

'It was my fault,' she cries. 'Forgive me, Martha. I didn't save you. I saw everything, but it was an accident. Joe tried to grab you and he fell in, too. It scared me. The ice cracked, and you both vanished underneath.'

I pull out a chair for her to sit on and she slumps down, her chin on her chest. Her eyes close. Lilith holds out her hands towards Rose and says, 'Your mother was the sweetest person, and I was cruel to her. Absolve me of my sins. Over there, in that chest. Open it,' she says, pointing to the wooden box in the corner of the room.

She closes her eyes, and Rose leans over and places the spell book on top of her. Charlie grabs a handful of papers from the container.

'Absolve my sins, Martha, my friend,' Lilith screams.

We stand around her bed, and Martha's energy fills me like a surge of electricity engulfing every cell of my body. I raise my hand. An iridescent beam shoots from my fingertips towards Lilith. I witness the story of her youth, the loneliness and envy. The room fills with glaring light, which bounces off the walls. The stench of burning rubber infuses the air. Rose opens the bottle and sprinkles the holy water over Lilith's body.

'*Lili, you have suffered enough. I forgive you,*' says Martha.

A dazzling beam blinds me, and I sink to the floor, covering my face.

Lilith holds out her hand. 'Pass me the crucifix.'

I edge towards her. Her features soften and her body relaxes. Lilith clutches my hand, as an image of her wrapping the book in a blanket and hiding it in a cot flashes into my head. She wanted it to be found. Taking a last breath, her eyes close.

The room is still. The energy whooshes out of me and floats away into the atmosphere. I shake my hands to release the tingling and take a deep breath. Charlie rushes over to me and places her arms around me.

'I saw her enter your body. It was unreal,' she says, shaking her head.

'Time to leave Lilith in peace,' says Rose, placing the crucifix in her hands and walking out.

Wrapping my arms around Nan, I guide her back to her room. She's shivering, and I help her into bed, placing a blanket around her shoulders. The corridor is silent. The malevolency has vanished, yet the stench of burning rubber continues to waft into my nose. Rose and Charlie are walking in front of me, close to the exit.

'Stop,' I whisper. They carry on, not hearing the crackle and bang. I spin around as a roar of intense reddish orange flames gushes along the passageway out of Lilith's room.

'Stop,' I say, speeding back towards it.

Charlie and Rose turn around.

'Leave!' screams Charlie.

I try to get closer, but the flames push me away from Lilith's door. The heat scorches my face. There's an ominous cracking, and I spin around as a wooden beam collapses and blocks me in the corridor.

Golden red flames leap towards empty rooms.

'Sienna!'

Silhouetted against the orange-red flash is Charlie, her hand reaching out towards me.

'Get out!' she yells.

In the darkness, black smoke twirls around me. My throat fills with ash and I retch. My eyes smart as I feel my way along the grittiness of the exposed brickwork. I'm hurrying away from the exit and Lilith's room, but I'm confused. My sense of direction gone. There's no light, and the fiery blaze roars behind me. I stop, look around, and see an ancient wooden door. In the distance, the flames are rocketing towards me along the empty corridor. My hand touches a round metal door knob. I push it and fall through space and slip on steep, damp steps. Grabbing a metal handrail, slimy with algae, I heave myself up. Nothing. Darkness, apart from the click of a rodent's claws scurrying across the floor, escaping from the smoke. I tread on the last step and my feet touch a cement floor. My eyes adjust to the lack of light and I find I'm in a large room with grey flagstones covering the ground. The air is cooler down here as water drips along the walls. An ancient stench of burnt wood lingers. A large brass bell, now cracked and scorched, is sitting in the middle of a circle of stones.

'Hurry, get out now,' says Martha, her hand on my shoulder, pushing me forward. 'This is where they summoned her, the wicked one – Biddy Bishop. Whatever you do, don't look in the corner of the room.'

The smoke is intense and I dash towards a faint chink of light. I whip my sweatshirt off and tie it around my mouth and nose. I'm in a narrow tunnel and can't stand up, so I crawl along on my hands and knees. Water drips onto my face. The stench of muddy pond liquid is overpowering. The tunnel is on an incline and I grab a handrail, pulling myself up till my hand reaches another door.

'Please be open! Please be open!' I shout.

A sharp pressure on my back and I'm pushed against the door. This opens onto the gravel driveway encircling the rear of Monkton House. I turn around and look in the corner of the room and I see her: Biddy Bishop, gliding towards me, her long dark dress buttoned up to her neck, her white cotton bonnet slipping down. Her head is tilted at an angle as the circle of rope twists into her throat. Her face ashen, her tongue swollen, and sticking out of her eyeballs are sharp metal nails.

Picking myself up, I slam the door shut and hurry over the dew-covered lawn towards the lake through the broken fence. The trees hide my friends. Matt is kneeling on the damp grass, his hands over his head, rocking backwards and forwards. Rose is rubbing his back, and Charlie is pacing up and down. I try to shout but end up squeaking. Charlie spots me first and they jog towards me. Matt dabs at my face, rubbing away the ash, while Charlie passes me a bottle of water and Rose makes the sign of the cross over me.

'Quick, we need to go... go... before she catches us,' I stutter.

The high-pitched squeal of a fire alarm rings in my head. As we buckle our seatbelts, Rose sticks the key in the ignition, but her hands tremble and keep slipping. Eventually, the tyres slide over the damp grass and the crunch of the gravel driveway signals our exit. In the distance, we hear the 'nee naw' of a fire engine.

Rose is hunched over the steering wheel, trying to navigate her way through the woods.

'Quick, before they catch us,' I say, leaning over the seat.

'What happened in there, Sienna? You're covered in ash. I should have been with you,' whispers Matt.

'No, you were the lookout and don't worry – the fire didn't spread to the residents.'

'Was it bad?' he whispers, turning towards me. 'Are the patients safe? What about Lilith Goldman?'

'I'm not sure about Lilith. But the sprinklers came on.'

It's late, and the road is empty as we drive along the highway.

'Dim your lights,' I say to Rose.

She twists the steering wheel into a layby and reduces the beam as the vehicle rushes past us.

'Fire engine,' says Charlie, biting her nails.

An ambulance and police car speed past us, their lights flashing and sirens blasting out into the still air.

'What have you done, Sienna? We need to hand ourselves in to the police station,' says Matt.

'No, we can't, because we have done nothing wrong.'

Matt turns to face me. 'Why didn't you want me in with you?'

'You're not a believer of the supernatural and you would have stopped me.'

He brushes a curl off my face.

'You know, Sienna, I'm not sure of anything now. It was surreal. The thunder was deafening as waves rippled from the lake and rose upward. Electric lightning pierced through the grey fog that surrounded Monkton House. White sparks flashed through the roof. Thank goodness you ran out in time. I wanted to follow you in but the others held me back,' he says, reaching for me. He lifts his hand and caresses my cheek, brushing away a smudge of ash. 'It worried me sick; I don't want anything terrible to happen to you.'

Rose drives home in silence. She stares straight ahead, concentrating on the road. The darkness of night is changing into the mauve light of dawn. No-one else is around as we arrive home.

'Rose, thank you again for taking me there. Few people would,' I say.

'I felt my mother next to me and I'm glad she's forgiven Lilith. Check your face. What do you think, Dr Matt?'

He touches my cheek and kisses my hand. 'Make sure you use a cold, wet compress to stop the heat and keep away from spooky things.'

One day I'll share what happened with him, but for now, it stays a secret.

CHAPTER 27

Next morning, I awake to my phone ringing and the stench of smoke in my nostrils. When I blow my nose, black mucus stains the tissue.

'What's wrong, Matt?' I ask.

'Have you heard the news? The care home contacted me earlier this morning. I'm there now and the place is in a right state.'

'I thought it would be.'

'Turns out that a malfunction from Lilith Goldman's heart machine started the fire. The staff raised the alarm before it spread towards the other residents. The firefighters had to remove a large beam blocking the entrance to Lilith's room.'

'What happened when you got there?'

'Anne was sitting in the lounge with the other residents. She took me to one side and told me you released Martha. I couldn't stay long because she had just taken her medication, however, she gave me a message.'

'What did she say?'

'That you need to tell your parents. Also, Mrs Jones has been gossiping to the other staff that you've been snooping around,' he says.

'Oh. Is she trying to get me into trouble? It's obvious she doesn't like me. What did she say?' I ask, as his phone cuts out.

My face throbs so I check in the dressing table mirror that it's not blistered. Last night, I slept with the cold compress over my cheeks and the patches of redness have died down. I stare at the birthmark which appears to have spread and is now an angry shade of scarlet. My clothes from last night lie on the floor in a jumbled heap. They reek of smoke, so they need washing before Mum spots them. I tiptoe downstairs, carrying the singed clothes, and notice my aunt in the living room, watching the local news on the television. She waves her hand at me. Stuffing my clothes into the washing machine, I switch the load on and enter the lounge.

'Come and listen to this. The police are at the care home and there's talk of arson. They want to speak to staff and volunteers,' she says.

Dad joins us and turns up the volume on the television. People are milling outside the care home. The scene cuts to the inside and pans along the corridors towards the statues, finally highlighting the inside of a bedroom.

'Ghastly place. I don't want you there again, Sienna,' Mum says and glares at Dad. 'It's your fault, James. You shouldn't have encouraged the ridiculous idea of her reading to your mother.'

He waves his hand at her. 'Hush, a reporter is speaking.'

'This is Jilly Metcalfe from Midlands Today, inside Monkton House. I'm standing outside one of the resident's room. A fire took place here in the early hours of today. Staff raised the alarm immediately, which activated the sprinkler system. This home cares for elderly residents, patients who suffer from advanced stages of dementia, and other medical conditions. Due to financial constraints, a skeleton staff was on duty when the incident took place.'

Dad stands up and cries. 'Oh my God! A fire! My mother there, all on her own. This is illegal. I must go there. Why didn't someone phone me?'

'There was one fatality, Lilith Goldman,' the reporter continues. 'She has been living here for decades and worked as the home's gardener, becoming a specialist in cultivating the *Lilliarosa Origianaus*, otherwise identified as the Lilliarosa flower, a hybrid of the lily and the rose,' says the reporter, glancing at her clipboard. Staring into the camera, she reads from her notes. 'The coroner will confirm the cause of death. Meanwhile, Gloucestershire Constabulary are continuing with their investigation.'

She thrusts the microphone at the woman standing by her side.

'Matron Roberts. What happened at Monkton House?'

'It was early in the morning and I was making a cup of coffee in the staff room when the fire alarm went off,' she says. 'I dropped my cup, hurried straight there, and found this.'

She gestures towards Lilith's bedroom. Her hair has escaped from its tight bun, and there are dark shadows under her eyes.

Dad shouts at the screen. 'I'll sue them. It's unforgivable they allowed this electrical fault to develop. Your nan will be worried sick with the noise and disruption. She won't understand what happened. It's preposterous her pension has been paying for this lack of care.'

His clenched hand punches the table, knocking over the dishes.

'Stop it, James. Your anger isn't helping,' says Mum.

'Mum, please.' I place my finger on my lips to quieten her.

'Inspector Griffin, a word please,' begs the reporter, gesturing to a figure waiting in the background. He looks at the camera. 'We are conducting our enquiries regarding the demise of Lilith Goldman, a resident and the owner of Monkton House, previously known as Monkton Abbey Orphanage. We shall question patients, staff and volunteers over the next few days,' he cautions, staring straight at the camera. My parents are listening on the settee and face me.

'Do you know anything about this, Sienna?' probes Dad. I ignore him and concentrate on the police officer.

'Inspector, what happened to Lilith Goldman?' the reporter asks.

'We are conducting further investigations and will provide an update later.'

'Thank you, Inspector. This is Jilly Metcalfe from Midland Today. We will be back as the story unfolds.'

Mum switches off the television.

'What did he mean, *further investigations*?' she says.

'Arson, maybe. Someone setting the building on fire for insurance reasons. Kids sneaking in and messing with matches. I don't know,' he says, rubbing the back of his neck. 'That's it. I'm transferring Mum to a modern nursing home outside the village. More questions need asking. What about the security system? Why was it faulty? Are there cameras in the home, and why were there so few members of staff on duty last night?' he asks.

'Dad, I need to tell you about Nan,' I say.

'Not now, Sienna.'

Dad stands up and paces backward and forwards.

'How much more can I deal with?' He slumps back down, his head in his hands.

'Who's that now?' he asks as we hear a car pulling onto the driveway. I go to the window.

'A police car,' I say.

'What are the police doing here?' he asks.

'They'll want to ask volunteers a few questions,' says Debbie, moving towards the front door. She stands up straight, smooths her clothes and tucks her hair behind her ears. I watch this unconscious action, reminding me that although she's my aunt, she is also a lawyer.

'Oh no!' My hands tremble, so I stick them in my pockets. My legs are twitching and I wipe away the beads of sweat gathering on my forehead.

'You're not involved with the trouble at the care home, are you?' asks Debbie, scrutinising me.

'Me? No.'

'If the police officer wants to question you, I'll help.'

'Yes, please,' I reply as the doorbell rings.

'Be careful what you say and don't mention spells, supernatural, or the old lady's ramblings about black magic and covens.' She laughs.

I answer the door. The police officer is tall and slim with glossy brown hair tied up in a ponytail and secured under her cap. Her uniform is pressed and the creases in her trousers sharp.

'Good morning. My name is Police Officer Fatima Kahn.' She inspects me, her dark brown eyes searching mine. Blood rushes to my face, and I try to hide my guilt by focusing my eyes on the wall behind her. My father strides towards her.

'Good morning, Officer. I'm Sienna's father and this is her mother,' he says, gesturing towards Mum who is biting her nails. My aunt steps forward and shakes her hand.

'Hi, I'm Debbie Powell, Sienna's aunt, and I'll stay for this meeting.'

'There's no need for a formal interview. I'm only here to gain an impression of the care home.' The police officer pulls out her notepad. 'Shall we sit?'

'Of course, officer. How about a cup of tea?' asks Mum.

'Black with two sugars, please,' she says, smiling at me.

My parents leave the room, and we sit down on the settee.

'Sienna, tell me about your time volunteering with the elderly residents.'

For the next ten minutes, I describe the home with the endless passages and religious statues. My parents bring in the tea tray and listen as I ramble on. I catch the officer examining me, and pinch the skin in between my fingers to stop myself blurting out. She studies my hands and keeps flicking back the pages in her notepad.

'Did you notice anything out of the ordinary at the home yesterday?'

I shake my head and splutter. I'm desperate for a drink. My mouth is dry. Can she tell how nervous I am? I won't bring up entering Monkton House with the others at night, but will *they* keep quiet? The police officer sits up straight, her eyes flicking from me to Debbie.

'How do you know she was there yesterday?' asks Debbie.

'There are a few security cameras in the home. We are asking all staff and visitors to account for their movements.'

I wipe my hands over my face. 'Can I get a glass of water, please?'

'Yes, of course. It's hot today, isn't it?' she says.

I go into the kitchen and lean against the work surface. There are cameras! What a fool. Why didn't I detect them? Sweat gathers at the base of my neck, so I wipe it away and splash water over my face. I catch my reflection in the window. No-one has mentioned my flushed cheeks. Taking a long drink of cold water, I reflect on my predicament. Have the police evidence of me being there last night? When I return, my aunt and the officer are discussing a colleague they know.

'Carry on, Sienna,' she says, opening her pad again.

'It was a volunteering job to read to the patients. Nan didn't need me, so I talked with the other residents and helped tidy the library.'

The officer is flicking back a couple of pages and studying her notes.

'Did you detect any abnormal odours in the home?'

'No,' I say.

'Why is that relevant?' asks Debbie.

The police officer stares at my aunt and turns to me.

'Did you smell anything electrical or like rubber?'

'Only lavender and talcum powder from the residents.' I try to laugh, but end up wheezing as my parents scrutinise me.

'What do you mean, a rubbery smell? Are you saying there was an electrical fault?' asks Dad, standing up and moving over to her.

'Mr Stevens, we will inform you when our enquiries are complete. In the meantime, this tragedy is under investigation.'

Dad tuts and paces up and down.

'Was anyone badly hurt?' I ask.

'No, but you will have heard on the news, Lilith Goldman died, and there'll be an inquest. The fire activated the smoke alarm, and the sprinklers sprayed her room and corridor before it could spread. The place is a mess, though. Here's my card – if you remember anything, no matter how insignificant, phone me.'

Debbie escorts her out to the car and stands chatting. I'm impatient to know what they're talking about.

'Phew, I'm glad she's left, but what do you think? That interview wasn't too dreadful, was it?' I ask.

Dad is standing at the window with a cup of coffee in his hand as Mum scowls at him.

'It's your fault, James, for making Sienna volunteer there.' He shrugs, hands her his cup and picks up his car keys.

'Yes, dear, as you keep informing me. I'm off to check on Mum,' he says as Debbie walks back in and glances at my parents.

'Wait a minute, Dad. They should be here soon,' I say, glancing at my watch.

'Who should? What am I waiting for?' he asks. 'Your nan will be distraught if I don't go soon.'

The doorbell rings, and I open the door to see Charlie and Rose waiting outside. 'Am I glad you're here. The police have been. Come in and join us in the living room,' I say, gesturing towards the chairs.

I wait till they're comfortable and the room is quiet before I start.

'Right, I have news that will interest you. I've told you about tidying the library at the care home with Matt. It was in an awful state, but we found a ledger written in a foreign language. Matt recognised it and we gave it to a resident – the author, Anne Duncan. She has a knowledge of basic Latin and invited her friend, a professor of languages, to translate more of it for me. Here are the notes,' I say, holding up a folder.

'Is this relevant? I need to see Nan. Although, of course, I'm curious why *you* have the notes, Sienna,' says Dad.

'You'll know soon.'

'Mmm… what's this about?' asks Mum.

'Do you remember my visions about the young girl?' I ask.

'Of course,' says Mum.

'You and your imaginary friend,' says Dad, standing up and jiggling the car keys in his pocket.

Aunt Debbie is sitting upright in the armchair with a coffee cup in her hand and is studying me. Rose and Charlie are next to each other and raise their eyebrows at Dad's reply.

'She isn't my imaginary friend. Martha existed and attended Monkton Abbey Orphanage, aged fourteen, from 1946 to 1948.'

'So, she was real?' asks Mum.

'Yes. Martha gave birth to a baby girl in 1948 and named her Rose.'

'Pretty name,' says Debbie.

'Rose?' questions Mum, twisting her body around to face her.

'An Irish family adopted Martha's baby.'

The frown line between my mother's eyes deepens as she concentrates.

'Carry on, Sienna.'

I collapse into the chair. The incidents during the past weeks have exhausted me. This is too much. They stop chattering. The whir of the fridge, the click of the water heater, and the ticking of the clock in the hall are at a standstill. Silence.

'Some members of the staff were unkind to the girls and Martha tried to support them. She had two friends, Lilith and Henrietta, but Lilith became jealous when Martha fell in love with Joseph Malone and had his baby.'

'What the heck, is this the storyline for a new Mills and Boon romance?' laughs Mum.

I scowl at her, and she looks away.

'Are you implying this Joe was Rose's father?' asks Dad.

'Yes, but it says here he disappeared.' I glance at the notes.

Charlie is holding Rose and sobbing.

I continue. 'We found a report of the accident when Martha fell off an icy wooden jetty into the lake. Lilith has been living at the care home all this time.'

Dad stares at me. 'You mean Lilith is the woman in the news?'

'Yes, and there's something else,' I say.

'No, what?' he asks.

'Have you wondered why Nan keeps saying, "Watch out for the lilies"?' I carry on, without waiting for their reply. 'She means, "Watch out for Lili." Nan is the third girl of the group and Lilith frightened her. Her actual name is Henrietta, but she shortened it to Ria when she left.'

'Hold on. Hold on. Ria came from an orphanage? That's impossible,' he says, pacing up and down before sinking on the seat next to Mum.

'Dad, think about it. Ria is short for Henrietta.'

My parents stare at each other. Rose is crying, so I rub her shoulder.

'This is too confusing. Have you figured it out?' Mum asks Debbie.

I look at my hands. No-one has noticed the scratches and I won't tell them what happened when I fell into the cellar.

'Another thing. While studying the Cotswolds hauntings, I've found out that people saw the figure of a young girl drifting around the grounds of the care home.'

'Why the hell didn't you tell me this before?' says Dad.

'You wouldn't believe me. Amongst my supernatural books, there's one written by Gordon Crowley, a psychic investigator. He wrote satanic rituals took place when it was a monastery. I've since found out that in Jewish folklore, the name Lilith means a demonic figure. It's not surprising she used the prettier name of Lili,' I say.

'Enough. I don't want to listen to anymore,' cries Mum, holding Dad's hand.

'It's true.'

'You shouldn't be researching spirits at your age, the way you are,' Dad says, rubbing his hands over his face.

'What do you mean 'the way you are'?' I ask, glaring at him.

'You know – sensitive. This information is changing my views on visions and psychic messages. We didn't understand the impact your hallucinations had on you, did we?' asks Dad. I nod. 'In the Greek restaurant, was Martha there?' I nod again. 'She has been trying to communicate. But why you? What's the connection between you and Martha?'

'Martha is Rose's birth mother, making her Charlie's great-grandmother, and I'm Charlie's friend. Through visions and whisperings, Martha told me to investigate Monkton House and tell Rose she was her mother. The connection is through Nan who was best friends with Martha and saw everything. The same as me and

Charlie are best friends.'

I pick up the ancient ledger. Yellow Post-it notes are sticking out of the side, with reams of pages written in Anne Duncan's frail handwriting.

'Some were destitute girls without relatives, while others came from moneyed families. The school took them in and organised adoptions. The orphanage benefited from extra money paid by the wealthy girls' parents. The young girls never saw their babies again,' I say.

'Is there any way to help those poor adopted children?' asks Mum, her voice shaking with emotion.

'If they survived, they're probably in their sixties or seventies now, possibly older, with families of their own,' Debbie says, regarding Rose. 'Isn't that correct?'

Rose nods her head and blows her nose.

'When Anne Duncan writes her next book about Monkton House, the proceeds will support a children's charity. I'm going to help her,' I say.

'Rose, it must be hard to find out you were adopted, at this point in your life, and Martha being your birthmother. It must be a massive shock,' says Mum, wandering over to her.

Dad is staring at me and his eyes sweep the room as if seeking the answers.

'Where is Joseph Malone?' he asks.

'No idea. There's no trace of him,' I say, glancing at the paper in front of me.

My aunt stands up and paces around the room.

'This treatment of young girls is appalling and needs investigating. I want to uncover them, the whole rotten lot, the establishment and their disturbing ways. Tomorrow I'll contact a friend of mine, an investigative journalist who will…'

I stick my hand up to stop Debbie from carrying on.

'Lilith started a witch's coven. She enlisted several girls and…'

'What happened?' interrupts Dad.

'…using the Ouija board, she summoned a witch.'

'Sienna! Witches? How on earth did this happen in quiet rural Cotswolds? That building has always been there, hidden in between the forest and the lake. When I was growing up, there was always a mystery surrounding it. Was your nan involved in witchcraft?' asks Dad.

'She witnessed the ritual. Anne Duncan explained how Nan ran back and asked the staff for help. She told Mrs Goldman about the accident. Unfortunately, she didn't believe her and accused her of being a liar.'

'How do you know this?' asks Dad.

'We've found torn out pages from the girls' diaries hidden inside the ledger. They probably smuggled them to the library in secret. There are loads of files with evidence about the treatment of the girls.'

'My head is whizzing with this information. I need to see if your nan can enlighten me about Monkton House. Are you coming, Tracey?' Dad rubs the back of his neck and rakes his hand through his hair.

My mother follows him, and he fumbles with the front door.

'Mum…' I say.

'What?'

'Your feet.' She glances down and gives a strangled sort of laugh and changes her slippers for shoes. I shouldn't let them walk away as they both seem in a daze.

'We need to go now,' says Charlie, looking at her gran.

Rose's eyes are red-rimmed; she clasps my hand and sniffs.

'Thank you, my dear, for everything you have done. You are a wonder. My nerves are all of a jangle and I can't think straight. I need some time to reflect on this information.' She kisses me on the cheek and they walk out the front door.

Debbie sidles over to me.

'Did Martha attempt to communicate with you at the care home?'

'Martha? Yes, she did. I carried out the job she asked.'

'Which was?'

'All she wanted was her friend's apology so their spirits can rest in peace.'

'Is she still in contact with you?' asks Debbie.

I wander away; heading towards the door.

'You haven't answered my question, Sienna.'

I turn around to face her.

'No, she isn't, but I'm not sure if the visions have finished,' I reply.

'I hope they have,' she says.

Later on, my parents return and I sit with them in the living room; the television is on, but it's just background noise.

Dad clears his throat.

'We underestimated your gift, Sienna. We spoke to Rose, and she told us your special powers will develop as you mature. I'm not sure what she meant, but it worries her that you may need protection from unscrupulous influences. We'll keep in contact with Rose in Ireland, and she can be your guide. I'm sorry I didn't believe you.'

'Oh, Dad,' I cry, rushing up to him and hugging him.

'Sienna. You must manage your gift wisely,' says Mum, clasping us both.

'I will,' I say.

Finally, she accepts her journey,' whispers Bella.

CHAPTER 28

There's a sense of excitement in the air. Dad has arranged a last-minute deal for a two week holiday in a Greek villa. I'm lounging on the settee, poring over the glossy holiday brochures and wondering about taking a holiday so soon after Bella's death. Charlie texts me to come round, so I drop the brochures on the settee and dash to her house.

Parked in the driveway is a large green van with the symbol of a shamrock and the name of an Irish removal firm.

'Charlie, what's this?' I ask, my back to her, gesturing to the van.

'Come in, Sienna.'

I turn around. 'Wow, what the...' I'm speechless.

Her black clothes have gone. She's wearing a white T-shirt underneath a multi-coloured floral jumpsuit with gladiator sandals. Her hair, now curled, is swept to one side with a clip and her goth make-up wiped off. In its place is a natural look with rosy pink lipstick and a tanned glow. I follow her into the large polished hallway. Two men are struggling down the stairs carrying boxes and placing them with suitcases, trunks, and plastic bags outside on the driveway. Her dad is shouting instructions.

Rose joins us and stares at me with downcast eyes. There's a sadness about her.

'Are you heading back to Ireland? You've loads of boxes,' I laugh.

'Yes, my time has finished here. I've found what I wanted.'

Poignancy sweeps over me when I reflect on what we've been through and the closeness we shared.

'We'll miss you, won't we?' I say, smiling at my friend.

'Sienna. I…' Charlie starts, but her gran places her hand on top of hers.

'Not now,' she says.

'In here, Sienna.' Charlie gestures to the conservatory.

We troop through the spotless kitchen, all evidence of them gone. She perches on a packing box and pulls out a raffia chair.

'Sit down.'

'What's the matter?' I search her face, trying to read her thoughts, but she looks away. Something is wrong.

'We're going back to Ireland with Gran.'

'For a holiday?'

'No, for good.' She clutches my hand and twiddles with my bracelet.

'For good? Why?'

Rose studies me. 'That's my fault, Sienna. My health is poor and I've been lonely on my own. My son's contract has completed, and he's secured another one in Dublin.'

'Oh,' I say. 'So does that mean we won't be going to college together?'

Charlie looks away.

'But what about my plan?'

'What plan? This is the first I've heard of any plan,' she says, and stands up, slamming the conservatory window shut.

'I thought we could, you know… I don't know… solve mysteries.'

'Don't be daft. I told you I'm not psychic.'

Rose walks over to Charlie and, putting her hand around her waist, manoeuvres her over to me and says, 'I'm happy now you solved the mystery of the spell book, but I don't understand how I ended up with it.'

'After your mother died and Joe went missing, Lilith wrapped the book in a blanket and placed it at the bottom of your crib. Your adoptive parents came for you at the orphanage and they took it with them, without realising it was there. Lilith wanted it found,' I say.

'That was a long shot. What if Gran's parents had thrown it away? How do you know this?' asks Charlie.

'I held Lilith's hand, and it came to me in a series of flashbacks.'

'I'm glad the fire destroyed the spell book. It must have been terrible for Lilith, being excluded from her mother's love and tormented by her own evil acts. My birth mother forgave her and I do, too. Here, I want to show you these,' she says, reaching for her large handbag. 'I carry these with me.' She withdraws a handful of envelopes tied up with a yellow satin ribbon.

'What are they?'

'All of them have "address unknown, return to sender" written on them.'

'Gran has been crying over them ever since I took them from Lili's chest.'

'They're letters from Lili, apologising to me and expressing how much my father loved my mother. They're tragic,' she says, wiping away a tear. 'She posted one every year on my birthday. I never saw them because we travelled around and they were sent back to her. In the letters, she regrets becoming involved with black magic and asks for my forgiveness. We must live our lives now, mustn't we, dear, and not regret anything?' says Rose, examining me.

I'm watching Charlie. Strands of hair drift over her face, hiding her gaze.

'Now you're leaving, what will happen to this house?' I ask.

'It's rented.' Charlie glances up, the hint of a tear glistening on her cheek.

I'm annoyed with myself for asking a stupid question, but introducing Lili's letters has stunned me. Now I have Charlie's attention. I lash into her.

'You're my best friend! How will I survive without you? We've solved the secret of the book and found out about your great-grandmother. Why won't you stay, and we'll investigate more mysteries?' I glare at her, anger growing in me. 'You took advantage of my gift to discover Martha and now you're leaving.'

Charlie pulls her hand away. 'We never intended to live here permanently, and I didn't deceive you.'

Rose has been listening to our quarrel.

'You have grown so much since I've known you. Your confidence has increased and your psychic gift is stronger than you comprehend. I predict you will be successful by using your power to help other people. Your guardian angel is by your side. Goodbye, my dear. We'll keep in touch.'

'Wait,' I say.

'Thank you for carrying out my mother's wishes. You're a special girl: brave, loyal and you radiate strength beyond your years. I hate farewells, but I must supervise the removal men. Until we meet again.' She kisses my cheek and wipes away the tear rolling down it. 'I will always look after you,' she whispers.

Charlie comes toward me, clutching a padded brown envelope in her hands.

'This is for you.'

'What is it?' I ask, wiping away my tears.

'It's from your sister. Isabella saw it on an antique shop website and sent it here. You were on study leave and she didn't want you to open it at home while she was at school. Can you wait till your birthday?'

'No, give it here.'

I rip open the brown jiffy bag and remove a white box. Lying on a bed of velvet is the shape of an eye made from lapis lazuli and attached to a gold necklace.

'The evil eye symbol to protect me from evil.'

'This stone symbolises strength and courage, wisdom, intellect and truth. Your sister will always be with you,' Charlie whispers, placing it around my neck.

We hold hands and stroll into the garden. In the distance are the woods where we first chanted that stupid spell to destroy annoying people. What a fool I was then. Will Bella ever forgive me? After the turmoil we've encountered, it seems immature and so long ago now. Charlie puts her arm around my waist and lays her head on my shoulder, but she can't see it.

Pale grey, ghostly mist.

A fluid form, swaying and undulating.

Her lips against my ear, and the voice of Martha whispering, *'My job is complete. Forgive yourself, my dear.'*

EPILOGUE

An investigation was conducted and found the electrical wiring from Lilith Goldman's heart machine triggered the fire. The coroner's report stated Lili died before the onset of the fire. The autopsy found tumours pressing on her brain, which could have worsened her mental state.

We transferred Nan to a modern nursing home with excellent security equipment. Her dementia is worsening, and she doesn't recognise us. Occasionally, I'll catch her staring into space and whispering the name *Biddy Bishop*.

The thought of working at Monkton House raised my anxiety levels, so I didn't return. However, not long after the fire, Matron phoned regarding a complaint about me. I didn't know what it could be, so Mum attended the meeting. It turns out that Mrs Jones had complained I was always 'sneaking around'. After I explained that my sense of direction was dreadful, we had a laugh about it and the management dropped the matter.

Mrs Jones retired. I asked for her address to send a card and realised it was the same as Octavia Hamilton-Jones. Mrs Jones still lives in the village. I want to tell her that her granddaughter's fall was an accident, but she always crosses over the road when I approach.

A ghost writer used Anne Duncan's research papers to produce a book. This became a bestseller, and she donated the monies received to a children's charity.

The results from my blood tests and EEG show no abnormalities. No petit mal. The medical centre arranged an appointment with a psychiatrist. They diagnosed schizophrenia, and the doctors prescribed antipsychotic drugs. Although my parents believe in my psychic abilities, they want me to follow the doctor's advice. I will, until another vision hits me.

Lili left a will where she donated Monkton House to a social housing development company. It's now a construction site – diggers, trucks, and men in hard hats wandering around, shouting out instructions. Whilst dredging the lake, they found the skeletons of a female and male. DNA tracing is being undertaken to establish identity, but we know who they are, don't we?

School is a distant memory. I'm nervous on the first day of college, but Matt holds my hand and I relax until the remains of Monkton House appear. As we pass it, the sparkle of the lake peeps through the gap in the trees and I hold my breath. A dark shadow covers the vehicle and the bus driver watches me in his mirror. I look out of the window as a song reverberates in my ear.

'Lavender's blue, dilly dilly,

Lavender's green.

When I am king, dilly dilly,

You shall be queen.'

Martha holds the hand of a young man and sinks into the depths of the murky water.

Finally, at peace. I breathe out.

THE END

ABOUT THE AUTHOR

P.J. Yardley's love of reading developed from an early age. With her head always in a book, she found words transported her to other worlds. After a successful career in education, she now writes stories that captivate her imagination, keeping her up at night. She lives in a small village outside the Cotswolds, close to a haunted pub. *Monkton House* is her debut novel. Watch out for the second book in the Sienna Stevens mystery series.